MAIN

LIES

Lies

By William Hoffman

River City Publishing
Montgomery, Alabama

Published in the United States by River City Publishing
1719 Mulberry St.
Montgomery, AL 36106.

Designed by Lissa Monroe.

First Edition-2005
Printed in Canada
1 3 5 7 9 10 8 6 4 2

Library of Congress Cataloging-in-Publication Data

Hoffman, William, 1925-
  Lies / by William Hoffman.— 1st ed.
      p. cm.
  Summary: "Wayland Garnett, a successful businessman, wants to come to terms with the past he has hidden from his wife and daughter. He attempts to shake off the chains of his poverty-stricken upbringing by revisiting the Virginia countryside of his youth for the first time in forty years"—Provided by publisher.
  ISBN 1-57966-063-0
  1. Businessmen—Fiction. 2. Fathers and daughters—Fiction. 3. Middle aged men—Fiction. 4. Rural families—Fiction. 5. Married people—Fiction. 6. Poor families—Fiction. 7. Virginia—Fiction. 8. Secrecy—Fiction. I. Title.
  PS3558.O34638L54 2005
  813'.54—dc22

                              2004024748

LIES

To my grandchildren
KK, Hunter, and Andrew

No mask like common truth to cover lies . . .
 —William Congreve

one

Wayland drove roads little changed from a time way back, though most were paved now, yet all still meandered and seemingly without purpose—soft, narrow asphalt strips squeezed between ragged stands of dusty Virginia short-leaf pines, which dropped a feeble shade.

The pines released their fumy scent of hot resin, and they bled yellowish white sap from bark-beetle wounds. He had suffered wounds to his body that had mended, but there were injuries inflicted on the self and psyche past all healing the years could provide as . . .

. . . the boy stands in the foot- and hoof-scalped yard beside the unpainted frame cabin set up off the ground at four corners by stones dragged from a field once cleared. This land has many stones, and distant clangs from the blacksmith's shop at the Ballards' big house ring all day long to repair blunted and damaged plow points.

Often the boy wakes to the striking of hammer against anvil as he lies on his thin, straw-stuffed mattress, the knelling of pounded iron preceding even the cock's crow, which lights the emerging dawn.

That light this July morning is coolly filtered by mist that rises off the Hidden River and hangs flat above the darkened shape of a hackberry tree. He can't see the river because the cabin sits isolated among cutover woods on a scrap of soured clay soil occupied down the family line starting with Grandfather Winslow Garnett, the name a sound that lacks a face, he spoken of occasionally at dusk as Wayland's mother and father settle with the boy's brothers and sisters on the porch steps and talk among the phantom calls of whippoorwills.

"My Uncle John it was who first come up to this country from the mountains with a team of mules, a sack of tobacco seed, and two redbone hounds," the boy's mama says. She's a tall woman worked lean. She wears a loose-hanging, faded cotton dress and uncrosses her ankles to flex toes of her long thin feet. A pall of dust resembles gray socks around her shins.

"What mountains?" Emmett, the boy's older brother, asks.

"Carolina hicks carrying Carolina ticks," the daddy says and grins because he loves to rouse his wife. His people has existed in Howell County, Virginia, since Grandfather Winslow migrated up from Tennessee.

Grandfather Winslow claimed to have used his pocketknife to hack free the remains of his own leg tore part off below the knee by grapeshot west of Atlanta and left dangling from tattered strips of shattered bone and bloody flesh. A notched, tarnished brass button from his uniform lies lodged in a King Edward cigar box kept on top a plank shelf the boy's daddy has nailed up.

"You Garnetts wont hicks?" the boy's mama asks and sniffs as if the hot, scratchy night air has become fouled.

"Granddad fought with General Joe all the way from Shiloh to Atlanta and left that leg planted in Georgia soil," the daddy says, he even taller than the mama, lank, his skin stretched taut, a man who moves easy, a hunter whose step is so silent he ghosts through woods never disturbing deer resting curled in beds of pine tags until he's upon them, the aged LeFever raised to deliver unerring death.

"And he carried a sword?" the boy asks, sitting on the bottom wooden step, slapping at skeeters. It's important to his vision of himself, which has taken shape from the yellowed picture in a school-owned history book of hollering butternut-clad troops charging a battery of firing cannons that line the stony ridge of a smoke-shrouded hill.

"Sure and General Joe ran 'em all to ground and ate their beans," the boy's daddy says.

"How you know?" the mama asks. "Your granddad never told a story straight he could make crooked. Like you."

"Fought with General Joe Johnson and the Army of Tennessee all the way to Atlanta," the father says. "Was one of General Joe's best boys."

"He come home crutching hisself and never done a lick of work ever again," the mama says. "It was up to the women. Always ends up on the women."

"He carried a sword," the boy's daddy said. "I seen it once before it got sold."

"Like everything else," the mama says. "All we get a hand on worth anything you sell or trade off. If he had a sword, he likely stole it."

"I ain't sold you yet," the daddy says, again grinning as he gathers his tobacco cud to spit aside.

"Prob'bly tried," she says.

"Couldn't get a nickel," the daddy says. "Have to feed and fatten you first."

"Fat's not fast enough to catch up with me," the mama says and sighs as a waning moon rises above the motionless pines. It glimmers on angles of her face.

two

Wayland steered the rented dark blue Sedan de Ville past fields grown wild with prickly bull thistles. What vanity or self-doubt had made him insist on a Cadillac rather than the Taurus? Neglected pastures sprouted a frayed ground cover resembling a crone's sparse hair growing from leached soil too anemic to eke out anything but sickly vegetation in this heat . . .

. . . of summer when the boy treads down from the canopy of shredded pine shadows into sunlight that smites and demands a squint. He shades his eyes to gaze across a flat expanse of low ground—broad cultivated acres astride the willow-lined muddy river, this soil not red clay but black loam yearly enriched by spring floodings. No need to spread manure or scatter fertilizer. Corn, wheat, oats, alfalfa, and most important of all tobacco nigh on to leap from this fecund earth.

During summer's heat the air above the bottom shimmies upward, and the southwest breeze, what little there be, bears odors of sultrily growing crops and the river weaving languidly between its moist and root-tangled banks.

He adjusts the heft of the hoe balanced over his shoulder, the blade sharpened the previous evening on a wobbly

15

whetstone wheel. His daddy rigged the wheel using pedals, a frame, and the seat wrenched from a broken bicycle discarded by Eugene Ballard to the burning pit dug for waste outside the wall behind the Ballards' house.

Two or three times a week the boy checks the pit to search for whatever the family could use. The Ballards toss away things others might give hard money for. He touches the bib pocket of his cutdown Big Boy overalls, which holds a bone-handled clasp knife he prizes, it too thrown on the heap because of a snapped-off blade. A second smaller blade of the best Solingen steel remains and will hold its edge 'til Doomsday.

The boy, his name Wayland, and his brothers Emmett and Ferdinand, poke sticks into the pit to draw out singed belts, gloves, and shoes from the forever smoldering fire. For their mama they rescue a straw hat with a broad yellow floppy brim—the kind Mrs. Ballard wears among flowers of a garden that draws bees over the stone wall to a drunkenness of heavy blooms. The boy's mama patiently mends the black ribbon and ties it in a bow under her chin to pose before her mirror.

Other field hands emerge from the fringe of pines surrounding the flourishing sweep of land. In this section of Howell County's lower end, few cash-paying jobs exist except at the Ballards'.

We like bugs, the boy thinks of himself and the stream of hired help converging toward the bottom, or ants streaming to and swarming around a dropped crust of bread, though likely no crust would stay long on the ground before being snatched up and eaten dirt and all. Hunger don't know dirt.

Miss Patricia Flowers, the boy's grade-school teacher, explained that because Yankee soldiers never passed through Howell County, Bellepays's white granite mansion escaped General Grant's plunderers and what she calls his "marauding scythe of war."

After Appomattox, the mounting demands for tobacco domestically and over in Europe paid for the plantation's survival through Reconstruction and again enriched the Ballards. The boy's daddy said, "Yeah, allowing that family to buy up even more acres from neighbors brought low by maimings, crop failures, and taxes."

The oak handle of the hoe that Wayland carries has been whittled and trimmed to size by his daddy. All the ditchers have their first hoes provided by the Ballards, not Mr. Henry himself, but a man years ago who would've been called an overseer and these latter days is spoken of as the farm manager, presently Mr. Wesley Rudd. If you lose or break your hoe, you are subject to do the repairing or replacing yourself. When you change jobs or quit, you turn in the hoe to Mr. Rudd, who makes a mark by your name on his book of records.

Mr. Rudd waits beyond the plank fence and broad gate where paths converge from the pines. Wagon roads spread along the bottom marking exact boundaries of the fields. Each fifty acres has been given a name—High Slant, Long Row, River Bend, Doe Run, Beaver Lick.

Mr. Wesley Rudd is a strong, heavy man who wears a white shirt and black fedora, its brim snapped up. He sits on an upended nail keg set outside his office doorway and checks off the names of hands who arrive to work.

"Morning, Mr. Wesley," the boy says. They all speak respectfully to Mr. Rudd.

"Wayland," Mr. Rudd answers, his voice not threatening, yet carrying the certainty of power beneath even a kindly greeting. He is hard but fair.

Mr. Wesley Rudd knows them all by name. He keeps account of the ten-cents-an-hour pay that Wayland and the other boys receive for a day's work. More mature youths, determined by size and strength rather than age, are assigned harder labor and carry home twelve to fifteen cents an hour.

During the growing and harvesting seasons, the Ballards also provide lunch brought down by house servants and laid out on a wagon bed. For most hands it's the biggest meal of the day—cornbread, 'taters, hog meat, mutton, and always beans—navy beans, snaps, or Jordans cooked with floating chunks of fatback.

Mr. Wesley Rudd assigns Wayland to River Bend, a planting of corn bound by ditches that drain to the river. If the ditches clog up, rain won't run off, and the corn droops and wilts like scrawny, wounded soldiers.

"Cook us today," Willie Meekems, Wayland's friend, says, a gangling redhead who lives at the upper end of Wildcat Creek. Willie looks at the cloudless sky where along the horizon the sun rises huge and blood red. Climbing, it will become a molten yellow that eats up the fleeting shade cast by the river's willows.

Wayland steps into the ditch where flourishing weeds and Johnson grass brush his legs. He wonders whether the grass was named after the general. The earth beneath Wayland's bare feet is spongy and bleeds black where hoe strokes cleave it. The soil oozes between his toes.

Other boys arrive, the pickaninnies from Tar Patch, an area of scrub pines, crooked garden plots, and moldering vine-claimed brick cabins that once housed slaves. They joke, laugh, and string out along the ditch.

"Dig Debbil time," a burrhead named Josephus calls. He's blacker than river mud, muscled beyond his years, eyes dark as nut coal set in egg whites. "Dig 'im up."

He and Wayland bump as they chop along the ditch's narrow course. Their hoe blades chime.

"Dig you up," Wayland says.

"Moufs never dug nothing," Josephus answers and the pickaninnies grin.

"Stay out my way," Wayland warns him.

"You way no way," Josephus says and ignites laughter.

Wayland might've swung his hoe but sees Mr. Henry Ballard skirting the corn along the wagon road. His young daughter Diana and his son Eugene follow. Mr. Henry rides his chestnut gelding whose flanks shine bright as a new penny, Eugene a dappled bay, and Diana a prancing white pony named Missy.

Mr. Henry appears every morning to eye the work being done on his plentiful acres. He sits erect in his McClellan saddle, not a big man, not nearly as tall as Wayland's daddy, but he believes himself large. A tan trooper's hat shades a face broad at the brow, narrow at the chin. His khaki shirt and whipcord britches are never smudged or sweat stained, and the spurs of his brown riding boots catch a glint. He served as a major in the cavalry during the Great War.

His son Eugene carries down the Ballard line the same broad brow and narrow chin. Like his father he wears boots and breeches but is hatless, his off-blond hair gleaming in sunlight. Wayland has hidden and spied on him racing across mowed fields, his body bent forward, head low while he waves an arm as if leading troops in the attack. Come September he's to be sent away to a New England private school.

Diana's yellow shirt has long sleeves to protect the fairness of her arms. Her brown riding pants are called jodphurs. When Wayland first heard his mama use the word, he believed they must've been made from fur of some kind of animals named jods. Diana's dark shiny hair hangs from beneath her derby to spread across her back. She has her mother's round face and small lips. In gloved fingers she holds a leather crop.

She smiles as she passes field hands, and Wayland hopes her eyes will light on and favor him. Sometimes he lies nights and imagines their meeting on one of the riding trails kept clear for her through Bellepays's woods. She may need Missy's girth tightened or the bridle adjusted, and Wayland will be quick to oblige.

She now rides between her father and brother. Her eyes seem to look at everything and nothing. Wayland watches her long after she passes and again turns to strike weeds of the ditch. Josephus smiles.

"Catch flies in your mouf," he says.

three

Wayland slowed the Caddy to glance at a half acre of stripped stalks drooping in straggling rows— the remainder of some poor farmer's crop of dark-fired tobacco.

"I won't have that stink around my new house," his wife Amy had told him in the den of their Fort Lauderdale bayside home.

"It's my house too," he'd answered.

"Inside is mine, outside is yours."

"Tobacco was the main cash crop buying food for people's bellies when I was a boy."

"Causing addiction and cancer, and you're no longer a boy but a sixty-three-year-old man who's supposed to have smarts."

"Nobody worried about those things back then. The old days tobacco was used for money. Planters paid their preachers in it. Poor whites crushed a leaf, mixed in kerosene, and fed it to children to kill worms."

"Worms, good Lord," she'd said. "I don't want to hear it."

And he hadn't to this day told her anywhere near all of it.

She was twenty years younger than he, had been a competitive swimmer and diver. He first saw her rising off the three-meter board to perform a full gainer, her body drawn into lines of grace so beautifully compelling he stumbled over a rubber float and bumped a poolside table, tipping a colorful umbrella and spilling the drinks of strangers.

"When and if a crop were brought to harvest," he'd said to her, "the Lord was thought to be good . . ."

. . . to those who own tobacco acreage like the Ballards, and Wayland believes God must look something like Mr. Henry Ballard. The boy has never been to the big house. From a distance among boughs of tulip poplars and thick-limbed, gnarled white oaks he's caught sight of the gleaming slate roof and the many flared chimneys, the smoke torn and snatched by winter winds.

He can't remember ever being told to stay away. He believes he was borned knowing it.

"They feed hounds meat we'd set on our table," his older brother Emmett says. Emmett's been hired for stable help and trudges home nights with tales of the big house. "You could raise hogs off they kitchen waste. Can't sneak nothing. Black Amos watching ever' step."

"No nigger's got the right to act that way," Wayland's daddy says.

"He got any right the Ballards give him," the mama says as she chunks up wood in her cook stove. She moves barefoot in the kitchen, the skin of her toughened feet whisking across wide unfinished but oft-scoured pine boards. Her free-flowing brown hair she's pushed back over bony shoulders. Her complexion is sun-darkened, her gentian blue eyes a reminder of a youth and beauty that once flourished.

The big house, a mile and a quarter off, has its own private entrance and drive. It's paved while half the roads in the lower end of Howell County remain dirt or washboard. Wayland keeps to a deer trail softened by the evening's cooling dampness and pine tags. He reins his breathing and moves as if stalking a deer to get a shot with his daddy's LeFever. The Ballards are hard on poachers. They fire them off the place and stand them before the county magistrate. Wayland has seen rocking wagons leave, mattresses and chairs twined down to bind and keep them from falling on the ground.

He believes terrible things must lie in wait down the road, not the private one to the big house, but the county secondary, which leads to an outer world he's never seen. The thought of what is beyond Jericho Crossroads has caused him to stare along the road's length and feel twinges of fear.

A black shape bursts noisily above him. For an instant he believes he's been caught and throws his arms over his head. He's already rehearsed what he'll say, the lie he'll tell. "Got lost and turned around in the woods, Mr. Henry. Honest to God I did." But no hands seize him, and he realizes the shape had to be a roosting gobbler that flushed from a shagbark hickory. Wayland waits for his heart to quiet and his breathing to even out.

Nearer the house, he lowers to his hands and knees, moves forward, listens, and lifts his nose to sniff. His daddy has taught him to scent both game and man. Wayland's approach is from downwind, and he picks up no smells carrying threat.

He moves among the grove of hardwoods, the land beneath kept clean of fallen branches by the Ballard help. No briars or wild grape vines tangle this orderly planting. He rises to part the leafy limb of a white ash with fingers that quake. He wills steadiness into them as he slips forward, halts, and lays his ear against the leaf-strewn soil to listen.

He drops belly down. To the north he glimpses the ghostly Kentucky gate, it always kept closed. His brother Emmett has told him that the gate is rigged with a wooden pull handle and an iron cannonball counterweight so that those on horses don't need dismount to open it and pass through. The gate swings shut of itself.

"Might get they pretty boots muddy," Emmett has said.

"None of that," their mama told him.

"Why none of that?" the daddy asked, straightening from the steaming mustard greens heaped in a bowl set on the oilcloth-covered table before him.

"Mouths eating off Ballards has best be kept closed," the mama said.

"What they feeding on is us," the daddy said, his narrow face angry, his reddish brown eyes catching a white glare from the Aladdin lamp.

"Tough chewing," the mama said.

"Damn right," the daddy said. "Break they jaws."

The boy lies flat and studies the gate. Beyond it alternate dogwoods and magnolias that line the drive to the big house. Golden light flickers from windows of an upper story of the white mansion hung with black louvered shutters.

The Ballards have been the first to install electricity, the old brass fixtures, Emmett has told, converted to use from water gas. At Christmas hands string bulbs along the lane all the way to the Kentucky gate, and when they switched on it's like seeing night come alive in brilliant flashes of colored fire. The lights cause the hounds to howl and crows to fly squawking off their perches. The first time Wayland saw it he took off his cap as if in church.

He crawls backward from sight of the gate until well away and again crouches as he works toward the stone wall. He scents the sweet odor of wisteria. He don't allow fright to direct his carefully placed steps.

"Waiting and easing's the way of the hunters," his daddy has taught him. "You got to be able to sit on a stand without blinking or swatting skeeters and when tracking set your feet down so soft you can slip by a copperhead without rousing him from his rest. Train yourself to it."

Wayland nears the wall. He again pushes aside boughs and holds them 'til they find their natural bend instead of releasing them to swish back into place. The gathering twilight seems not to lower from the sky but seep upward from the ground like a mist rising.

Again on his belly, he squirms to the wall. It's reared before him blacking out all sky, and his fingers touch the cool slickness of moss growing up the quarried stone blocks. He lies listening for barking—not from meat dogs like Triggs, blueticks, or redbones that give voice in wavering cries but glossy English foxhounds kept in a roofed kennel with concrete flooring, water spigots, and fence-enclosed runs. The English foxhounds give cry in different voices as if more properly brought up.

All the Ballards hunt. They are raised to it, even the women. It's told they have brought harriers from across the sea, though the boy has never seen the ocean and can only picture it like a great river stretching all the way to Tobaccoton, Lynchburg, or Danville.

The Ballards run bird dogs too, Irish and Llewellin setters bred so fine they go on quivering points, tails lifted and rigid, their sleek bodies so tensed up it seems they will crack apart like delicate glass. Emmett claims when they retrieve birds their mouths are gentle and leave the feathers undisturbed and barely moist, no tooth ever puncturing flesh.

The Ballard women and female guests ride out on a farm wagon fixed with bolted-down benches set crossways to the bed. They wear floppy hats, bright dresses, and shoes not boots. Wooden racks holds their shotguns upright, and Black Amos drives a mule named Sleepy who never blinks when shots are fired over his head.

The men mount horses also trained to the sounds of shell blasts. Their guns are side-by-sides holstered in leather scabbards. Mr. Henry Ballard sits astride his chestnut gelding and don't dismount to shoot when his dogs point. He has a fine eye and uses a twenty-gauge Parker, always seeming to bring it to his shoulder kind of dreamily and firing as if he has all the time in the world and's above caring. Partridges hit the ground, bounce, and feathers settle after them.

Black Amos wears clothes finer than most whites, owns a Chevrolet automobile, and strings a gold watch chain across his vest. He unleashes the dogs from a box at the rear of the wagon. They course ahead of the hunters and jolt to shuddering halts among lespedeza, their lips twisting over teeth, eyes bulging, paws caught midstride lifted as daintily as ladies' hands holding teacups.

On covey rises Mr. Henry Ballard permits guests the first shots. The women stand in the wagon and raise their guns. Mrs. Isabelle Ballard appears as outfitted and refined as if on her way to Tobaccoton's St. Luke's Episcopal Church. Her Holland & Holland has been fitted to her by a London gunsmith. The Ballards believe everything English is quality and automatically better than anything that can be bought at their store or from Sears & Roebuck.

Mr. Henry's son Eugene rides beside his father while Diana stays on the wagon with her mother. She fires her small cutdown .410-gauge L. C. Smith with a seriousness that seems shocking after her usual gaiety. When she drops a partridge, she laughs, and her father permits her to step off the wagon and take the bird for the retrieve. Diana tenderly strokes its feathers before handing it to Black Amos to place in the canvas bag hooked under his spring-supported seat. The bag swings in time with Sleepy's slow pace.

The hunt over, they drink wine and liquor that Mr. Henry offers around in bottles and glasses lifted from wicker baskets. Eugene and Diana are allowed cider. At the big house the birds will be plucked, gutted, and washed by kitchen help before being served on a large silver platter among rice, butterbeans, and sugar-cured ham.

"You can see your fingers through the ham they slice it so thin," Emmett has said.

Wayland pulls back from the wall, listens, and quietly shinnies up a tulip poplar, keeping the trunk between himself and the wall. He peeps around and pushes away branches to peer across a darkening lawn greener than any pasture that ever grew grass. It has a shimmer from its own depth. Do the Ballards order the help to wipe and wax each blade that produces such a sheen?

He stares at a fountain crowned by a copper fish from whose gaping mouth water falls onto the top tier of three that overflow and splash into a rounded stone pool beneath. The disturbed surface catches fleeting specks of light from the tall, broad windows, each overhung by white molding.

The granite mansion rises three stories, and its chimneys poke high among the massive, lichen-splotched oaks. Wisteria vines climb and tangle the limbs, the dangling purple blooms hanging heavy and perfuming the evening.

Yellow, blue, and red flowers flourish in oval-shaped brick borders, and slate walkways wind among box bushes that grow only a couple of inches a year and are now ten feet or more tall. Ivy encircles a sundial.

White iron chairs and benches are set under the oaks and in a rose arbor. At the far side of the property is the family cemetery enclosed by black iron pickets. Striped gaily-colored mallets and croquet balls lie strewn on finely mowed grass.

Wayland listens to three notes from a piano, the beginning of no tune he knows, played as if a hand is just passing by on its way somewheres else. A bird sings an intricate song, one the boy's never before heard, but Emmett has told him of Diana's canary whose cage she hangs in sunlight of her window.

Wayland hears what he believes are shrill cries of "Help. Help." He's about to flee when he makes out the bird strutting through silky shadows—a peacock dragging its feathered train. For a moment the fan of those brilliant tailfeathers opens and glitters in shafts of light thrown from the house.

Wayland glimpses a chandelier, the bulbs shaped like flames at the end of upcurved golden arms. The corner of a blue rug has yellow fringes. A silver basket holding ripe fruit sits on a polished table under a lamp whose glass shade casts color of many different tints.

A shape crosses past a pink glowing window on the second floor. Diana's room, he guesses. If so, it's nothing like the cabin where his sisters Lottie and Pearl May share a bed, those walls not plaster but untrimmed planks insulated with tacked up newspaper never purchased but recovered from the Ballards' burning pit.

Those walls are also decorated by cutouts from magazines the Ballards throw away—Greta Garbo, President Roosevelt, a beautiful radiant Jesus, an outdated calendar from the Planters Bank in Tobaccoton featuring two wasp-waist ladies wearing ankle-length dresses and sitting on chairs with twisted wiry legs set around a marble-top table. The ladies sip dark Coca-Colas through white straws.

Closing darkness transforms the big house into an island of light. He hears laughter and again a begun yet unfinished few notes from the piano. A hound barks, and others take it up. Maybe they've caught his scent on the breeze, which shifts the white oaks' leaves. He's seen enough and lowers himself among the tangle of tulip poplar limbs.

"Got ya, boy," the huge black-within-black shouts. Hands grab Wayland's ankles, tug, and drag him down the grainy trunk. The bark skins his arms, legs, and belly. He wails, and the hounds answer.

Black Amos, whose bald head is like a cannonball, has snuck up beneath the tulip poplar and pulls Wayland to the ground, twists him about, and presses him against the tree's trunk. Wayland's fright causes him to foul himself.

"Who-ee, boy, you stink worse'n a hog in heat."

Black Amos is Mr. Henry Ballard's man, follows him about, does his bidding. He has borrowed of Mr. Henry's power and assumed authority over the house. Even Mr. Wesley Rudd treats him like an equal. When Black Amos speaks, he's voicing Mr. Henry's commands and is obeyed.

Wayland tries to kick free, and Black Amos slaps him. Black Amos straightens him, shoves him hard against the wall, and punches a knee into Wayland's stomach. He leans his shiny pocked face close, his teeth seeming big and square like dice men toss on the ground behind the Ballards' store. Wayland hears the tick of the gold watch, a lump snug in a vest pocket of the dark serge suit. Black Amos's breath smells candied from sucking on peppermints taken from the big house.

"I know you," he says. "I been seeing you stealing around like a rat in the corn crib. I been waiting."

"Turn loosa me."

"What if I hauls you up 'fore Mr. Henry? What if Mr. Henry call Sheriff Calvin who carry you off and put you to work on the road gang? What you think of that?"

"I didn't mean nothing. I just lost."

"Lost up a tree. That's something. I see you when you don't know I seeing."

"Won't do it no more. Promise you I won't."

"No more slipping around and spying on your betters. You don't belong on high ground. You hearing me, boy?"

"Yes, sir, Mr. Amos, please turn loosa me."

"Next time I gonna haul you up 'fore Mr. Henry, and he call Sheriff Calvin. Put you on the road gang."

Black Amos pulls the knee from Wayland's stomach and stands away. Wayland dodges around him and runs through the night woods. Boughs whip his face. He jumps Weeping Creek where his father often seines shiners. He runs among tobacco plants drooping and torpid under a sliver of moon.

He crawls between rails of the fence his father has split by pounding iron wedges with an eight-pound sledge into cedar trunks uprooted by a north wind. He's so scared he claws beneath the cabin and lies trembling beside Reb, his daddy's redbone. He now knows how a treed coon feels peering down from a limb at jumping, snarling dogs as night hunters raise their shotguns and take aim.

Later his daddy holding the lantern finds and calls him from under the cabin. His daddy smells of soured sweat, his narrow face shadowed by beard stubble. He hugs Wayland, listens to his quaking voice, quiets him by taking the trembling into himself. He blows out the lantern, and together they hunker in moon shade from the hackberry.

"I'da got us out long ago if there'd be anyplace to git to," he says. "But you stay away from up 'er. The woods is where you and me belongs. And they's other ways."

Jostling Wayland, the daddy laughs, his snaggled teeth lit by moonlight.

four

Wayland drove a stretch of road flanked by the splintered desolation timber companies had left blasted behind as if war had been fought through here—another Hürtgen Forest after the battle.

During his youth the Ballards allowed people to swarm over the unmarketable broken trunks, shattered limbs, and laps remaining on the ground. Whole families carried axes and crosscut saws to lay in fuel for winter. Black Amos passed down the permission from the Ballards.

Wayland had flown to Richmond from Fort Lauderdale to attend a meeting of the Southern Automobile Dealers Convocation, put up at the Marriott, and meant to return on Sunday to Florida. A photograph and article on the State page of the Richmond *Times-Dispatch* announcing the opening of the Danville tobacco market had triggered an impulse that made him break his sworn oath never to return to Howell County. He pictured himself walking not to the back entrance at Bellepays but up the front steps, a man with every right to knock on that door.

"I'll be staying an extra day," he'd told his Amy over the phone.

"If you're fooling around with another woman you can't hide it from me, and I'll kill you slowly," she had said and laughed. "I'll feed you into a meat grinder starting with your toes."

"It's an opportunity to bring more business to the company," he had lied, hating to do it, but to tell her the truth might open doors he had kept closed all the years of their marriage. There were good and bad lies, those meant to hurt, others spoken out of love with resulting consequences that harden into a sort of truth that abide so many days it's impossible to reverse course and turn back to a time . . .

. . . Wayland is poked during the night. His daddy rouses him and his brothers Emmett and Ferdinand from the bed all three sleep on. The bed is rough-hewn oak, the adz strokes visible on the square headboard. It has been in the family even farther back than Granny Ruth, his daddy's mother, could remember, she, the bed, and her kettles hauled up from Tennessee on a wagon drawn by a plodding Percheron mare that lay down and died with a long sigh the minute they stopped for good in a pool of thin shade dropped by the immature hackberry tree.

The bed's stringy mattress is laid on planks and stuffed with shifting, crackling corn shucks and wheat straw. During summer's heat Wayland and his brothers sleep crossways instead of end to end in order to gain the cool from the single uncurtained window. Not 'til winter winds blow and the aged hackberry bows before it do they lay their bodies under a patch quilt end to end. Whoever snores receives a kick or elbow jab, and often they scuffle for territory.

"Let's get to work," Wayland's daddy says, whispering 'cause he's not told Wayland's mama what he's up to. Tired, worn as always from a woman's endless chores, she sleeps across the hall in another bed, this one brought along with her marriage—brass, once her mama and daddy's precious piece, people who after trekking up from Carolina had crossed the Hidden River and into Howell County to work Ballard tobacco.

The daddy, Wayland, and his brothers don't leave by the cabin door. They drop barefoot out the window, which has no screen and allows in skeeters, greenies, and deer flies whose bites become so regular a part of night and day that the family slaps at them not with anger but resignation, knowing a squashed and splattered kill solves nothing 'cause skeeters, greenies, and deer flies be like the poor that the Reverend Arbogast preaches is always with us.

Reb waits below the window and wags his tail. He noses Wayland's bare legs. The hound whines happiness as the daddy shushes him. In the yard no grass grows underfoot, no attempts ever made at planting it, the packed ground worn bare as bone by the feet and hooves of chickens, livestock, and the hogs that will be slaughtered annually at first kill frost, the scalded carcasses hoisted by block and tackle, scraped, and hung clean and bright as newborn flesh from a lower limb of the hackberry.

The daddy leads them to the dilapidated shed behind the cabin where he stores firewood and tools. From the single cobwebbed stall he passes out folded burlap feed sacks. He also pulls down lengths of miller's twine hanging from a ten-penny nail.

"What for?" Wayland whispers.

"Hush," his daddy says, and they follow him along the dark lane to the dirt road rutted from wheels of Ballard farm vehicles. No moon this night, no shadows, the dust roused by their feet unseen, though its dry, prickling scent is, like the skeeters feeding, unrelenting.

"We take Reb all the way?" Ferdinand asks. He walks with a hitch to the left because he was borned with a withered leg. From the ankle to the knee of that leg the muscles never filled out and look as if the skin covers little more than a tobacco stick.

"We tie the dog," their daddy says. It's the kind of night he's been waiting for, darkness so dense it seems Wayland can reach out to gather it in his hand and shape it to a ball.

"How come Wayland's along?" Emmett asks.

"Time he learns," the daddy answers.

"Learn what?" Wayland asks.

"How it be," the daddy says.

They traverse the road to the line of woods marking the western edge of Ballard property where they troop single file along the same deer trail Wayland followed when he dared stalk the big house and climbed the tulip poplar to look over the stone wall. He thinks of Black Amos who in darkness of this night could be invisible and waiting.

But they don't go near the big house. At Wildcat Branch that runs dry during summer's heat they descend toward the low ground. The daddy knots two lengths of twine and loops it over Reb's head before tying the hound to the trunk of a hickory sapling.

Reb whines after them as the daddy keeps to the edge of Wildcat Branch 'til it levels out at the first fence. They stand crouched and listen while the daddy sniffs the air.

"Smell them fancy peppermints if that nigger's around," he whispers.

"Where Mr. Wesley Rudd?" Ferdinand asks, also whispering.

"Mr. Wesley Rudd," the daddy says, hissing the words and drawing out the name before he spits. "Thinks he something. Worse than the nigger. Them Rudds wont nothing when we owned all our land. They begged our bread."

Wayland has heard the story, 'specially when his daddy's drinking and sprawled on the cabin porch, not only his voice but also his eyes catching fire.

"How much we owned?" Wayland had asked the first time he heard the story, a Fourth of July while they was firing off skyrockets at the big house—red, white, and blue bursts shooting skyward and falling apart against a glooming blackness.

"Seventy acres oncet," the daddy had answered, lying on his back, his legs hinged at the knees and dropping from the porch's ledge.

" 'nuff," the boy's mama had said. She'd come from the kitchen after washing the tin plates and cups in well water heated on the wood stove.

"Good land," the daddy had said. "So rich rocks'd grow. Had a spring that run pure and cool. That land gave way before a plow blade easy as a honed knife through a pail of lard."

"Don't do no good to go back," the mama had said.

"My pappy loved that land," Wayland's daddy had said as if she'd not spoken. "He'd stop, reach down for a handful, and run it through his fingers like grains of silver and gold."

"Where'd it git to?" Wayland had asked.

"Land don't go no place," the daddy said. "Land is. It was thieved from us."

"Paid for," the mama said.

"Stolen when I was a tyke and my daddy got struck down by the fever. He kept on plowing sick. Had the reins 'round his neck and under an arm. The mule dragged him 'til dirt clogged his ears, eyes, and mouth. Never no good after that. Lost his strength. Hardly sit in a chair without toppling."

"It don't do no good," the mama said.

"I tried to keep things going," the daddy said. "I was a tyke, and me and Granny Ruth tried to hold it. But the drought burned us off. Dry fields broke with cracks big enough to fall in. The sun stayed red all day long. Nights so hot cattle laid down and died, tongues hanging out. Bawling and dying ever'wheres."

"Pure pitiful," the mama said.

"Pitiful except for the high and mighty Ballards," the daddy said. "They could pay to truck feed all the way from Pennsylvania. And when my daddy walked to the big house to ask for a stretching out of money owed at the store, he got it but had to put up all his land but the pitiful patch we got left. By the time that drought quit, them Ballards took everything except ground what wouldn't grow nothing but thistle and slash pine. A starving rabbit couldn't make it on soil so poor. They owe us. They got rich on us. Bled us out."

"But it don't do no good," the mama said.

✦

They wait at the fence, hunkered now, the rolled feed sacks laid on the ground before them. Wayland hears the river's quiet drag against its banks, the throbbing insects, the bewonks of frogs. His daddy bends low so he can see any shapes that moves against lights from the big house, their sparkle marking and defining the obscured black horizon.

"Mr. Henry ever do it?" Emmett whispers.

"He don't," the daddy answers. "He be lying up in that big soft bed on them slick white sheets. He sleeping with a full belly while them who he pays for it does his guarding. Got enough money you can get ever' damn thing in the world done for you and still lie in the bed."

"Black Amos?" Wayland whispers.

"Nah, not that high-toned darky in his gent'men clothes. He sleeping too, got him a room in the house up on the third floor, his own indoor crapper, and a fancy white bathtub."

"It's fact," Emmett says.

"Thinks he one of them," the father says. "Believes he white and got Ballard blood."

"But never sits at the table," Emmett says. "And eats leavings."

"Hush," the father orders.

They quiet, though the boy hears nothing more than a rustling of corn as a breath of breeze rises off the river and stirs stalks and their fronds. But his daddy's sight goes beyond eyes and ears. He draws from the air and ground messages others can't detect. He senses game and is able to settle among sumac or hawthorn for hours until what shifts in the forest is not wind driven and the LeFever speaks death.

Deer, turkey, squirrel, and rabbit he takes mostly off the Ballard land, and the Ballards know it. They conspire to catch him and send Sheriff Calvin to the cabin. The sheriff drives a black Model A that has a gold star painted on two of its doors. The daddy and the sheriff chat under the hackberry, a shade slight 'cause the hackberry's not much, the leaves thin and ragged, the wood unfit for a hot fire, the trees spread by bird droppings on land that has been cut over and neglected.

"Now, Larkin, I don't mean to come out here again and warn you," the sheriff says. His high-top black shoes, brown suit, and a brown felt hat are dusty. He swats at his clothes to batter the dust from his trouser legs. His face is ruddy, his eyes nearly without tint and watery.

"Calvin, you welcome here anytime," the daddy answers.

"I know times is tough," the sheriff says. "I tell you I understand how hard it is for a man to feed his family. But I don't want you in my jail living on the county either. Howell County too is poor."

"Ain't nothing taken off the Ballards they'd ever miss," the daddy says.

"Maybe that's true, but it's their'n. They got the law."

"They got everything, including you."

"That's right, they got me when you go wrong. That's how she works. Now you could go down and speak to Mr. Wesley Rudd. He'll put you to work in the fields. You strong and smart and can earn your beans."

"You work for the Ballards, they earn the beans."

"You keep off them or you studying jail. Who gonna feed your family then?"

"I ain't studying no jail."

"The jail might be studying you," the sheriff says. "My best to Miss Winona."

He hitches up his pants over his belly, crosses to the Model A, and drives off, leaving a swirl of aroused dust. Wayland's daddy grins and does a jig that causes Reb to bark and the mama to turn away.

⚛

They lie low along the Ballard fence. Wayland sees nothing pass in the hot blackness but hears the sound of a single step, a clod of soil dislodged, the brushing of a corn frond when all breeze has died.

Skeeters cover his face, yet he gently brushes them off. Nor do his brothers shift their bodies. The daddy, who has taught them silence and the sanctuary of immobility, rises slowly. He continues to listen and scent.

"Not yet," he whispers and eases down.

Wayland thinks of himself as a soldier. So many times his daddy has told them of Grandfather Winslow who fought with General Joe Johnson down in Tennessee. He wishes he held a rifle.

"They was never beaten," the daddy said. "General Lee got cornered but not Joe Johnson. His army held and stood ready to keep fighting. Your granddaddy never give up. He come back carrying his rifle. Wouldn't let no bluebelly take it from him. Nobody ever whipped him. He didn't know no whipping."

The King Edward cigar box on the cabin shelf holds the tarnished notched button the father tells them is from the grandfather's uniform. When Wayland fingers it out and strokes it, the button seems to give off a power.

The box also contains a steel pocket watch that still works, the head of a buck deer carved into a knob of its leg bone, dice, a meerschaum pipe which has an S crook in the stem as well as a flared bowl that fills the hand, and a copper coin advertising Green River whisky. The daddy often lifts the cigar box down, places each item on the kitchen table, and treats them as if they are pieces of great value.

He again rises to his knees to sniff and taste the air. He could be licking a lollipop on a stick. Slowly he collects his body to stand.

"Now," he whispers. "Wayland, you stay."

The daddy and Wayland's two brothers leave him and slip between fence rails and amongst the soughing corn. Wayland listens and can just make out sounds of ears being ripped from stalks. His daddy returns bearing a sack heavy with pickins and shows Wayland how to shake the ears down and bind them with a miller's knot.

The brothers carry him sacks and fade back among the corn. As Wayland waits he looks toward the big house and the lights, some blocked by shifting leaves of the great white oaks. Even while people sleep, the big house is never dark.

Seven sacks are filled, Wayland to carry one, his father and brothers two each. They work up the slope toward cover of the pine woods. Wayland struggles under the weight, trips, falls, and the miller's knot gives, allowing ears to spill. He gathers and tries to stuff them back.

"Halt right where you are up there," a voice calls from darkness below.

"Leave the rest," the daddy orders, and they climb running 'til they reach the pines. Wayland is sweat slick, his teeth biting for breath. Flashlight beams sweep side to side among the corn rows.

"Halt, this the law," the voice, Sheriff Calvin's, shouts. He fires his World War I .45-caliber revolver.

They don't halt but free Reb and jog through the woods. The corn they carry not to the cabin but a ferny spring deep in the forest where the daddy does his cooking. What he don't drink himself he sells to both whites and niggers he's known all his life—rarely for money because most money during tight times seems to have been swallowed up. Rather he trades for bacon, shotgun shells, an axe, which he again might barter for shoes, a frypan, a tattered army blanket somebody brought back years earlier from France. Trades never stop trading.

Wayland and his brothers help the daddy shuck the corn and twist the ears to spill kernels into the metal drum he keeps buried when not used, wrapped in heavy canvas 'til he's ready to mix and stir his mash. He fastens the lid on the drum for now but will fill it by dipping and dumping in buckets of spring water. Lacking sugar, he'll chop and add sorghum stalks that'll commence to work a quiet, bubbly fermentation. The sorghum too comes from the Ballards.

Wayland's daddy leads them through the dark back to the cabin where they climb through the window. Each night the daddy will sneak into the forest to visit the spring. When the mash is ready to fire, he'll remain for days to connect his coil, tend the fire, and fill Mason jars with drippings. He'll leave false trails to baffle those who try to track him—not only the law and hounds, but also the hobos who roam the country and camp in the woods.

Again Sheriff Calvin comes calling, this time along with a deputy. The Model A shudders to a stop before the cabin as the daddy prepares to eat an apple, the peeling dropping away in one long whorl as if of its own will from the sharpness of his Barlow blade.

"Thought you might could use this sack we found," the sheriff says, thumbing up his hat. It leaves a deep red impression across his brow. "Oh yeah, one of these days we having us a big party down to the jail."

"I always been liking parties," the daddy answers. He sits on the porch's one chair, which Ferdinand, who's handy with tools, made using lengths of cedar he split and nails he later snitched from the Ballards' equipment shed.

"Oh you particu'ly be invited," the sheriff says, spits, and ambles to the Model A. He spits a second time before driving away, rousing more dust.

Wayland's mama comes from the cabin and stares at the daddy as if blue eyes could strip off his skin. He winks and grins.

"Making thieves of our children," she says. Behind her are the boy's two sisters—Lottie and Pearl May, girls in their early teens— Lottie spare and rangy like the mother, Pearl May already heavy and not as smart, though her fingers are keen with thread and needle. The sisters have the job of tending the garden behind the cabin.

"Thieves beget thieves," the daddy says. "Them that steals gets stolen off of."

"You want them working on the road gang?" she asks.

"I want them to stand up like men," the daddy says as the peeling drops free from the apple to the porch floor.

Her eyes flay him until she wheels back to her kitchen. In the past he has hit her. He will hit her again if she unleashes her tongue too freely. Wayland hates it but believes such is the way everywheres except the big house. At the big house there's no want or need for hitting.

"Come here, son," his daddy says and motions Wayland with a sweep of his hand.

Wayland crosses to him. The father's overalls smell of the woods, smoke, and sweat.

"Us Garnetts has always kept it going," he says. "We been in wars down with General Joe Johnson. We been in fire, flood, and drought. We been in the land of the empty belly, but we always kept it going. I can guarantee you as long as this old world lasts, they'll be Garnetts. You remember. Keeping it going's in your blood."

five

Eighteen miles back Wayland had turned off the dazzling new four-lane highway to gas up at a sun-speckled superette where a gristmill once stood. The mill had vanished, and an Amoco sign rose forty feet above rows of glittering pumps and stainless steel vending machines. No mules now, no wagons hauling wheat, barley, oats, or leaf tobacco but snarling trucks that had more power under the hoods than a hundred teams.

As he rounded a tight curve the Ballards' store took shape, what remained of it still standing at the fork called Jericho Crossroads. The building had partly tumbled down as well as been climbed over by creeper, honeysuckle, and poison oak. Weather had honed and the sun baked all paint from the plank siding. The porch's rusted tin overhang beneath which tenants gathered evenings to sit and swap stories had collapsed.

Wayland's stomach tightened as he remembered and pictured a November day there. He gripped the wheel as if the Sedan de Ville were trying to turn aside and bolt free of him . . .

. . . and Mr. Henry Ballard who Wayland sees close up at the store on election day. The Ballards not only own the store, they issue private money, scrip, so if you deal with them, you take your change in their paper and wooden coins and are bound by it to return. The scrip's printed in Philadelphia, and a fierce green eagle, wings outstretched, soars over a golden field of flourishing tobacco ready to be pulled.

White folks get time off from the Ballard fields and sawmill to hike to the store and mark their ballots. Mr. Luther Blackburn operates the store. His grainy skin is rutted, and seemingly he has no eyelids 'til he blinks. That act startles and makes Wayland want to step back as if from a wind.

Mr. Blackburn wears a white apron over a white shirt buttoned at the collar. He never rolls up his sleeves during the blaze of summer when the pine boughs droop as if grieving and hounds lie panting in whatever shade that can be sought out. He parts his white hair in the middle so precisely it looks as if it's been axed in place.

On election day he climbs a ladder to set the American flag in the bracket over the store's steps. Mr. Blackburn rarely speaks, and when he does his voice sounds like it's about to seize up from rust and in need of a squirt of oil.

He knows his customers, those who pay on time and others who are owing and will be penalized by interest added to their accounts. It's said Mr. Luther can see into the pockets of all who enter the store and judge to a penny how much each is able to spend. He's a patient man because he's certain all customers will meet their due bills eventually, one way or another, even beyond the grave.

He has also tacked up the ELECTION sign on a porch post. No candidate posters are displayed. Mr. Henry Ballard is a Democrat and who isn't? He serves in the General Assembly as well as entertains the governor at Bellepays. Bird-hunting senators are guests, and Mr. Henry's picture appears in the *Times-Dispatch* standing with other prominent men alongside smiling President Franklin D. Roosevelt on the front steps of the capitol building in Richmond.

Mr. Henry arrives at the store in his LaSalle sedan driven by Black Amos. November's hot and still, and he wears his white shoes, white suit, and black-banded Panama hat. Though short and becoming portly, his posture remains militarily erect, and when he walks among those he calls "my people," they appear to compress and he to grow.

He greets them by name. He's up-to-date on accounts, and his people are aware he bears that knowledge. He asks about wives, who don't vote, as well as their kin and infants. To the gawking chaps he passes out cherry suckers usually sold two for a penny and are displayed protected from flies in a gallon glass jar that has a large screw-on top.

Wayland receives a sucker and speaks his thanks. He does not look into Mr. Henry's face or eyes. He fears them. He sees only as high as a silver belt buckle that has letters entwined on it he don't yet understand how to make out. He's never heard of English script.

Mr. Henry walks from the porch into the store. Wayland's daddy opens the screen door for him. The daddy's name is in the ledger.

"Just once in my life I'd like to be off that goddam book," Wayland has heard his daddy shout.

"Sign on with Mr. Wesley Rudd," the mother tells him.

"That don't get you off. You just dig yourself deeper and deeper 'til you can't see no more sky."

"You can't eat sky," she says.

Mr. Henry stops and turns back to look at the daddy. Mr. Ballard is not greatly disturbed by the puny thievery. He knows that in the end, one way or the other, he'll prevail. He allows himself a smile.

"You voting right, Larkin?"

"I'm with you, Mr. Henry," the daddy answers, and Wayland sees the bobbing bend, the subservience his daddy can't control, an inability to stand straight eye-to-eye in the presence of the other man, though hating his body's submission, shamed by it.

"Figured you would be," Mr. Henry says and laughs, causing other men to join him, requiring it as if commanded. He continues on into the store where salt-cured hams hang from ceiling beams and deer heads with sad, dusty glass eyes have been mounted. Shelves hold tools, harness, canned goods, and fabrics the women can buy to make they dresses.

At the center of the room is an iron stove set in a box of sand and flued through the ceiling. The men spit onto the sand, though not Mr. Ballard who smokes cigarettes during the day and, Emmett says, cigars at night inside the big house.

Mr. Henry walks to his desk at the rear of the store, a rolltop set sideways to the front entrance. No chair has been placed beside it for men to sit, talk in leisurely fashion, and waste Mr. Henry's presence.

They stand passively, hats removed, as he opens his ledger at settling-up time and traces down spidery written names, his clean stubby finger sliding along the ink that holds the threat of judgment. Always on election days he examines the ledger to remind his people what is due. The land holds them no matter what their color, and Mr. Henry Ballard one way or another owns that too.

The boy watches his daddy take his turn at the desk. Mr. Henry leans back in a chair that squeaks like a shriek of pain. He holds a black Parker fountain pen. He hasn't removed his hat. His pale green eyes narrow, and his expression tightens.

"You still behind, Larkin," he says. "Been a while since you put anything down in the book. And I been paying your poll tax."

"I'm working on it, Mr. Henry. Things turning 'round for me."

"I know what's turning," Mr. Henry says, and again causes laughter among the other men. "What goes in corn turns out lightning."

"Not me, Mr. Henry. Whoever told that about me's lying."

"Sure, Larkin, I know you'd never dip your fingers into anything that'd soil them. I'm surprised you didn't grow up a preacher."

More laughter. The daddy takes it, the bend still in his spine, both hands holding to his hat, blood coloring the back of his neck.

"Now if you can't put a little something down by the end of the month, I recommend you report to Mr. Rudd and work off your debt. I'm certain Mr. Rudd can find something for you."

"Yes, sir," the daddy says. "If things don't turn better, I surely will do that thing."

"End of the month, Larkin. Got me?"

The boy sees the hardness under Mr. Henry's pinkish flesh, a firming as if a resting creature has stirred beneath his skin. His gaze focuses, and his eyeballs seem to enlarge and to send out the light rather than take it in.

"Yes, sir, Mr. Henry," the daddy says, his fingers crimping his hat brim.

"Good then," Mr. Henry says, leans forward, and makes marks in the ledger. "I got your word."

The daddy knows he's dismissed. He turns, blood flushing his face. He moves to vote at the counter where Mr. Luther Blackburn passes out the ballots and watches where the Xs are marked. The daddy doesn't look at those men he passes but walks rigidly out the screen door and down the steps.

Wayland follows silently. Away from the store and along the road his daddy slouches. Then he straightens as if each stride is a pounding to hammer the curve from his back. At the side of he road he snatches up dirt in both hands and flings it at the sky.

"What kind of God You be to do this to a man?" he shouts into the disturbed dust.

six

Once the Ballards' store had been not only the center of a community but also appeared to Wayland to be the wagon hub of the world. Had he looked at a map of the entire United States, he would've expected to find Jericho Crossroads located right smack dab in the middle with all other life extending out in spokes.

"Getting you to talk about your boyhood is like pulling teeth," Amy had said to him, slim in her black exercise tights as she stretched to her toes and did kneebends in sync with the TV's musical aerobics program.

"A simple rural life, not much to report," he'd answered and looked out the French doors to gulls floating with bosomy unconcern on the slight chop of the tropical blue bay. A white yacht maneuvered among buoys of the intercoastal. His own forty-foot Morgan bumped softly against padded piles of his dock. Amy was a much better and bolder sailor than he.

"I'm sorry," she'd said. "That was very insensitive of me."

They had driven from Fort Lauderdale to Decatur, Georgia, and their daughter Jennifer's graduation from Agnes Scott. Amy had worn a lemon-colored linen suit and a pale pink silk scarf. Though nineteen years younger than he, she fretted about wrinkles spreading upward along her neck and out from her eyes and the corners of her mouth.

A warm early June evening, they had nibbled Brie and cold boiled shrimp on the college's emerald lawn. Tuxedoed musicians played Schubert's "Trout" Quintet under candy-striped tents. Jennifer and other seniors, each holding a lighted white candle, sang the college hymn on steps of a columned mansion, their faces aglow in nimbuses of flames that made them appear spiritually devotional. Above shadows fluttered as if alive and reaching down for them.

Never in Amy's or Jennifer's lives had they witnessed squealing hogs cut and butchered, felt hot spurting blood, or slung slimy intestines into the dented galvanized tub dragged from the shed behind the cabin. Wayland had cleaned guts, funneled well water into snaky sections and squeezed them inch by inch to milk them down and free them of lodged feces. Not soap but time alone wore the stink off him.

He had needed to explain to both Amy and Jennifer just exactly what chitlins were when his daughter read about them in an assigned book at Agnes Scott.

"Ugh, you actually ate those things?" Jennifer had asked.

"Not me, but the poor folk considered them fine in the mouth," Wayland had lied.

"Poor folk, not folks?" Amy had asked.

"You could usually tell by the way they talked," Wayland had said.

"Gross, intestines fried in hog lard," Jennifer had said and looked at her mother. They had made faces.

So much they didn't know . . .

. . . about Wayland, his brothers, the daddy, and Lonnie Tyler hunkered under the hackberry. Each looks at the ground. Ferdinand uses a twig to draw circles within circles in the dust. They do not raise their heads at the scream.

"Need rain," Emmett says. He's barefoot, no shirt, and his skin catches a weak gleam from fading yellowish light of the sinking day. He swats skeeters. Ridges of lumpy muscles flex along his tanned arms. Though he works at the Ballard stable, he's never ridden anything except a plow mule.

"Always rains," the daddy says, and again they hear the scream, yet don't acknowledge it.

The locusts are quieting, the gloaming absorbing their plaints and reducing them to a weltering purr except for a few last screeches along the low grounds. Wayland absently picks their fragile husks off the scabby trunk of the hackberry and spits on a finger to wipe over and shine their empty eye sockets.

A new moon rises as they wait. Kerosene lamps have been lit in the cabin, and shadows of the women move beyond the open door and windows. Those shadows slide quickly across walls. There are sibilant voices, the words not fully shaped, utterances which have no entrances or exits.

Reb lies close to Wayland. When anyone speaks, his tail flops up dust. The boy pinches ticks off the hound's ears. A fat, heavy one's attached to the dog's sagging lower lip. Wayland squashes the tick between his thumb and index finger and cleans the blood off by dragging his hand across the ground.

Talking stops, and they stare along the lane. Lonnie Tyler sighs and bows his head to his arms that rest across his knees. He's married Pearl May, Wayland's younger sister. She's fourteen. Supporting her as she listed and stumbled, Lonnie has brought her to the cabin and given her over to Wayland's mama.

Slim, tall Lonnie is sixteen and has quit school to work the Ballards' dark-fired tobacco. He checks temperature as he tends smoldering hickory fires burning on the floors of the curing barns. His fingers test for moisture in tied leaf hung drooping from sticks laid in rows across rafters. He has a deep knowledge of tobacco passed on to him by his daddy. He sleeps little 'til the crop is right for the Danville market.

The wedding happened fast, a Saturday afternoon, the bride and groom gathered at the Healing Spring Baptist Church. There were no guests, and footsteps resounded in the frame building's near emptiness. Pearl May, close to weeping, hung her head and kept her glances lowered. Lonnie appeared dumbstruck and uncertain of his whereabouts.

Preacher Ernest Arbogast raised his long veined hands over the new altar he'd fashioned out of sawmill pine donated by the Ballards and coated white with oil-base house paint.

"Lord God," he called with his eyes clenched and face drawn tight as if he strained to lift a great weight, "bless these children of Yours as they set their feet on the path of holy matrimony. May they hold fast to Thy righteous ways and thwart Satan's snares that wait in ambush at every turn for all us human beings."

After the ceremony they ate cracklings and slices of cake Wayland's mama has hurriedly baked, an angel food set on the tree stump behind the church, it a narrow, single-story clapboard structure that has been whitewashed, the roof tarpaper, an iron bell in its rickety steeple that had edged off plumb.

Wayland's daddy cut the cake with the Barlow frog sticker he always carried in his right-hand pants pocket where it would be close and quick to his fingers. He wiped the blade clean first on the heel of a hand. There being no plates, slices were balanced on leveled palms. They drank water pumped from the well where a tin dipper hung from a loop of fencing wire.

The Tylers had brought nothing. They stood apart and left as soon as Preacher Arbogast's words were pronounced. Icing stuck to Lonnie's lips. He wore his dark woolly Sunday suit, Pearl May a yellow bonnet tied under her chin and a calico dress buttoned at the collar. She wiped his mouth with her handkerchief as she tried to smile, and her eyes shimmered.

She and Lonnie walked off hand in hand down the winding dusty road to a Ballard tenant house. Arrangements had been made with Mr. Wesley Rudd about rent. They owned a bed, a stove, a chair.

Wayland's daddy has gone to see the Tylers. Hard words got spoken. The daddy drew the frog sticker, and Mr. Tyler sidled to the corner of the kitchen where he keeps his shotgun propped. Mrs. Tyler grabbed and hugged him, stayed between the men, and used her bitter tongue to drive off Wayland's daddy.

"Them Tylers think they something," Wayland has heard his daddy tell his mama. " 'Cause they got that Model T that won't run half the time. Just sitting in the yard for chickens to scratch around and nest in."

"Lonnie's a nice boy," the mama said. "He works hard."

"Oh nice as pie slipping around with Pearl May in the bushes and singing loud in the church. They acting like it was Pearl May, like she oughten to bear the blame."

"Blame don't get into it. The Lord God works it out. Like with you and me and Emmett who was borned of it. Nobody ever had a finer son."

"Nobody ever had to come catch me neither. I coulda run, but I wanted you. And after you and me stood before the preacher man, ever'body ate the cake and drank the lemonade."

"More than lemonade. You was so drunk I had to throw a bucket of water on you. Well, I got a pot and pan for them to start a kitchen."

❧

Under the hackberry Wayland's daddy is first to raise his face and again peer into darkness. Ferdinand and Emmett lift their eyes. Lonnie still bows his head to his arms. Wayland sees the figure take shape—Aunt Lulu, the black midwife who's ancient and humpbacked. She has crossed among the pines. She's bound her head in a white cloth and carries her satchel. As she passes the hackberry, she doesn't answer the daddy's greeting but enters the cabin as if no one has spoken.

They wait. The shrill of locusts has been replaced by crickets and tree toads rousing to fill the night with a pulsating cadence. The tree toads bring the promise of rain.

"Seen a gang of turkeys feeding through the lespedeza," Ferdinand says. He's no hunter, has never taken to the gun. He puts this information out for the benefit of Emmett and the daddy, knowing it will please them.

"Plenty of turkey and squirrel but rabbits is scarce," the daddy says.

"Hawks," Emmett says. "Too many hawks."

"Some without feathers," the daddy says.

A sob and wail from the house. The women's shadows move more swiftly. Unearthly light from the kerosene lamps splays into darkness where it exhausts itself.

Another scream. Except for Lonnie the men don't move. He stiffens, yet never looks toward the cabin. Wayland tries to ape his daddy's and brothers' unconcern. He stares at the ground and mentions bear tracks seen by field hands near the river.

"They's always bears," the daddy says. "Come up from the swamps. They see you, but you don't see them."

"I never et of the meat," Emmett says.

"Strong and greasy," the daddy says. "But good for the blood."

Another scream, this one longer and louder. For a moment it halts the night sounds. Then the crickets and toads seep into and fill the silence. A whippoorwill tunes up.

The screams come more rapidly, shorter, more abject. Lottie walks out on the porch, then crosses back inside and lets the screen ease to. Wayland sees tears on Lonnie's face, which catches a moist gleam from the kerosene lamps.

"I met a bear face to face oncet," the daddy says. "Down to the mill race I was walking along the path where it bends to the pond, and here come the bear. We stopped and just stood there looking at each other. Then we both turned and run."

"How come you didn't shoot him?" Emmett asks.

"Didn't have no rifle along."

"You was in the woods, wont you?" Emmett says and snickers. The daddy has taught them never to enter the woods without carrying a gun.

"I was aiming to fish," the daddy says.

"Shoulda jabbed him with your pole," Emmett says.

"I wouldn't mind being a bear," Ferdinand says. "Eat all summer, sleep all winter. Way I see it, bears have it good."

" 'Til they make somebody a fur coat," the daddy says.

More screams and sobs. Lonnie has turned his face away from the cabin. The shadows rush, and the white agitated light flickers. The screaming breaks off of a sudden. Quiet is followed by a small different cry.

The daddy, brothers, and Lonnie slowly stand. They shake Lonnie's hand and slap him on the back and shoulders. Wayland touches him too. Reb's tail wags. Lonnie grins weakly and totters toward the house. The light from the doorway causes his shadow to shorten behind him on the ground.

The baby stops crying. Wayland's mother brings it out wrapped in a towel. She shows it to Lonnie, doesn't allow him to hold it, then carries it back inside the cabin. Through the windows the pace of action slackens.

"Got me a split tail," Lonnie announces.

The daddy steps behind the hackberry and returns. He has collected many jars from the Ballards' pit. This one he holds held sweet pickles before being emptied in the big house and tossed on the smoldering heap.

After unscrewing the cap, he passes it to Lonnie. Lonnie sniffs of it, drinks, and says "Who-ee." He gives the jar back to the daddy who helps himself to a swig and hands it to Emmett.

"Fire in the blood," Emmett says after swallowing.

Ferdinand lifts the jar. He don't want to drink but understands good manners means he's required to. Wayland's allowed a sip. The liquor burns all the way down his throat to his belly and glows there like a hot coal. He's breathless and tries not to gag. His mouth opens, his tongue licks out. It's all he can do not to run to the well for water. They laugh and poke at him.

"Get a hose pipe," the daddy calls.

"Steam blowing from his ears," Emmett says.

"Burn warts off a hog," Lonnie says.

Emmett, the daddy, and Lonnie drink. Ferdinand smiles, but he turns the white liquor aside. He's a quiet brother. Despite the withered leg, he's risen to doing most of the maintenance work on the Ballards' farm machinery. Mr. Wesley Rudd says that Ferdinand was born with a wrench in his hand.

The daddy's jew's harp lifts and fits to his mouth. He plays "Ole Dan Tucker." Lonnie and Emmett dance, their feet disturbing dust that spirals in the kerosene light. Wayland too stomps out a hoedown. Reb circles and barks. Emmett hoots and hollers.

Aunt Lulu leaves, again without speaking. Wayland's mother steps out on the porch. His daddy stops playing but doesn't move toward the cabin to extend the jar to her. He knows she won't drink of it.

She speaks Lonnie's name, and her voice carries a note. The daddy lowers the hand holding the jew's harp. Emmett sets both feet on the ground, and Reb's tail stills. Lonnie stands in front of the mother and listens as she speaks. She hugs him before going back inside. He looks after her, the intense white light shining through the doorway making his skin appear white as leprosy.

They bury the baby the next evening in the Healing Spring Baptist Church cemetery—no marble or granite marker but a slab of fieldstone that will be set upright in the ground.

The baby wrapped in a white cotton cloth is so tiny she hardly fills a shoebox. Preacher Ernest Arbogast lifts the box to the Lord, his hands raised as if the baby is an offering on his upturned palms. Neighbor women weep and keen. The men have removed their hats. Lonnie holds Pearl May to keep her from sinking. Her eyes closed, she moans. The Tylers do not attend the service.

Ferdinand plants the scoured stone. It's been plowed up and heaved to the side of a Ballard field. There are many stones, and it's the custom to save the flat ones that can be used. The Ballards don't object.

Ferdinand writes on the name, date, and saying. He has a fine hand with a brush as well as tools. He dips into the bucket of white house paint left over from putting a second coat on the reverend's new altar:

Baby Ellen

July 7, 1936

God Wanted Her

So Bad He Took

Her Early

seven

ayland saw a truck pull from the woods ahead and turn toward him. It was a banged-up, filthy GMC loaded with timber, and he recognized the logs as red oak. Taught by his daddy, he'd been able to walk through the woods and name every kind of tree that grew in Howell County.

The two black men in the cab returned his wave as the truck passed by, wobbling under its burden and leaving tracks on the asphalt, though the land was dry. They must've loaded up in the wet low ground. He hoped they'd get a fair price for their haul.

He'd felled lots of timber in his day, back then using a crosscut saw and a double-bladed axe because no chainsaws were owned during that time even by the Ballards. After hot flaying work in the woods when he was almost eaten up by greenies, he'd gone to the river, stripped down, and splashed around in the cooling water like a hound seeking relief after a run.

Water made him again think of Amy and the full gainer she'd performed at Fort Lauderdale's city pool. He'd observed she had a daily swimming schedule but not discovered her name. Each afternoon she'd arrived slim and tan, changed into a sleek black latex bathing suit, and swum laps to loosen up before climbing the high board. She'd arched off the board, and the sun glazed her lithe body, which for a moment seemed to defy gravity before knifing the blue water and creating hardly enough splash to fill a teacup.

Wayland had asked the lifeguard about her and learned her name and that she worked at a realty firm on Broward Boulevard. Under the pretense of wanting a property listing, he'd entered the sunny office decorated with hibiscus growing from red outsized ceramic urns.

While talking on a telephone and nibbling a yellow pencil, Amy had lounged in a leather desk chair. Her ash blond hair was cut short, and her sleeveless white blouse set off the lengths of her smoothly muscled swimmer's arms. She touched an earring, which was a lacquered coquina shell, and turned to the counter to find him staring.

"Help you?" she asked and tipped the chair forward.

She held the phone at her breasts. He felt unable to speak, shook his head and left, yet still took time off from his office to spy on her at the pool. Not only was he awkward around women but even a little fearful. He rehearsed opening remarks to her like, "Excuse me, Miss, I don't know how to get myself introduced to you except by just stopping you and telling you my name and hoping you'll tell me yours."

She beat him to it. He nearly bumped into her along the dank corridor that led to the locker rooms. She was rubbing her wet hair with a yellow towel, and beads of water along her body made her skin glisten.

"Mister, you think I don't know you been hanging around eyeballing me? Now just what's your problem?"

"My problem is I think I love you," he said, the words this time taking charge with no forethought from him.

"Oh, Lord, deliver me," she said and laughed as she dabbed at wetness along her thighs, which were goose-bumped. "Tell me it's for my mind, not my body."

"I got to start somewhere," he said.

"You were at the office."

"It's like an affliction," he said.

Again she laughed and snapped her towel at his ankle as she passed on by. She called back to him, "You're telling me I'm an affliction . . ."

". . . is the Lord God's way of herding His children to righteous living," Preacher Ernest Arbogast calls out over the pulpit of the Healing Spring Baptist Church. "Affliction and suffering are His message to man he can't stand alone. The proud and stiff-necked will be smited, their backs bent, their cries for mercy and grace sound into the swallowing darkness."

To Wayland affliction seems a daily chore. He works in the Ballard fields where drinking water is supplied in twenty-gallon wooden casks carried down from the big house on a wagon pulled by mules.

It is Ballard water, during early mornings still chilled from being pumped from Bellepays's deep well, and it tastes of the casks' splintery oak staves. That well doesn't run dry even during droughts so lasting that every breath drawn is invaded by dust that rasps the throat and clogs the nose.

The casks are unloaded along the way, the last two left on the wagon unhitched under willows that grow close to the river. Despite the shade the sun's rays seep through and steal the water's coolness. The enlarging heat dries condensation on the iron bands, and by noon a drink brings only fleeting relief to parched throats and panting tongues.

The casks sit on separate ends of the wagon. From each hangs a tin dipper, one for whites, the other for coloreds. No field hand need be instructed which dipper to reach for. Knowing is like knowledge in the blood.

Except for burrhead Josephus Blodgett. Wayland has seen him eyeing the casks. Josephus's blackness sinks deeper and deeper as if he's layered in wraps of it. Strong and heavily shouldered, he's several times bumped Wayland in narrowing passages of the drainage ditches. Blades of their hoes clang like swords clashing.

"Debbil down, Debbil down," Josephus chants. "Black man hoe, white man slow."

"Black man brag, white man drag," Wayland answers. "You best not swallow what your eyes has been drinking."

"Water got no color. Same down the gullet."

"You know why you black?" Wayland asks as he drags dock weeds aside. "When you made, God forgot to wash you off."

"You know why you white? God figure you ain't worth a coat of paint."

Wayland resents being put into ditches alongside the darkies. He believes they oughten not be assigned by Mr. Wesley Rudd to the same fields. Yet Josephus is a good worker. Side by side they rhythmically and in tandem chop the weeds and wild grass, each not allowing the other to move ahead and show himself better with his hoe.

"That's how the Ballards and Mr. Wesley Rudd fix it," Wayland's daddy has said. "Get us going head to head with the niggers and squeeze the last drop of sweat and blood out of both. The Ballards sit up in the big house around that table loaded with silver and figure it out. Talk about us like we stock in the pens."

Josephus drops his hoe and climbs from the ditch to cross to the wagon for a drink. He cuts his eyes around as he stands under the stringing willow boughs, and from the white-man cask snakes down the dipper to hold under the wooden spigot. He drinks fast, spits, and rehangs the dipper.

When he swaggers back, he's smiling. He believes nobody's seen. His sweat and teeth glitter.

"I be telling Mr. Wesley Rudd," Wayland says.

"You telling what?"

"Your black mouth been on the white dipper. I telling Mr. Wesley Rudd we need a clean one."

"My mouth clean as yours."

"You a son of Ham and cursed. Preacher Arbogast tells it's in the Book."

"White preacher tell it."

"You made for dark, to hide in the night."

"You belong under a rotten log like them white bugs never seen the light."

"You a nigger."

"You white trash."

They throw down their hoes and spring at each other—fists swinging, arms flailing until they stumble, fall, and roll along the ditch. The fight draws other hands who have straightened to watch.

Wayland breaks loose from Josephus, and they stand to circle up from the ditch to the field. He tries to get a hold on black skin so slick there's no grip to be had. His fingers slip off Josephus's short wiry hair. They grapple, struggle to throw each other to the ground, and tumble back into the ditch. Blood squirts from Josephus's nose, and Wayland tastes it as they knee, kick, and bite. He spits and wonders whether he's poisoned by nigger blood.

They back off as they realize Mr. Wesley Rudd is approaching across the field. He is as unhurried as a man out for a Sunday stroll, his hightop black shoes setting down with a methodical swing of the legs, his face partially shaded by the brim of his fedora.

Wayland and Josephus wait. Soil and weed clippings stick to their bloodiness. Flies seek the blood. Mr. Wesley Rudd pauses, gazes at them, and slowly scratches his neck.

"Finish it," he says, his voice easy like he's passing the time of day, yet the words are a command.

Again Wayland and Josephus fight, this time beside the ditch, which edges oats nigh ripe enough to be threshed. Blood, grain, and dust coat their bodies. Not only boys holding hoes but also older field hands gather to watch. They line up along the ditch, the coloreds one side, whites on the other. No one speaks. Mr. Wesley Rudd calmly nurses his tobacco cud, which bulges a cheek to an apple-like shine.

Wayland feels himself giving out. His arms become so heavy he can just lift them, and he totters. Josephus too falters. They stop hitting and lurch about rassling, then stagger, collapse, and release. They lie heaving. Wayland tastes vomit mixed with his own blood.

"Had enough?" Mr. Wesley Rudd asks.

"Up to him," Wayland gasps, pushing to an elbow.

"Up to him too," Josephus says, rising to a knee.

"On your feet," Mr. Wesley Rudd says.

They sway as they right themselves and stand. Each swipes at the flies hungry for blood.

"Get at it again," Mr. Wesley Rudd says.

They fight but are drained and no longer hurt one another. Their fists sweep too slow and aimlessly to inflict punishment. They hold on, droop, crawl, feebly strike out. They pant and gape. The blood drips, and the flies spiral to resettle.

"All right, wash up," Mr. Wesley Rudd orders. "Rest of you back to earning your pay."

Wayland and Josephus reel along the ditch to the river. They unhook shoulder straps and let their Big Boy overalls slide down over their hips and legs. They flop into the sluggishly flowing brown stream.

The water soothes their hurt. They sit in shallows and splash their bodies. Disturbed crows fly up cawing from scaly birches, and a heron squawks and flaps up, its shadow tracing the course of the river.

The river carries off dust, sweat, and blood. Wayland pukes and watches the yellow excretion spread and float away. Josephus touches a flap of a torn ear. He dips his face in the water, sucks up a mouthful, sprays it out.

"You still a nigger," Wayland says.

"You still white trash," Josephus says.

"Reckon Mr. Wesley Rudd dock us?"

"Lessen we get a hoe in the hand," Josephus says.

They rise dripping, fling water from their nakedness, and climb the bank. They shake out and pull on their overalls. Their hoes lie in the ditch, and they take them up. The sun burns not yellow or red but a high molten white. Wayland, his eyesight clouded, keeps dropping his hoe and battles letting down as he chops poisoned oak tangled with Johnson grass. Josephus shuffles as if he's an old man and his feet won't lift off the ground.

They make it through the afternoon. Mr. Wesley Rudd don't dock them. As they leave, he sits in his office doorway fanning his face with the fedora.

"Happen again and you gone," he says.

eight

Wayland drove in silence past a scattering of unpainted cabins set back deep among the dusty pines. Colored children stopped their play and stood motionless to peer at his car. They never knew what good or bad the road might bring them.

As he drew closer to the home place, his stomach felt unsettled, and he realized his palms were moist. He became angry at himself. What did he have to fear or be ashamed of? He'd established a substantial business in hydraulic presses, married a classy loving woman, fathered a beautiful daughter, built a Mediterranean-style four-bedroom house on the Florida intercoastal, and moored that Morgan named *Pilgrim* to a piling of his own dock.

He wasn't the same person who had left Howell County, Virginia, forty-seven years ago. He could stand tall, knock on any man's door, meet him eye to eye. He'd shaken a Florida governor's hand and been invited to the inaugural ball for which he bought and wore tails. He and Amy played golf at El Cielo, an exclusive country club with two eighteen-hole courses, an Olympic-size pool, and a ballroom lighted by a dozen chandeliers.

He glanced to his left where a horse stood dozing and soaking up sun, its head hung over a honeysuckle-tangled barbed wire fence that surrounded a thin pasture—an old roan long in the tooth and forsaken by the plow, the animal's coat dull and mangy. Maybe it remembered or dreamed of another time when its blood still ran hot and encroaching tractors were not on their way to conquering all . . .

. . . the land he and Willie Meekems leave Saturday afternoon after Mr. Wesley Rudd blows his whistle to signal they are finished work 'til Monday morning.

"They gonna do it today," Willie tells Wayland. Willie's red hair has a natural curl and sticks in ringlets to the gummy sweat of his freckled brow.

"Do what?" Wayland asks his friend.

"The thing with the horses. My Uncle Allan fixed it with Amos Feathers. Heard them settling the deal at the stable. Amos coming to bring his mare."

As they walk up the loamy slope from the bottom, Wayland wonders whether he can break away from home. His mama likely wants him to help Lottie work the garden or split stove wood. Willie keeps talking to him about the horses, and Wayland's interested but can't get it exactly fixed right in his mind.

"I'll try to sneak off," he says.

"I'll be looking for you at the head of Uncle Allan's lane," Willie calls back while they take different paths at the fork in the road, and he moves away in long, looping country strides.

Wayland's mama's boiling clothes behind the cabin—a ring of fieldstones contains the fire and supports the black kettle. She pokes his daddy's roiling overalls with a broken, bleached length of broomstick. The lye soap bubbles and churns up brown. Reb lies watching, his tail flopping at sight of Wayland.

"What you and Willie up to?" she asks, studying Wayland out of her gentian blue eyes.

"Just messing 'round," he says as he draws up a bucket of water from the well. Washing his face, neck, and arms keeps him from having to confront those eyes that he sometimes feels are able to pry all the way into to his skull and finger his thinking.

"Messing 'round sometimes leads to mess," she says.

"We might set us a fish trap in the river," he says. It's not exactly a lie. He and Willie have done so before and could again this afternoon, though it's unlikely. Still the answer has at least a chance of being the truth.

"Want you back here by supper," she says, again punching the overalls. Steam has strung her brown hair straight. She pushes it back, but it swings forward. "You hearing me?"

"Yes'm."

He doesn't allow himself to run 'til he's beyond sight of the cabin. Wildcat Creek is three miles away even taking the shortcuts over Ballard land. He don't have a watch but figures time from the sun as his daddy has taught him. Wayland thinks of what Willie has claimed: "Hit's a big show and it's free."

The late afternoon's burning hot as Wayland jogs across cutover woods grown up with briars and broom straw. Beggar lice cling to his overalls, and the brushing touch of a bull thistle prickles a finger. He stops to suck at it.

A good thing because a shiny writhing copperhead coils at a tree stump, its forked tongue flicking at him. He circles the snake, but then his foot dislodges laps and disturbs a yellow jacket nest. He runs swatting at them and using the cuss words he and Willie has practiced when nobody's around to hear. Cussing, they believe, requires thought and training.

Wildcat Creek is nearly dried up. He dabs mud on the yellow-jacket stings. During early spring the gigging's been good, but the frogs has had to move down closer to the river. On the other side of the creek is land belonging to Willie Meekems's Uncle Allan.

Uncle Allan is considered lucky. He got himself gassed over in France in 1918 and wheezes like a steam engine if he walks more than a dozen steps. The government pays him a pension so he don't have to work if he don't feel like it. There's lots of men around Howell County that would count the wheezing a good tradeoff if they could make a deal from it.

Uncle Allan owns eighty-two acres of land all paid for, a board-and-batten house painted white, and is able to hire help to keep his fences in repair. He owns cattle, hogs, a mule, and also a Clydesdale bought at a farm auction in Tobaccoton. He's no lover of fine horses like the Ballards, but figures the Clydesdale's an investment that will return his cost and make him a profit from the ten-dollar stud fees.

Willie Meekems sits on a chestnut fence rail under a cedar tree at the head of the lane. Willie is beanpole tall and shows his tushes when he grins. He and Wayland has smoked corn silk after rolling it in old newspaper. They next tried tobacco, snitching leaf from the Ballards' rustling crop and sun curing it by flattening it with stones on roofing tin of an abandoned shed that'd half blown over during a winter wind.

They'd also chewed their first Brown's Mule together, each carving a corner section off the nickel plug and setting it in his jaw. Wayland, uncertain about how to handle the cud, choked and accidentally swallowed juice. He became so sick he feared he'd die. It was worse than overeating crabapples, and he pulled his knees up against his stomach to ease the pain.

"You honest-to-god has turned green," Willie had said to Wayland as Wayland sprawled retching on the riverbank.

As Willie shifts off the fence rail, a black Hupmobile rolls down the lane from the house. Driving is Uncle Allan's wife Miss Thelma Dawn and beside her the widowed mother Miss Linda Sue. The car stops beside them.

"What you boys doing here?" Uncle Allan's wife asks. She has sagging doughy cheeks and a small set mouth. Her white-haired mother peers around her.

"Just messing," Willie says.

"Mess somewheres else or I'll tell your ma."

"We going down to the river," Willie says.

"See that you do," Uncle Allan's wife says.

The Hupmobile, the only one in the county, drives on and turns at the head of the lane in the direction of Tobaccoton. Willie spits and winks. They've both worked on their winking and can use either eye.

"They always go to town when Hector does his job," Willie says.

"Hector?"

"Uncle Allan's Clydesdale. Come on. Just act like you got business 'round here."

They start along the cedar-hung lane toward the house. A Model T clatters by, slows, and backs up. Driving is Mr. Randal Fenton, a barber, coffin maker, mailman, and deacon at the Healing Spring Baptist Church. He's so skinny you can hardly see him when he turns sideways.

"You boys get on away from here now," he says and scowls at them 'til they turn and walk back to the road. He then rolls on toward the house.

"We got to do some circling around to the barn," Willie says.

They hurry along the road to woods at the corner of Uncle Allan's property where Willie climbs the fence and Wayland follows. They move among pines 'til they reach barbed wire strung along a pasture spotted with cow pies Uncle Allan's Guernseys has dropped. They duck through the wire, and Willie leads as they run hunched among the staring cattle. The land dips to an acre pond that has a skim of algae on it. Willie studies the barn set on the rise behind the house.

"Just keep low," he says.

They skirt the pond. A bullfrog plops in, causing the algae to part and close over it. Orchard grass has been grazed down to hard clumps. A mule watches them, and a flock of cowbirds scatter, their wings a whispering.

They approach the plank barn from the rear. It is weathered, has settled to one side, and is no longer used for stock but just the storing of hay. Wayland and Willie stand puffing and feeling the sun's heat reflecting off the planks before gathering themselves to sneak past the silo to a feed bin under the rusted tin overhang. They climb over the bin and up a ladder to the loft.

Pigeons roosting among trusses flap out through broken ventilation louvers. Willie kicks and highsteps through loose hay to the front of the barn. The loft door's latched closed by a twist of baling wire through a hasp, but they can look between gaps in planks toward the white stable, which has a red roof.

Men are collecting about. They stand in shade of a persimmon tree talking and smoking. Uncle Allan wears rubber boots, a cowboy hat, and uses a cane. He moves slow, saving every breath he can as if air's money in the bank.

Others arrive, a few in Model Ts, buggies, some on foot. They greet each other, shake hands, spit. They having fun like at a church social or barbecue.

"Here come Amos Feathers," Willie says.

Amos Feathers, who holds a railroad job, rides his piebald mare bareback. The toes of his brogans hang nearly to dust of the lane. He resets his brakeman's cap, dismounts, and the men make way for him as he crosses leading the piebald to Uncle Allan. The animal is skittish, stomps, bends away. Amos Feathers jerks the bridle.

He and Uncle Allan talk, and Amos draws the mare to the near side of the stable where two sawed sections of a creosoted power pole set deep in the ground are crossed by a third cut which has been bolted through at the ends to form a strong hitching rail.

Amos Feathers stands holding his piebald there. She walls her eyes and kicks back, though nothing's behind her.

"She scents him," Willie says.

"Huh?" Wayland says.

From the stable a darky carrying a bucket leads out Hector. It's Josephus Blodgett's daddy, who helps Uncle Allan on the farm. The sorrel stud is heavy, huge, excited. He holds his head high, arches his thick neck, struts, and snorts.

"He's winded her too," Willie says.

Josephus's daddy leads Hector to the opposite side of the hitching rail where he sets aside the bucket. The mare rears, but Amos pulls her down. Hector whinnies, sticks his head across the rail, and bites at her stomach. She squeals and tries to twist away.

"Don't he like her?" Wayland asks.

"He's teasing her," Willie says.

"Biting's teasing?"

"Look at that thing of his. How'd you like to have one of them?"

That mottled thing is Hector's pecker, only it's too thick and long to be called just that. The word just don't cover the situation. It's an unnatural splotched pink and brown, like a swaying club, a weapon. Hector keeps leaning across to nip at the mare. Each time her rear hoofs spring off the ground. Despite the heat, she's shivering. Suddenly she shrieks, and her hind end squirts.

"What?" Wayland asks Willie.

"She's getting hot."

At a nod from Uncle Allan, Josephus's father brings Hector round to her side of the rail. Amos Feathers holds the piebald while she stands trembling. Hector wants to get at the mare. Josephus's daddy lines Hector up. The stallion's still snorting and trying to bite.

"He ain't going to put that great prong in that small mare?" Wayland asks.

"You just watch and see."

Josephus's daddy slacks off the lead line, and Hector collects to lunge onto the mare. She seems tiny, frail, and her legs give a little, yet Hector's the one that screams this time. His teeth gnash at her neck.

"Why don't she kick or bite him back?" Wayland asks.

"I tell you she likes it."

"How could anything like that?"

Josephus's daddy grabs Hector's prong and guides it. Hector hunches forward. The mare goes to her knees but recovers. Hector humps hard, still biting. He bangs the mare into the hitching rail, yet she submits. That's the thing Wayland can't figure—her just letting it happen without a fight.

Hector shoves one last time, then sort of goes slack, his head drooping, his forelegs straddled over her as if he's using them just to hold on. He slides off her rump. The mare rights herself and stands calmly, her tail swishing. Josephus lifts the bucket and tosses water onto her hind end.

"Make her close up and keep it in," Willie says.

"Keep what in?"

"The jissum he's shot into her."

"But whyn't she fight more?"

"I told you she liked it."

"Nothing could like that."

"Women does."

"They couldn't. It ain't possible."

"How you think you got borned?"

Wayland knows he's come from something secret his mama and daddy do, and he's heard them at night rustling and rattling the brass bed, but he's never been able to picture it exactly, and whatever they did to get him born could be nothing like it was with horses.

Josephus's daddy leads Hector back into the stable. The men that has gathered 'round to see what'd happened turn away smiling and laughing. Amos Feathers pays Uncle Allan and shakes his hand before throwing a long leg over the mare and riding her off down the lane.

"Some show huh?" Willie asks.

"Appears cruel to me that big lug of a horse treating that little mare that way."

"It's ever'wheres. You seen chickens doing it and dogs hopping bitches."

"People not chickens, dogs, and bitches."

"Got to be something like that. And the thing about it she whupped him. That's the way women get even with their men. She won."

"Won what?" Wayland asks and won't accept it. He's awed, a little sick, sorry he's seen, yet strangely drawn. Terrible what Hector done, yet Willie grins and points at Wayland's Big Boy overalls. Wayland turns away aware and ashamed his own pecker is hard.

"Let's go to the river and set us a fish trap," he says, feeling guilt and wanting a truthful answer to give his mama when he returns to the cabin and she set her eyes on him and starts the questions.

"Don't have no bait," Willie says.

"We can watch the buzzards and find us a piece of dead possum or coon. Catfish eat anything."

They sneak from the barn to the pond and across the pasture to the fence along the woods.

"You best not get that poke-out you still carrying caught on no wire," Willie says as they duck through.

He again points, giggles, and keeps at it, his tushes uncovered, until Wayland punches him.

"No call for that," Willie says and walks off mad. He stays that way 'til Monday when they are again chopping in the Ballard ditches.

nine

As Wayland drove, a curling rooster tail of dust pursued the Caddy. How often had he walked this route both in reality and his mind? He'd remembered the taste of Howell County dust hundreds of miles distant, once on a freezing snowy morning during the Hürtgen Forest campaign and another time as he bit into a Memphis barbecue sandwich. He and Amy had celebrated their tenth anniversary in Charleston, her favorite city, and while they'd strolled along the Battery in the sunny and sea-washed air, the taste of Howell County's dust had resurrected itself in his mouth.

"Tell me about it, the place you grew up, this Howell County," Amy had asked, a July day as they lounged on the beach, the ocean just able to mount a few swells that ended with a languid splash and a curling slide of foam across the white sand.

She was a Florida native, a rarity among all the come-heres like himself. Wayland had first felt the draw of the lush tropical land during basic training at Camp Blanding even as he endured the weight of a full fieldpack on a twenty-mile forced march among Spanish bayonets, rattlesnakes, and beneath moss hanging listlessly from stunted, twisted live oaks.

When Amy had learned he hailed from Virginia, she envisioned fox-hunting country, white plank fences, manor houses set on sloping expanses of bluegrass, belfried stables, the gleam of brass buttons, sounds of baying foxhounds, and the distant call of the huntsman's horn. If he didn't encourage her to believe that, he at least allowed it with no avowal.

Moreover he'd deceived her by telling her he'd attended the University of Virginia a year and had his education interrupted by the war. He was living in the downtown Fort Lauderdale apartment he'd just moved to—a towering white highrise that had swift elevators, underground parking, and from his living room a distant view of the glittering blue Atlantic. Gulls swept past and sometimes hovered just beyond his bedroom window.

He hated lying but felt he had to deceive Amy in order to win and keep her. It wasn't only that he was so much older but that he sensed she was uncertain about him. He would catch her eyeing him as if weighing his worth. He had become very careful of his English, attempting to see words before he spoke them to make certain he made no mistakes. He felt both she and her father were suspicious and detected the redneck in him.

She'd remained slim and compact, her posture good, her features tending to keenness, the ash-blond hair she refused to let grow out because of her love of swimming. Twice he'd feared losing her to other men—the first her bronzed diving instructor at the pool, the second a charter-boat captain whose *Buccaneer* held a seasonal record for the catch of blue marlin.

While on a selling trip to Georgia, Wayland walked the old village area of Savannah and turned into a narrow side street flanked by small shops. An antique store had a sign shaped like a frightened black cat over the doorway, and in a narrow window that needed washing stood a spinning wheel.

The shop smelled of mold and was little more than a hole in a wall housing a jumble of dusty silent clocks, pewter tableware, and iron kettles, though a grimy display case held badly tarnished pieces of silver. He leaned close to focus on a ladle, its stem gracefully curved, its flared handle etched with a faint engraving.

"May I see it?" he asked the dwarfish woman who sat on a stool, her feet hanging free like a child's. She wore a blue smock and a crocheted shawl around her shoulders, her yellowish white hair was tangled, her glasses smeared. She stroked a calico cat.

It was an effort for her to slip off the stool to the display case. She carried the cat along. Her small stubby fingers lifted out the ladle, which she set on the counter. The piece had weight, and he was able to detect the maker's hallmark on the handle's underside.

"Which means?" he asks.

"English, a London silversmith, likely Edmund Pearce," the woman said, her voice not much more than a croak, her breath smelling of chewing gum. "Brought over here after the war when people was selling out by the barrelful over there."

"How old?"

"Seventeenth century."

He wiped his thumb across the top of the handle. The entwined initials in English script were so badly worn he held it to light from the grubby window to make them out.

"Is that a *G*?" he asked, showing her the ladle.

"Appears to be," she answered and stroked the cat, who dangled limply over a chubby arm.

He placed the ladle back on the display case, thanked her, and turned to leave. *G* for Garnett, a family initial on English silver from the seventeenth century. It seemed providential. When he turned back and paid her eighty-six dollars, the woman examined the traveler's check and gave him a sly look as if they now shared a secret. He carried the ladle away not wrapped but in a brown paper bag.

He discovered the portrait at a Beaufort auction house specializing in estate sales. Just to kill time until he kept an appointment with a Buick dealer, he walked among rows of stacked furniture, oriental rugs, china, mirrors, figurines, bric-a-brac. Sticking from a pigeonhole of a scarred mahogany secretary was a rolled canvas loosely tied by a single strand of twine.

He slipped off the twine and unrolled the flimsy torn portrait of a Confederate wearing a gray uniform with braided cuffs and a high collar. His black leather belt supported a holstered revolver, and his long hands cupped themselves over an ornate saber guard. He had long reddish brown hair, a full mustache, and a sharp goatee. In murk of the cracked oil paint, his eyes were amber like candlelight seen through dusk.

"Who was he?" Wayland asked the passing auction supervisor, a dark-complexioned man who hurried about holding a clipboard and pencil preparing for the night's sale.

"Don't know. Found it in the secretary's drawer."

The Confederate's buttons were dully depicted, whether brass or not, and Wayland had learned from his continued nightly study of the encyclopedia that while Union officers displayed rank on epaulets, the Rebels used their uniforms' collars. He made out three nearly indistinct gold stripes, the sewn replicas of a captain's bars.

"I'd like to bid on it," Wayland said.

"I'll tag and put it on the block," the manager answered.

Wayland bought the portrait for forty-seven dollars, the only other offer coming from a young woman he believed to be a shill planted to raise prices for the house. He carefully rerolled the canvas, wrapped it in tissue paper, and again bound it with twine. The Levantine who took his money smirked and said, "Have a good ancestor."

Wayland set on his apartment mantel the rolled portrait alongside the brass button from the cigar box and the ladle he'd polished. He invited Amy to come advise him how to furnish the place. She arrived during the afternoon wearing a yellow sunsuit, her hair still damp from swimming, her teeth seemingly unnaturally white against her tan. She immediately spotted the ladle.

"Why it's beautiful," she said as she lifted it. "Such a lovely curve of its handle. And is that a G for Garnett?"

"It's the only piece of family silver saved from the fire," he lied.

"English?" she asked.

"Seventeenth century."

"The silversmith?"

"I believe I heard the name Edmund Pearce."

She set the ladle back and picked up the button, which she held close to her turquoise eyes.

"And this?"

"From my great-grandfather Winslow's uniform. He was wounded at Shiloh in Tennessee."

Wayland had learned from the encyclopedia that there was no General Joe Johnson at Shiloh. In fact there was no Johnson at all. It had been Albert Sydney Johnston in Tennessee and later Joseph E. Johnston in Georgia.

Lastly Amy touched the rolled-up portrait. He lifted it and untied the twine.

"Torn out of its frame at the fire," he said.

"Your great-grandfather was a handsome man. You can have it repaired and reframed you know. There are experts who do that. It surely ought to hang over this mantel."

She told her father, who was impressed. She also helped Wayland furnish his apartment, and some months later it was on the spool bed she'd chosen for him that he first made love to her and asked her to marry him.

"What the hell, might as well," she said. "You've seen everything I have to offer and still hang around. On the other hand you're old enough to be my father and might break down on me. I'd hate to be taking on a nursing job. Course you're still looking damn good, no gut, and stepping into the money too. Plus the question of love. All in all I think I probably come out a winner. I'd like to go back to see where you lived in Virginia."

"Not me."

"The fire you mean?

"Yes."

"It must've been terrible. I can see it on you whenever you talk about it. You seem to draw into yourself."

"I don't like to talk about it. Over the years I've tried to put it out of my mind."

"If it hurts that much, I won't speak of it again ever . . ."

. . . closer Sheriff Calvin and his deputies move in on Wayland's daddy 'til he has to leave the ferny spring deep in the woods. First he wraps the copper still, worm, and his barrels in the tarred canvas, buries them, and smoothes over the ground by dragging pine boughs across it. He's been forced to take field work in order to keep his account open at the Ballards' store.

"I been trying to remember when I wont paying," he says as he sits on the cabin steps, hunched forward, his long hands limp and resting over his kneecaps. "Reckon the day I got borned into this world I started at the store or the store started on me. Reckon they'll be a Ballard at the pearly gates to take up admission."

"You'll never see no pearly gates 'lessen you change your ways," Wayland's mama says.

"My runs is honest. Nobody ever got a burning gut from what he took from my hand. Don't a man deserve a little release from the killing troubles of this world?"

"Don't a woman?" the mama asks and throws out a pan of dishwater that sends her Dominickers squawking across the yard. Her mouth has tightened to a grim slit.

It's haying time. Alfalfa and timothy are hip high to Wayland, and wind welters the green sea of stalks coming to seed as if ruffled by invisible fingers. Those stalks give way before teeth of honed clacking mower blades. The Ballards operate only the latest and best equipment, which is kept oiled and repaired by Ferdinand.

Heavy-footed, patient Shires are no longer used, replaced by green Oliver tractors that have no need of blacksmiths and shod hooves. Machines don't become weary and drop their heads. At the stable Emmett has only riding horses, ponies, and hackneys to look after.

Wayland's daddy goes to Mr. Wesley Rudd for a job. He hates the asking, and his fingers grip his removed hat as if he will rip off the brim. Mr. Wesley Rudd is amused. He knows men. His wife uses a Mason jar of the daddy's clean, pure run cooked from stolen Ballard corn in her Christmas fruitcakes. He has seen the daddy fade into and emerge from shadows of the woods.

"Well, Larkin, that well of yours must've dried up," Mr. Rudd says.

Wayland's daddy answers nothing. The wind has quieted, yet he stands and waits as stiff as a planted post.

"Been good rains of late," Mr. Wesley Rudd says. "Most wells running full and fresh. Funny about yours going dry."

Still the daddy does not speak.

"Guess we can put you on a wagon if you got a mind to it," Mr. Wesley Rudd says and smiles.

During haying time, loading the wagons and storing hay in the barn are the hardest work. A single man braces his legs on the swaying bed as the wagon swings among rows of bales dropped by the new machine. They are lifted to the loader by boys walking and flanking him as he stacks them head high.

At the barn he must heave bales up to the loft. Chaff burns the skin and blurs the eyes. Mucus clogs up lungs, and muscles ache to the point of giving out. Even if protected by gloves fingers become raw on the wire which binds the bales.

"I'm a tractor driver," Wayland's daddy says.

"Sure, Larkin, but we got us plenty of tractor drivers already," Mr. Wesley Rudd says. "If you was a regular I'd set you on one, but they is already spoken for and worked up to. Stacking's not too hard for you, is it?"

"Nothing's too hard for me."

"Good 'cause that new baler packs them heavy," Mr. Wesley Rudd says, and his mouth squeezes as he positions his chaw in his cheek.

The sun burns off the slight morning coolness and rises to become a fuming planet that appears about to boil over and drip red fire. It seems to lodge in place forever and not allow the day to proceed to an end. Draining sweat attracts flies and bees. Strength seeps away as if the body has leaks, legs wobble, and thirst claws at the throat past anything that water can quench.

Always haying is hurried because of thunderstorm threats, causing Mr. Wesley Rudd to keep his eyes on the horizon. When white clouds with dark underbellies take shape, build, and billow, he stands from his nail keg to climb on the back of a saddled mule named Pompeii. As he rides among hands, he calls, "Let's gather it in, boys. Let's get it all to the barn."

Mr. Ballard too might appear on the terrace in front of the big house, and often his son Eugene walks beside him. Watching from high ground the harvesting is a pleasing picture. The mowers leave behind orderly fragrant cuttings, the hay lying flat, bright, and fresh, the bleeding juices capture shifting glints. Rabbits scamper and zigzag for their lives before the slashing blades.

The clattering rakes gather the hay into long windrows that curve slightly and become bright stripes laid across the land. The clamorous, pounding new red machine gathers up the stripes, digests them, and dumps bales out in precise patterns as if dropped and arranged for pleasing the eye.

Mrs. Ballard strolls out. Black Amos carries her easel, and she settles before it on a folding canvas chair he opens for her. Her straw hat creates a broad shade that protects her milky skin from the sun as she paints the scene.

Occasionally Ballard guests arrive and observe. Black Amos places lawn chairs in front of the wall under a massive water oak. The summer colors of visitors' clothing resemble flowers on the terrace. Shafts of sunlight reflect from cooling drinks being raised to lips, and bamboo fans flap to cool faces that open like blooms.

The new baler that has replaced the unbound storing of hay in barns becomes jammed. All hands welcome the rest. Wayland's daddy slides down from the wagon, his overalls sweat darkened, his jaw's heaviness dragging his mouth open. Strength of his youth has waned, and what's kept him working are the mocking eyes.

He wipes his forearm over his face and crosses to the baler. The machine is the first in Howell County, an invention so recent and productive other planters arrive to watch it feed on the windrows. Envious of it, the men nod their reluctant approval.

Hands crowd around the baler and offer suggestions to Lamanuel Hovey, who drives the tractor that pulls the baler. He's lifted the cover off the compactor, which had become tangled by twisted stalks and wire. He tugs and tries to free it.

Wayland's daddy hopes if he fixes the baler, Mr. Wesley Rudd might take him off the wagon and put him on tractor driving. Instead of waiting for Ferdinand, who understands machinery, the daddy unclasps his frog sticker. The baler's gasoline engine is still chugging. As he reaches inside to cut stalks free, a gear falls clanking into place, and the compactor's piston plunges downward.

The daddy screams as he pulls out the brilliant spurting stump. When Wayland runs to him, the men push him back to keep him from seeing. They lift his wailing daddy to the wagon bed where two men kneel beside him and press him flat. They tie his leather belt around the stump while the daddy kicks and screams as the wagon rocks up the slope toward the big house.

"Where they taking him?" Wayland cries.

"Easy, son," Mr. Wesley Rudd says, holding him. "They carrying him to Tobaccoton."

"His arm?" Wayland asks, crying.

"You run see you mama," Mr. Wesley Rudd orders him. "You tell her there's been an accident."

There's something else. Men have collected around the last bale dropped from the machine. Among the tightly packed flakes of alfalfa are the crushed length of the bloody arm and the white gleam of shattered bone.

"What we do with it?" the men ask. They have stepped away from the bale. Already flies have found the sunny redness of flesh.

"Make way," Mr. Wesley Rudd says.

He works the arm loose from the bale and wraps it in a burlap sack that has been folded over the seat of the tractor to soften the ride.

Wayland flees to find his mother. She's setting cornflowers in colored bottles on the sill of her kitchen window. Over the years she's collected the bottles, many lifted from the Ballards' pit.

"Look after things," she orders him and rushes apron flapping to the road where Emmett meets her. He's driving a Ballard truck. She climbs in, and they speed away, the dust rolling after them. He's carrying her to the Tobaccoton hospital.

Only later as Wayland hunkers at the side of Ballards' store and waits word does he learn about the arm. Men sit on the porch trading talk. As twilight settles in, he overhears voices not intended for him.

"Throwed it in the river."

"Had to be got rid of somewheres."

"Catfish having themselves a time."

ten

Wayland stopped the Caddy and looked about him. He wasn't lost. He'd been expecting to see the one-story school building where Miss Flowers had taught him up through the sixth grade. Had he been gone for so long that the land or his mind could fool him? No, this had to be the place, three-quarters of a mile beyond Jericho Crossroads, yet there were no remnants of a structure. Merely a desolate field grown wild with broomstraw, dwarf pines, and honey locust trees.

"It's a shame you didn't continue your college education on the GI Bill after the war," his wife Amy had said to him.

"The war was enough education for me," he'd answered.

"If only you'd been able to save some photographs. It seems some of your *kin*, as you put it, would've kept snapshots tucked away in a drawer."

He'd never told her there were no snapshots or photographs. The Caddy's trunk held a Sony camcorder that had cost a thousand dollars, but who during tight times of his childhood earned money for cameras or film? Only the Ballards and their like.

Amy had never withstood want or a depression. She'd been born into and grew up among the industrial prosperity that followed World War II. Even during the worst of times her father, a respected postal inspector not anywhere near rich, had been able to provide his family a good home, food on the table, and insulation from economic hardship.

Wayland met her parents in their Melbourne bungalow set on an acre of Bermuda lawn. Amy's mother raised tropical flowers and kept them arranged in vases around the house shaded by two live oaks. The pipe-smoking father mowed grass in leisurely fashion and tended to his orange and lemon trees. Amy's parents were clean, orderly, dependable people who sang in the choir of a Methodist church.

Wayland hedged answers when speaking of family and avoided telling that his mother had often gone barefoot draped in an undyed cotton dress that hung loosely over her thin, insect bitten body bare of underclothes as she worked suckering, dosing, and pulling tobacco.

He never mentioned the privy or hogs penned behind the cabin or his daddy's increasing gauntness, the haunting despair that lived in eyes, which shone like the swabbed steel grayness of his Enfield rifle's barrel. Wayland had told Amy's parents his father had been a Virginia planter.

"Planter of what?" Amy's father had asked.

"Dark leaf tobacco mainly," Wayland had answered, thinking of . . .

. . . Tobaccoton where Emmett drives the Ballard truck to the hospital and brings their daddy back. His stump is wrapped in taped gauze. When the mama boils rags to replace the gauze, they glimpse the red, angry skin folded over bone and stitched as neatly as a flap of repaired harness leather.

The daddy has stopped speaking. Wayland's mama fixes chopped pork, butterbeans, and turnip salat from the garden. She serves him tea flavored with mint and precious sugar. Emmett, Ferdinand, Lottie, and Pearl May stand about ready to help. The daddy eats and watches them but has no words. He uses his left hand to feed himself. His spoon trembles, but he won't permit them to succor him.

Daily at first light he leaves the cabin, setting out in paced strides to the woods and shadows of the ferny spring. He receives no insurance payments for the loss of the arm, no compensation, though Mrs. Ballard, driven by Black Amos in the Packard, stops at the head of the lane and honks for Wayland's mama to walk to the car and accept ten dollars worth of store scrip from a white-gloved hand.

Evenings the daddy returns. They see him take shape out of dusk as if formed from it. Pulsing fireflies glow around him. He moves slowly, unsteadily, yet is determined. His eyes gleam with a kind of craze in light from the kerosene lamp and seem not to comprehend what they fasten on. They burn not only from the wick's flame but also dug-up runs of white liquor. The eyes become embers.

The mama talks to him as she changes his bandages and lays food before him. Wayland's sisters chatter around him while they wash his clothes and make his bed. Emmett and Ferdinand bring what little money they can spare to help out. Wayland keeps a bucket of fresh well water and a dipper on the back porch to slake his daddy's constant thirst.

For three days the daddy doesn't return. The mama stands on the porch as darkness seeps over the land and looks down the lane for him. Her entwined fingers grip, and she sighs before sending Emmett, Ferdinand, and Wayland to search. They have no luck, and her face tightens.

Saturday afternoon when Wayland finishes work in the Ballard ditches he walks to the river for a swim and cooling wash. A pocket of his Big Boys carries a chunk of soap his mama made from hog fat, lye, and wood ashes. Reb tags along, his head drooping, his ears nearly dragging the ground.

In dust of the path lowering toward the water Wayland comes across the print. He hunkers and recognizes the faint Cat Brand trademark of a heel. He searches each side of the path 'til he discovers a broken sycamore twig.

"Hie on," he orders Reb.

Reb sniffs, circles back, and courses through the woods. His tail beats side to side and quickens. Wayland picks up more signs—a flattened fern, a dislodged chunk of rotted log, a wild grapevine dragged out its length. He and Reb move alongside the river and through stringing willows that close behind them like green curtains.

He discovers a cleared shelf of bank. His daddy lies on his side, his one hand under his cheek, eyes closed. He's dead, Wayland thinks, his heart gripping, but stoops to a soured breath exhaling with a fitful snore. Spit dribbles from a corner of his daddy's tobacco-stained mouth. Reb sniffs at him.

"Pa," Wayland says.

His daddy don't move. Red ants scurry across his face and into his beard. He moans, yet his eyes remain shut. His stump bandage is soiled, and flies excitedly circle a bloody splotch that has turned brown.

Wayland stands and runs home. His mama is killing a Dominicker. She has the chicken laid across the top of a fencepost, its neck stretched, the axe raised.

"At the river, Mama," he tells her.

She turns the Dominicker loose, and it flutters away cackling. With a quick stroke she whacks the axe blade into the fencepost where she leaves it stuck. Wayland leads as she hurries behind him and Reb. She shoves aside brambles and whipping tree boughs.

The daddy hasn't moved. She kneels and lays a hand on his brow. She feels along his body, and her fingers touch the stump lightly, but it's enough hurt for the daddy to open his eyes.

"We going home," she says.

Careful of the stump, they raise him. His feet do little more than scuffle so that most of the weight hangs on Wayland and his mama.

His daddy's eyes again close, and his head hangs forward as if his neck has become hinged.

At the cabin they settle him on his bed. The mama removes his clothes and washes him with a rag dipped in a bucket of water that had been placed in the sun to warm. She patiently removes the soiled bandage to clean away the crusted blood, dabs on pine pitch, and wraps the stump using a torn strip of a worn-out dress boiled for that purpose.

She spoon feeds him bean broth, which the daddy accepts without opening his eyes as she urges the spoon to his lips. She covers him with a sheet patched after being thrown out by the big house and salvaged by Ferdinand from the pit. The sisters and brothers take turns standing watch. They fan the daddy to shoo away greenies and skeeters. He opens his eyes but still won't speak. The eyes take them in as if he doesn't know their names. Lottie shaves him, trims his hair, and kisses his cheek. He'd not respond.

"He's been shamed," the mama whispers in the kitchen. "Without his arm he don't feel a man."

Yet under her care he becomes stronger. He rises to sit on the side of the bed and looks out the window toward the hackberry. The Reverend Ernest Arbogast arrives. He wears his black preaching suit, black hat, and white shirt buttoned at the collar beneath the lump of his Adam's apple. He carries a Bible. He too sits on the bed.

"Well, Larkin, looks to me like you got a few good years left in you," he says.

The daddy stares out the window.

"You had a stretch of bad luck there, but it ain't nothing like what Job went through. It ain't a sliver of what our Savior suffered on the cross to bring us eternal life."

The daddy's eyes drift upward. Crows have lit high on hackberry limbs where they flutter and caw. In the kitchen the mama, Lottie, and Wayland stand listening.

"The Ballards'll find work for you," Preacher Arbogast says. "I talked to Mr. Henry at the store. He told me he'd tell Mr. Wesley Rudd to make you a place. Now let's have us a prayer here. Let's thank the Lord we got a roof, food, and breath in our bodies, all of which in time is perishable as the grass of the fields."

Mr. Wesley Rudd arrives the following Sunday evening. He drives his new Model A, which he keeps as slick and polished as licked licorice. His stride is slow and steady, a man always testing the land that lies before him.

The daddy has left the bed to sit on the porch. Mr. Wesley Rudd joins him and talks of tobacco, blue mold, the damage done to the crop by a thunderstorm that shot hail from a flashing purple sky.

"Cut up the leaf bad, but the price is high in Danville," Mr. Wesley Rudd says. "Larkin, things even out."

Mr. Wesley Rudd leans sideways to spit over the porch. He is careful, not wishing to foul the railing.

"Plenty of work around," he says. "Always something I can use a good man to help with. More than shake a stick over."

Yet Wayland's daddy doesn't return to the Ballards' fields. He sits on the porch days and most nights. He won't speak. Wayland carries him cool water from the well. The moon glazes his daddy's eyes as he drinks and watches the boy over the dipper's rim.

Early September when the listless dry air flays the skin, the daddy stands and walks behind the cabin to take his bamboo fishing pole from the shed. He uses a foot to shove aside logs of the woodpile, and his fingers sift out worms that have found refuge in the damp, black decay beneath. He drops them into a coffee tin.

The mama lets him go without questions. Wayland carries his own pole and trails along. The daddy returns to his shaded hideaway by the river, and they sit at the top of the bank to drop lines into the water. For bobbers they use squirrel-cracked, dried-out hickory-nut shells tied to and made adjustable on their lines by slipknots.

Yellowed birch leaves flutter down and settle to trace the river's idle flow. When the boy stops breathing, he hears its quiet drag against the bank. A heron flaps inches above the pale green water, its upside-down reflection keeping pace. A smallmouth bass breaks the surface to snatch a snake doctor from the air. Ripples bend away.

The daddy baits his own hook one-handed. He holds a thrashing worm against a rock with his thumb and used his index finger to work it over the barb. Blue cats and suckers bite. They catch a mess and string them through their gills on two stripped weeping willow branches that has snags at the ends to keep the fish from slipping off.

They carry home their catch. Wayland scales and guts the fish, and the mama fries them in the larded iron skillet she sets on coals of fire in the circle of field stones used for outdoor cooking, washing, and soap making. The good odor rises on smoke, which layers and settles above the cabin. Reb's tail wags.

Lottie, Pearl May, Lonnie Tyler, Ferdinand, and Emmett join the fry. They pinch up hot fish from the skillet and dip forward to eat and keep grease from dripping off their chins to their clothes. They talk to the daddy, who watches when they speak but won't answer.

Emmett loosens his belt to relieve the pressure of a full belly that pushes out rounded and tight. When he pats it, the belly thumps like a ripe melon. Ferdinand plays his harmonica, and the daddy watches Lottie and Emmett dance. The mama's the first to see the daddy's fingers keep time against a knee. She stands behind him and smiles.

Each day the daddy fishes at his river hideaway. Wayland hurries there afternoons when work's done. Sometimes his daddy is stretched out sleeping, his pole stuck into the soft bank, a hooked blue cat on the line already worn to half a wiggle. They sit together and fish, their lines hardly moved or swayed from the vertical by the listless current. A buck glides through shadows to drink on the far side, spots them, bounds away. A mockingbird dives at a crow and raps its head. A beaver swims upstream and smacks his tail against the surface to scare away intruders from his den.

Wayland's daddy might look across the water at the sycamores or up at a flight of doves whistling above the birches. His face don't change. He seems to be listening for something he never quite hears. The stump's healing.

To make up for the daddy's loss of earnings, the mama sells eggs to Mr. Luther Blackburn and tacks up a notice on the store's porch offering to do sewing and housework. Ferdinand has penciled it for her. Emmett will see to butchering the hog, an annual chore usually tended to by the daddy.

During the late afternoon as shadows slide across the unruffled water, the daddy speaks to Wayland.

"Us Garnetts always been fighters," he says. "We always come out swinging."

"Yes, Pa," the boy says.

"You got fight in you if'en you know it or not. In the blood."

"Yes, Pa," the boy says and waits for more. His daddy stares across the river, lifts the rod to check his bait, lets it sink back.

The last Saturday in September Wayland walks to the river and finds his daddy gone. The fishing poles are lying on the ground, the worm can is empty. My daddy, Wayland thinks, quit early and headed home.

The daddy's not at the cabin, and Wayland's mama hasn't come from beating rugs and cleaning house for Mrs. Wesley Rudd. Wayland questions Lottie, who is baking spoon bread. More and more she has his mama's brown hair and lean body.

"Don't mean nothing," Lottie says. "Daddy could be anywheres."

They see the mama coming down the lane. She carries a paper sack, which she empties on the linoleum of the table the daddy has hammered together when they first married. Mrs. Wesley Rudd has paid her with six slabs of ham, six potatoes, and six oranges.

The mama waits supper. She removes her shoes, washes her hands and face, and ties on an apron she had made herself from a throwed-away shirt of Mr. Henry Ballard. On the kitchen windowsill she's rearranged the empty multicolored bottles she's rinsed out that once contained Little Bo Peep bleach, hair oils, tonics, and perfumes. The sun lights the blues, greens, yellows, and reds that dapple their hues along her hands and arms as she works at her sink.

Often she will stick sprigs of cornflowers, wild daisies, or Queen Anne's lace into the bottles. Wayland has seen her stand looking and smiling as if in communion with them and receiving a private message that pleases her. She waits before them now. October's approach is stealing the light.

At dusk the mama, Ferdinand, Lottie, and Wayland eat without the daddy. Ferdinand does the praying. He feels the call of taking up the Word and helps Preacher Arbogast at the Healing Spring Baptist Church. "The mark of God is on him," Preacher Arbogast claims.

When they finish the meal, the mama stands and looks out the door into darkness. "I'm going to the river," she says.

"I'll come along," Wayland says.

"You and Lottie keep a watch out for him," the mama tells Ferdinand.

She fills the lantern with kerosene and touches a match to the wick. Wayland holds the lantern to lead her, and their shadows lurch side to side as they work down the path among the pines. They hear a cry like a woman screaming—a wildcat disturbed during its night hunt.

Wayland stops and examines the ground for prints. Twice he backtracks. The dark has transformed familiar land into alien country. They pass under willows whose leaves drag and rustle over them. The lantern pushes away the darkness at the daddy's hideaway. He's not lying there. The mama stands by the edge of the river and looks across water, which steals light from the lantern.

"Larkin?" she calls. Frogs quiet, and the chirring of crickets and katydids becomes silent

"Pa?" the boy shouts.

They wait standing by the river. The night creatures again take up their throbbing plaints for the season's end.

"We mighta missed him," the mama says. "He could be home."

They hike back to the cabin. The daddy hasn't returned. Lottie has washed the dishes and cleaned the kitchen. She sits with Ferdinand on the porch steps. The mama takes off her shoes and lets herself down to the chair Ferdinand has made.

"Maybe he's got turned 'round in the dark," Lottie says.

"Never been lost in his life," the mama says.

She sends them to bed, and they hear her rocking—not the long slow crescents of a person relaxing, but abrupt starts and stops. She comes in finally, yet her bed is not quiet. Shucks of her mattress rustle like squirrels scratching among leaves. At first light she's on the porch peering through a shredding mist toward the lane. She and Wayland go to the river hideaway. Nothing's changed.

"You run check his private place," she tells Wayland.

The boy circles and doubles back through the woods to keep anybody from tracking him. His daddy has ordered him never to come to the ferny woods where the copper still's buried. The ground is now covered by the softness of pine tags, and there is no sign of recent diggings or footprints.

They wait a second night. At first light the mama walks to the big house where the Ballards have a telephone. They've strung wire to a junction with a trunk line that reaches Tobaccoton. Black Amos talks to the sheriff.

Sheriff Calvin questions the mama. He also stops at Mr. Wesley Rudd's office. Wayland is called from the field where rows of tobacco droop heavy. He won't start school 'til the last leaf is pulled and hangs curing in the barns.

"Now, son, you can tell me and it won't hurt you daddy none," the sheriff says and tips up his fedora. "He doing any cooking?"

"My mama does our cooking," Wayland says.

"Sure and tasty too from what I hear, but has your daddy dug up his special skillet?"

"I don't know nothing about special skillets."

"You been there, ain't you?"

"I don't know nothing."

The sheriff and deputies search but don't find the still or daddy. An old darky named Josiah, the uncle of Josephus Blodgett, spots the body as he wets a line the following Sunday afternoon. It floats face down, a shoulder strap of his Big Boys snagged on the branch of an eroded and toppled birch.

It threatens a shower the morning of the funeral. Wind gusts from the southwest. No canopy has been raised and anchored by iron stakes in the cemetery of the Healing Spring Baptist Church. No funeral home from Tobaccoton has been retained either. Local women help Wayland's mama wash, dress, and lay out the body in a cedar coffin hurriedly knocked together by Ferdinand.

Pallbearers carry the coffin from the cabin to the bed of a Ballard Reo truck, which then winds among blowing pines to the church. The coffin is left propped open on sawhorses set before the altar. Wayland endures only one swift glance at his daddy whose skin looks powdered. The women have rouged his cheeks.

Preacher Arbogast climbs to the pulpit, his face long and solemn. He holds a Bible he doesn't read from. He raises his face and closes his eyes.

" 'The people is grass,' " he recites from Isaiah, his favorite book. "Just like we reap the corn, wheat, and oats, the Lord God sends his angels down here to bring in His crops."

The church is filled. The Ballards allot time off and no docking of pay for hands to come to the funeral, so even those who hardly knew Wayland's daddy would rather rest in pews than labor in the fields.

Mr. Henry Ballard and his wife Isabelle sit in the front row. They do not attend the Healing Spring Baptist except for weddings and funerals. Sundays Black Amos drives them to Tobaccoton and St. Luke's Episcopal.

There is no choir. Anybody who feels like singing can stand, give voice, be joined by others. Mostly these are the women, and the hymns shrill on high wavering notes of "I Come to the Garden Alone," "Jesus Loves Me," and "Rock of Ages."

Mr. Wesley Rudd, who also does not attend Healing Spring Baptist regularly but Tobaccoton's St. Andrew's Presbyterian, sings bass. Men whisper he sounds like a bullfrog on a log. The Ballards have donated hymnbooks to the church, not new ones, but castoffs when replaced at St. Luke's. Mrs. Isabelle Ballard has presented an upright piano that has come from her daughter Diana's room in the big house. Miss Diana now has a spinet. Neither she nor Mr. Ballard's son Eugene attends the funeral.

White mourners occupy pews on the right side of the aisle, which runs straight down the middle of the sanctuary, coloreds on the left, Black Amos among them. The darkies sing louder, and their women insert grace notes and exclamations not in the hymnals. One skinny young black girl named Viola Spain sends her soprano up bird high. No other voice can reach hers.

When Preacher Arbogast finishes preaching and praying, the people sing "Tell Me the Old, Old Story," and he steps down from the pulpit and closes the coffin.

Six men who have known Wayland's daddy stand to carry it out. They are not close friends because he's had none. Larkin Garnett has always kept to himself, a man apart, a rover of the woods, swamps, and rivers.

Wayland believes that generations before in Tennessee his daddy would've been a frontiersman, a hunter and slayer of Indians and panthers instead of a trifling cropper who never fully paid his bills at the Ballards' store.

The pallbearers carry the coffin to the grave, which has been dug by men of the congregation who brought shovels along to the church. Emmett and Ferdinand walk on either side of the mama. She has wept so long she seems to have no weight but to float upon their arms. Wayland follows, attempting to be manly, yet his eyes wet and his vision veils as if moving through rain.

Preacher Arbogast stands at the head of the grave. The coloreds line up on one side, the whites at the other. Men remove their hats. The mama slumps, held up by Emmett and Ferdinand.

As men slip hemp ropes beneath the coffin, Preacher Arbogast raises his arms and eyes to the clearing sky and calls out, "Lord God, we send You back Larkin Garnett and ask You find him a fine and easy place to live out eternity. Yes, Sir, Lord, indeed we do."

The men slowly pay out rope to lower the coffin into the hole. Wayland turns his eyes away from its wet red-brown ugliness. His mama sags between Emmett and Ferdinand. People sing "Amazing Grace," and Viola Spain's voice trills. The Ballards edge off. Wayland has seen they're anxious about muddying they fine leather shoes.

eleven

Wayland stepped from the Caddy and crossed to the field where the school had been. No cornflowers grew along the ditch, only briars and poison oak, and again he felt sorry he had come on this journey. Howell County was no longer his and hadn't been for forty-seven years. It wasn't too late to turn and go back. What good or obscure justification could he expect to find in this forsaken place?

Amy had asked about what she called his forebears, not his kin—people in fact he'd learned little about. His daddy had spoken often of Grandfather Winslow fighting with General Joe Johnson but given no details of particular battles, just that the grandfather had hacked off what remained of his own leg left dangling from a cannon blast. Wayland couldn't be certain any of it was even true.

He remembered only two of what could be called living forebears—an uncle with a yellowish white beard that itched like dry straw against his face and Granny Ruth, an ancient woman whose cheeks and neck were lined deep as a rutted road. Her kiss smarted from snuff, which she nursed and tongued between her lower lip and toothless gums. She smelled of wood smoke as well as the coal oil she rubbed on her legs to keep off ticks and ease the stiffness and pain of her aching knobby knees.

There'd been vague talks of other Tennessee and North Carolina kin, though no letters ever arrived from those places and no portraits existed like the ones Emmett said hung in the Ballard house. Certainly none of Wayland's forebears had kept slaves. Nobody in the family had ever been rich enough to own another person.

"My mother traces her line back to a German paper maker who arrived from Frankfurt in 1840," Amy had said. "Daddy to a Scotch schoolteacher who came on a ship to South Carolina in 1794 to tutor six children of a sugar-cane plantation owner's family."

Wayland stood beside the ditch and pictured the school as he could best remember its . . .

. . . square white frame structure, which has a tin roof painted bottle blue and topped by three spearlike lightning rods. The building sits on two acres of red-clay land and has only a single doorway. Each of the three rooms holds two classes, and all are taught by a single teacher. The windows lack screens, and when the weather warms, bees, wasps, and June bugs fly in to ping against walls and rafters. The boys use their rulers to swat at them. The girls are more cautious and dainty.

The darkies' school to the other side of Mud Creek looks the same except that tin roof is black. Their teacher is a heavy Negress they call Miss Penelope who has come from Hampton Institute and pays for room and board in the house of Sampson Bacon, the colored preacher at the Beautiful Plains Baptist Church.

Miss Penelope speaks better English than the local whites except for the Ballards, Mrs. Wesley Rudd, and Miss Patricia Flowers. At all times during school hours Miss Penelope carries a switch cut from a pussywillow, and it whisks through air to snap against stubborn flesh. The pupils are afraid not to learn from her.

Wayland's teacher is Miss Patricia Flowers, a starched young female just graduated from the State Normal School in Farmville. She has a soft, flowing body and wears her sandy hair cut in bangs. Her mouth doesn't seem large enough for her to speak loud, yet if aroused she knows how to holler.

She lives in a guest cottage inside the Ballards' wall. She don't eat at their table except when invited to the big house on special occasions like Thanksgiving, Christmas, or Easter when the Ballards open their doors for major celebrations.

Miss Flowers's boyfriend wears a straw hat and drives down from Lynchburg in a red Dodge to spark her. Wayland tracks them at every opportunity and catches them among willows down by the river where they believe themselves hidden. Peeking from among arching green branches Wayland sees the boyfriend kiss her bowed lips, hates him, and thinks of putting sand in the Dodge's gas tank.

Miss Flowers wears starched colorful dresses, bracelets that jingle, and perfumes herself. When she calls out instructions, her voice is a song to Wayland. Angered, she breaks chalk by banging it against the blackboard and even throws it, though only at the boys. The girls giggle.

She stops by Wayland as he sits at his bench alongside the other fifth-graders.

"Who helps do your math?" she asks, the words more an accusation than a question.

"Nobody, Miss Flowers," he says, half turned to gaze up at her. He looks at her lips and thinks of them being kissed among the willows. He feels he can hardly breathe.

"Somebody in your family, a brother or sister?"

"I do it myself 'fore I get to bed," he says and senses the sweet heat from her body.

"Don't you fib to me, Wayland," she says as other students watch, the girls serious, the boys grinning. Miss Flowers carries no pussywillow switch but punishes pupils by ordering them to stand facing a wall and wear a sign around their necks that reads, "Fool." The girls never misbehave.

"You can ask my mama," he says.

"Which I shall do," she says and does and then keeps him after school to stand him before her desk. She taps her pencil against a bottle of black ink and eyes him, her chin slightly raised, causing her nostrils to appear larger.

"You have a way with numbers," she says.

He don't answer and waits to be scolded.

"What do you expect to do with your life after you finish here?" she asks.

"Drive a Ballard tractor for Mr. Wesley Rudd when I'm old enough," he says, that job as far as he's allowed his ambition to extend.

She laughs, leans forward, a hand held across her bosoms, which shift mysteriously when she strides about.

"That's your great aim in life?"

"Maybe someday become one of they field bosses."

"Not 'they' field bosses."

"No'm."

"You know better."

"Yes'm."

"You might consider continuing your education."

He says nothing. Emmett, Ferdinand, his sisters, none has gone past the sixth grade. Attending middle school requires riding a county bus to Tobaccoton and using up an entire day, meaning no money for work in the fields.

"Give it thought," Miss Flowers says.

He craves her nearness. She is his first love, so fresh, airy, and perfumed. Thinking of her makes getting through work and chores easier. As he stretches Ballard barbed wire or mauls an iron wedge into a section of a wind-felled oak to be split for stove wood, he imagines himself talking with her. Her name escapes his mouth.

"What you just said?" Ferdinand asks as he passes carrying two buckets of water to the cabin to heat for a bath.

"Nothing," Wayland answers and keeps his face turned away.

And then a second love named Lucy Randolph, who sits across the aisle at her bench on the girls' side. Her daddy tends the Ballards' sheep. She has dark blond hair she ties with bows of bright ribbons at the top of her head. Her eyes are bluer than the cornflowers that grow wild bordering the roads.

Wayland has never spoken to her, but at recess while the boys race and rassle, he's aware she and other girls who skip rope and play hopscotch among themselves watch him. For Lucy Randolph he runs and wins races around the building.

He carries to school a sugar cookie his mama has baked. She believes he's eaten it, but he has slipped it into a gap between buttons of his shirt. Walking to school he protects the cookie so it won't break or crumble. He intends to give it to Lucy at recess if he can speak to her away from the eyes of others.

He has no chance. She's always among girls. He waits 'til she starts home and trails her and her friend Jennette Bains. When they are well down the road, he catches up.

"Here," he says and hands Lucy the cookie.

"Why thank you, Wayland," she says and smiles over teeth as pretty and moistly clean as kernels of fresh shucked corn.

"What about me?" Jennette asks. She has a pug nose and red hair worn in pigtails.

"We'll share it," Lucy says.

"His hands is dirty," Jennette says.

"It'll taste fine," Lucy says and turns to smile again at Wayland as they walk away.

He looks at his hands. They are ink smudged.

His mama finds work wherever she can and is often gone before he leaves for school. She drags home at dark and lowers herself slow to a chair where she settles and sighs as if she means never again to move. Lottie does most the cooking, and Wayland's left to look after himself. He takes better care washing his hands.

He sits on the school bench and thinks how much he loves both Miss Patricia Flowers and Lucy Randolph. He's unable to choose between them and repeatedly scratches his hot itchy scalp. He's already finished the numbers problems Miss Flowers has written on the blackboard in her beautiful handwriting.

He waits for the dizzying moment she will bend above him to check his work, but this time she draws back from looking at the lined tablet paper and his decimal answers. She peers at and parts his hair with prying, fussy fingers.

"Lice," she says and stands away quickly.

Laughter escapes covered mouths as Miss Flowers flees to pour water from a pitcher into a white porcelain bowl kept in the cloakroom. She soaps and dries her hands before sitting at her desk and writing a note to Wayland's mama. She sends him home carrying it.

He believes his mama'll whip him because she has trusted him to keep himself clean. Emmett returns from work at the Ballards' stable, reads the note, and takes sheep shears to Wayland's head.

Wayland cries inwardly not at the loss of hair snipped and falling down his neck and around his shoulders but because the students' snickers and giggles continue to knell off the long chiming blades. He dies from the way Miss Flowers was repelled by him and what Lucy Randolph has seen.

"Why that'd be a two-bit cut anywhere in the world," Emmett says, uses stinging lye soap to scrub Wayland's scalp, and finishes off the job with slapped-on palms of kerosene he rubs in. "Little brother, you one handsome dog now."

twelve

As Wayland drove on, the air was so thickly humid he checked the car's windows to make certain they fitted tightly closed, reached to the dash to finger and adjust the air conditioner's controls, and felt for a flow of coolness on his palm. He used his handkerchief to dab at his forehead. Was it only the southside Virginia heat?

He thought of the aged roan horse he had passed earlier. When his golden-haired daughter Jennifer learned to ride, she'd always chosen a spotted pony named Tinkerbelle at Fort Lauderdale's Palmetto Stables. Jennifer had been a small erect beauty sitting helmeted and proud atop a child's saddle. It had made him think of Diana Ballard and wonder whether that memory had been part of the reason for his encouraging Jennifer to take lessons taught in the English style of riding.

"Did you ever ride horses?" his daughter had asked, a leather crop gripped in her delicate hand. When she strapped her helmet under her chin, she did have a regal bearing.

"When I was boy not much older than you," he'd answered.

"You had a pony?"

"It wasn't a pony but a black horse, a thoroughbred."

"What was his name?"

"Midnight Baron."

"Did he go fast?"

"It seemed very fast to me at the time," he'd said . . .

. . . and stops behind the cabin, his hand holding a five-gallon lard can nigh to filled with butterbeans picked in the family garden. Movement catches his eye. He peers down through a gap among pines to a wedge of Ballard low ground, which is a sea of tasseling corn and languorous tobacco.

The shape a second time. It slides into shadows along the river and disturbs crows perched in the willows. A hound dog, he thinks, or buck deer rooted up by a pack from its bed in the woods, or maybe a heifer from the Ballard herd that has found a gap or sag in the three strands of barbed wire.

He squints to make out the fleeting shape, but birches shelter it. If a calf, Mr. Wesley Rudd will send men after it. Mr. Rudd has every head of stock the Ballards own numbered and described in his ledger, and when an animal's sold or slaughtered, he places a ruler across the row and draws a line through it with his ink pen.

The Ballards eat hog meat too, registered Berkshire swine fed by Black Amos, who also sees to the brick smokehouse where each year dozens of hams hang curing from hooks bolted to the sooty rafters. Leisurely burning hickory curls upward around the hams and escapes by drifting from portals beneath the cedar-shingled roof.

The Ballard hogs eat no slop as do the rambling razorbacks Wayland's daddy has slaughtered but corn and peanuts. Emmett claims the flesh is so white and tender a knife isn't needed at the table, that the meat separates as easily as a fork sinking through batter bread.

"Live better than most people," Emmett says of the sleek, squealing Berkshires.

The shape again, an instant of it—dark, large, vanishing. Wayland shields his eyes against the sun's aching glare. Through the lids he sees his own blood's redness. A bear, he wonders. Paw prints has been discovered along the river's banks.

Reb crawls from beneath the cabin. The days and nights are so hot the hound rouses reluctantly to eat scraps the mother tosses into the yard for him. Mr. Wesley Rudd loves the heat because it causes crops to flourish in the steamy bottom that stays moist from the river's seepage. Nowhere in Virginia does corn stand taller or tobacco grow ranker than on Ballard land.

"You hunt down that darn bear for me?" the boy asks Reb, who drags along, his brown eyes sad. He moves no more than the day calls for, conserving his energy, though the morning is still fresh from a shower upriver. Wayland has heard thunder grumble in the west and watched lightning ignite black departing clouds. The rising sun will steal all that is cool.

He crosses to the well dug by his daddy years earlier. Ferdinand, using his carpenter's talent, has repaired the peaked tin roof above the well and installed a new windlass carved from an oak chunk. The color of the frayed hemp rope reminds Wayland of Lucy Randolph's hair. He cranks up the bucket, which drips into a resounding blackness.

From an eight-penny nail he lifts the dipper, fills, and tips it to his mouth. This water tastes of earth and is different than that drunk from kegs in the field. The Ballard water comes from a deep well lined with concrete, not unmortared fieldstones that leak soil through green mossy joints.

Wayland allows Reb to lap from the dipper, and as they walk back toward the cabin he sees the shape is a horse and rider, the animal's black coat casting a gloss of sunlight.

The animal canters along a wagon road gone to pokeweed before slipping out of sight among the dusty pines. It's not Diana Ballard unless she's been given a new horse. She still rides Missy, her white pony whose mane and tail she braids like a girl's hair. Emmett brings word of her. He oils her saddle and bridle.

Wayland carries the lard bucket toward the cabin. His mama, who with other women is picking rows of Ballard tomatoes and packing them for the Richmond market, has told him to shell the butterbeans and bring in okra she'll fry up for supper.

Reb becomes alert. He hears something, and Wayland too—a faint drumming, like a grouse that's wandered into low country from the hills. His daddy has taught him to listen to and identify all voices off the land.

"Land talks," his daddy has said. "It's always telling you something if you got ears to hear. It might be wind or rain or just quiet, but it's giving tongue."

This drumming is different, not the mating strut and breasting wing beat of a grouse. Crows caw in the woods. Perhaps a great horned owl or red-tailed hawk has invaded their territory. They'll dive and fuss to drive it off. Crows are the poor man's watchdogs. Learn their language and you can judge what's happening in places far beyond reach of the eye.

Chickens circle Wayland, keeping their distance but hoping for a feeding of grain. They have seen the axe taken to their brethren. His mama has taught Wayland to soothe the chicken by stroking its feathers before laying it across the stump and using a quick, short chop to cleave the head. Stand away to avoid the mad flopping and spurts of blood. Reb always gets the heads.

Wayland empties the butterbeans in the chipped, stained kitchen sink and crosses back to the garden. As he passes the rail fence, he hears an approaching rhythmic beat, which grows louder and becomes a pounding that fills his ears. He wheels and sees God gigantic and soaring. Wayland drops the lard can, throws up his arms, and believes he will be taken by the angel of death.

Not God, not the angel of death but a vast black horse and its rider—a lady tall and white, a giantess she appears sitting calmly and gazing down at him as the horse arches past and lands in the yard.

Chickens fly squawking and scattering feathers. Reb's so scared he yelps, tucks tail, and squirms under the cabin. Hooves strike and spume dust, the horse heaves about, and foam flings into sunlight.

Wayland lowers his arms to gawk at the lady, who wears a black derby, a white shirt, tan britches, and long black boots with silver spurs. She reins the lunging horse to a circle and orders it to stand. The horse paws dust and snorts. It walls frantic purple within black eyes. Wayland backs toward the cabin.

"It's all right, little boy," the lady calls. "He won't hurt you. What's your name?"

"Wayland, mam."

"Well, Wayland, do you know how to reach the Ballard house? I seem to have lost my way."

"Yes'm."

"Think you can show me?"

"Yes'm."

"All right, climb on the fence and give me your hand. Don't be afraid now."

When he obeys, she reaches for him, and her long gloved fingers fasten tight around his wrist. She drags him upward across the horse's flank. Wayland scrambles to get a leg over the animal as it twists and prances. The lady holds the reins with one hand and settles him behind her with the other.

Wayland's bare legs squeeze the hot, sweaty horse as it sidesteps and tosses its head. The lady smiles back at him, this white woman so foreign and beautiful he thinks she's got to be from a picture book. She smells of lilacs, or maybe lilies, like Heaven itself must.

"Little boy, wrap your arms around me now," she says as she draws the reins and turns the horse toward the low ground.

He holds on for his life as they lunge at the fence and surge upward. The lady seems to lift the horse by using her hands—as if the great animal is a puppet to her fingers. It curves over the rail, lands, collects, and they race ducking pine branches along the trail.

He closes his eyes, clenches them, his cheek pressed to the scented female silkiness of her shoulder.

"Which way, little boy?" she asks, slowing the horse.

Wayland fears letting go and indicates with a quick stab of one hand, causing the lady to laugh. A hank of her yellow hair escapes and falls from beneath her black derby. She wets her lips, the reddest he's ever seen on any woman, as she spurs the horse, and they rush toward the low ground and river, the speed bending pines, sycamores, the land itself. I know now, Wayland thinks, what flying's like.

They approach another fence, and Wayland feels the horse gather. He hides for protection behind the lady's back. They hurl into the air, and the horse stumbles on landing but levels and bounds onward.

A second time the lady laughs. I have, he thinks, my arms around a being from another world who I'll never again touch or be near.

The lady spies the Ballard house, which commands from the high ground, seemingly suspended above the fields as if removed from all bonds to the earth. The horse scents the stable and gallops faster. Field hands laboring among corn and tobacco straighten to watch them pass.

The land slopes upward. Wayland peeps over the lady's shoulder as the house grows larger. They clatter through the stone wall's gateway and into deep shade from overreaching white oaks that barricade sunlight.

The courtyard whirls. Iron shoes clang and strike sparks on cobblestones at the side entrance. Black Amos hurries from a door to catch the reins of the blowing, excited horse. The lady reaches around to Wayland to help him slide off against the sweating flank. He releases his hold on her waist.

While Black Amos holds the horse, she swings down and removes her derby. The rest of her yellow hair falls free.

"You wait, little boy," she says, this fair kindly lady who he later learns is Mr. Ballard's new wife from up north. She strides into the shadowy hallway at the side entrance, where bulbs of a chandelier burn pale orange in bluish gloom.

"Well you done had yourself a ride," Black Amos says.

"I didn't have nothing to do with it," Wayland answers and looks down at the swept cobblestones to evade the Black Amos's bulging consuming eyes and their depths of darkness.

"Don't need to tell me that," Black Amos says.

The lady returns, her chin lifted to catch air on her long white throat.

"Hold out your hand, little boy," she orders, and when Wayland obeys she presents him a reward. Awed, eyes bugging, Wayland's fingers close over it and grip so tightly they hurt.

"Thank the lady, boy," Black Amos says.

"Yes'm," Wayland says.

"And put your feet on the path," Black Amos orders.

Wayland scampers away hearing the lady's laughter. He runs from the big house down to fields of torpid tobacco and jumps ditches without opening his clenched hand. He squeezes the wealth it holds until edges dig deep into his skin. He runs faster and leaps farther than ever in his life 'til he nears the cabin and stops panting in shade of the hackberry.

He needs the fingers of one hand to pry open those of the other. His clasp doesn't want to reveal the sheen of a pure silver dollar, a coin he's never in his life looked upon until the lady placed it on his palm, hardly knew it existed, like a magic ember.

Before his mama comes home, he hides the dollar by wrapping it in a Bull Durham sack and burying it in a Clabber Girl Baking Soda can at the base of a Judas tree well back of the woodshed. At each day's end during weeks following, he slips to his cache to uncover this treasure, take hold of and feel the power of it, allow it to capture a last blushing light from the setting sun.

He breathes on the coin and with the cuff of a clean work shirt wipes it tenderly. The dollar seems to spread a force into him, and he performs a silent hoedown with it lifted toward the sky before again sacking it, tightening the drawstring, and covering the baking soda can with soil he pats as lovingly as a mother might a child laid to rest beneath a blanket for the night.

All during August and September the sky forgets how to rain. The unyielding sun bakes the ground until it cracks, and crops shrivel. Gusts of wind lift swirling red dust. The Reverend Ernest Arbogast preaches that sin has overrun the land, causing it to steam, break open, and bring forth fiery days. Cattle low and bawl through strangling nights. The river runs low, stinks, and becomes filmed by a green scum. Frogs no longer bewonk along the banks, and corn bows as if before the passage of a conqueror.

Wayland sees his mama in the garden where even weeds wither and die. She claws the soil to bring forth a misshapen turnip, a shriveled yam, a galled potato. She rises nights, her cotton gown hanging loose, to stand shoeless by the window and look toward the river from which direction the rain most often arrives.

Hunger and guilt gnaw Wayland's belly like rats feeding on it. Unable to hide the coin any longer, he digs at the Judas tree and carries the silver dollar to her, presents it on his washed raised palm. She stares as if she's witnessing the dead rise from their graves on the Day of Judgment.

"What?" she asks. Her hard, thin hand reaches out timidly to touch the coin and draws back. "You stole it?"

"No'm," he says.

"But, Wayland, how?" she asks.

He tells her of the beautiful lady, the wild galloping ride, the burial of the silver dollar at the base of the Judas tree. His mother asks when did it happen, and he admits he's hidden the dollar all these many long days. He's shamed, can't meet her eyes, but she holds him tight, kisses him, and breathes into his hair.

She ties on shoes, and they walk to the Ballards' store where on the porch men, also bent and withered, speak kindly to her. She stands before the counter to buy dried beans, a slab of fatback, flour, cornmeal, and a penny purchase of horehounds, the candy further thanks to Wayland conferred not in words but a trembling hesitant release of scarred, leached fingers from the delicate paper sack.

She and Wayland watch Mr. Luther Blackburn accept the silver dollar, his fragile arthritic hands considerate upon it. He places it in the crank-up cash register that rings like a prizefight gong.

"Not many these passing through here these days," he says, his white hair blowzy, the watery pinkish eyes still unblinking because they have seen all there is to see.

"Wayland earned it," the mother says.

"Musta did powerful work."

"He's a good boy," she says.

"I been knowing that," Mr. Luther Blackburn says and counts out change to the mother—forty-seven cents' worth.

She and Wayland hurry back to the cabin where she pushes off her shoes. The bottoms of her feet have become tough as cowhide. She crosses into the kitchen to fix their supper. When she serves the plates, the air is so laden with dust it flavors the food as if sprinkled from a salt shaker.

"Reckon it'll ever rain again?" she asks and looks at a sky the color of a glowing horseshoe drawn from the hissing forge of the Ballards' blacksmith shop.

Wayland wakes during the dark of early morning to hear the throbbing plaint of tree toads and see his mother standing at the window. She believes him asleep, and her eyes lift to lightning flashes that shatter across her face. She raises her hands to her seemingly fragmented cheeks. Wind stirs dry crackling hackberry leaves, and distant thunder rolls along the river bottom.

It's a while before he hears the approaching rain, which first whispers its advance up from the river and over the land. Drops begin to smack the seared stalks of blasted corn and the dwarfed collapsed leaves of thirsting tobacco, arousing a strong scent of wetted dust.

His mother stretches her arms before her and dangles her fingers as if the rain falls from them. She turns to him. He pretends to sleep. She lets her arms droop and among lightning bursts, thunder, and the jubilant croaking of frogs she chokes back weeping that becomes submerged in the cool rapping of the rain.

thirteen

Wayland slowed the Caddy. Ahead in shade that cedars laid across the road, turkeys crossed—a bearded jake and three quick-stepping hens. They were aware of the car but not greatly disturbed by it. His daddy had brought home many a gobbler taken from the Ballard woods. When the family finished a meal, all bones of the bird's body had been gnawed on and licked so clean there was no meat left on them for Reb.

The turkeys merged into shadows. Wayland thought that it wouldn't be long before he sat with his wife and daughter at the antique cherry table in the dining room of their Florida house to celebrate Thanksgiving. They'd attend church first, not the Baptist, Methodist, or Presbyterian, but Episcopal, the denomination which Amy had chosen, though not reared to it. From her he had learned to say "reared" not "raised."

"I remember that first day you came in the office, the way you gawked and talked," she had told Wayland before they were married.

As a result of wearing braces during her childhood her small, brilliant teeth were perfectly aligned. She followed daily complex routines for cleaning them—not only floss, but also red-, yellow-, and blue-handled brushes, each used at specific hours of the day.

During his early years he'd not thought of or cared for his teeth. One of his incisors was snaggled. At the most he'd sharpened a sassafras sprig with his Barlow to pick at them after a meal. His daddy had claimed tobacco burned the mouth clean, making a tooth doctor wasted money. His daddy had also used a crumpled and cured dark-fired leaf cut with kerosene on wounds and claimed it killed all belly worms.

Wayland and Emmett had grown up chewing. They'd held spitting contests behind the woodshed, which Emmett mostly won. Wayland had accuracy, Emmett distance, and Wayland had never seen a dentist close up 'til his hitch in the army.

"And you were trying to look up my dress," Amy had said.

"With legs like yours, who wouldn't?"

"The devouring way you stared at me."

"I told you I was smitten at first sight of you."

"Sex starved is more accurate."

"Don't they go together?"

"And the way you talked. I believed I detected submerged hick."

"Virginia gentlemen have levels of dialect suited to the propriety of the occasion," he'd said.

She was so young, fresh, and lovely that the sight of her caused his stomach to flutter, his mouth to feel seized up. He tripped over words.

"When you asked me to dinner, I couldn't believe I agreed to go out with this bumbling, muscular man old enough to be my father and whose eyes burned with lechery."

"Don't confuse lechery with the devotion in my . . .

. . . own eyes I seen 'em," Willie Meekums says and adjusts the single suspender that holds up his loose-fitting Big Boys. He and Wayland wander home from school on a May afternoon as doves flit among the pines, their white tail feathers streaking among tree limbs. Wayland spots turkey tracks in the road dust, and Willie finds a j-hook dropping, which indicates a male gobbler. He hunkers to roll it in his fingers.

"Fresh," he says.

"Lucy wouldn't have nothing to do with Mud Dog," Wayland says. "He don't even smell good."

Mud Dog has bullied them for years before graduating from the sixth grade after being held back a year. Older, larger, stronger, he hid along the road to jump out at smaller boys and make them turn out their pockets to see whether they held gum, horehounds, or a limp slab of potato sandwich not eaten at lunch. He'd not rob direct. He forced boys to accept bets only he could win—a footrace or lifting a log or throwing a rock the farthest. He might rise from a bramble bush, slip up behind you, and grab you in a stranglehold. You had to play by his rules or get hurt.

"Reckon he's learned to wash up and now he's riding that Rollaway Runner," Willie says.

Mud Dog, who got his name 'cause he liked to slog around the swamps searching for turtle eggs, beaver, and snakes, has saved himself enough money working at the gristmill to buy the Rollaway Runner bicycle. It is fire-engine red with chrome tire rims, a sprocket chain guard, and has a bell clamped to the handlebar. There are other bicycles around, but none newer and shinier than his Rollaway Runner, which before mounting Mud Dog strokes like a hot-blooded horse that needs to be quieted.

"Never get all that stink off him," Wayland says. "Smells worse than a wet skunk."

Mud Dog took a tiger-eye off Wayland by forcing him to play a game of marbles. It was Wayland's choicest breaker, and when Mud Dog walked away whistling, Wayland felt a part of himself had been hollowed out.

"Well I seen him and her together," Willie says. He is speaking of Mud Dog dressing in his go-to-meeting black suit to call on Lucy

Randolph, she with the dark blond hair tied by colored ribbons and eyes bluer than cornflowers growing wild in the ditches.

Lucy has changed, grown taller, and her hair lies long and gleaming down her shoulder blades. She walks different too, not hurrying with small purposeful steps, but moving in a kind of lingering gait. Her lazy smile indicates to Wayland she possesses a special knowledge boys are too dumb yet to understand.

Wayland still loves her. He can't look her way without feeling his face heat up and remembering the shame of his appearing sheep sheared in front of her because of head lice. He believes she thinks of and pictures it ever' time they meet. She treats him nice but moves on by instead of stopping to pass the time, which is what he always hopes for.

She's forever on his mind, and that's the reason he can't keep from playing with hisself, though it wont exactly play, and doing so causes him guilt miseries because Preacher Ernest Arbogast has warned boys should always sleep with their hands outside the covers to avoid the filthy sin of self-befoulment.

And Wayland can't get it straightened out in his mind that pretty, sweet-smelling girls would like that aching part of his body stuck in them. Girls wont animals like mares. At least nice dainty girls wont.

Wayland couldn't refuse seeing and accepting that's how babies was made, yet no way the act could be pleasurable for women. Willie was just wrong about that. If good women did it at all, they just had to suffer the shame because it was their Biblical duty as wives to submit to their husbands.

"I'd sure like to get that damn Mud Dog," Wayland says.

He and Willie had once teamed up and fought Mud Dog when he stopped them to inspect their pockets. Wayland sprang on Mud Dog's back and bit his neck while Willie rassled him. Mud Dog flung them off like leeches and left them battered and plundered at the side of the road.

"Must be some ways to fix him," Willie says.

"Let the air out of his bicycle tires," Wayland says.

"He guards that bike. Sleeps with it alongside his bed."

"His mama wouldn't let him do that."

"What I hear she does. Tells he reaches out and touches it in the night. Like he wants to do to Lucy Randolph."

"How you know?"

"Told you I seen them when I was over at the house with my daddy. Mud Dog rides her on that bicycle, and when they sit on the porch swing evenings, he tries to inch his hand up and work it 'round 'til he can drop it on her shoulder. He has to be quick 'cause ever' once in a while Mr. Randolph peeks out to see how they behaving. Mud Dog he grabs that hand back."

"Lucy Randolph'd never want his warty hand on her."

"She loves riding on that bicycle," Willie says. "He lets her ring the bell."

"I'd like to bust his head open with a hoe handle," Wayland says. He spits long.

Willie stops walking. He's thinking, and it wrinkles his freckled face. He sucks at a corner of his mouth.

"Maybe they's something," he says. "Mud Dog's over there most ever' night. I snuck around and spied on them. You know the thing I do best." He grins. "Might catch them right."

"The thing you do best?"

"The thing I the champ at."

"How you get close enough?"

"I got me a plan," Willie says. They reach the fork in the road. A buzzard skims the treetops, its shadow following. "Meet me tonight just 'fore dark."

Wayland watches Willie walking away before continuing on to the cabin. That afternoon he plants two rows of snap beans, carries in stove wood, and washes up before he eats cornbread, gravy, and collard greens flavored with a chunk of ham hock. He tries to ease out of the cabin.

"You going messing again?" his mother asks, turning from the sink, her eyes boring into him.

"Me and Willie might stroll down to the store."

"Might again huh? Either you is or you ain't."

"Yes'm," he says and slips off before she can shoot more questions at him.

"*Might* don't mean nothing," she hollers after him.

As he reaches the fork in the road, the sun lowers. A coon traveling through the woods gazes at him and continues on as if it has every right in the world to take its time and do whatever it damn well wants. Nothing more sassy than a danged coon.

Willie appears around the bend, that stride of his long and gangly. Like Wayland, he don't wear either a shirt or shoes, and the pants legs of his Big Boys pull up over his skinny shins.

"We doing what?" Wayland asks.

"We lucky no moon tonight," Willie says.

"How's that lucky?"

"Come on, you see."

They walk a quarter mile toward Jericho Crossroads but turn off at a dirt road that leads to the Ballards' sheep farm. Willie sidles into the pine woods, hunkers, and scratches his back against the trunk of a persimmon tree.

"Get yourself comfortable," he says. "We got a wait."

"For what?"

"You'll see."

The wait's not long before Willie raises a hand, and Wayland hears the whir of bicycle tires along the road. Mud Dog passes on the Rollaway Runner. They see his white shirt and red bow tie. His black shaggy hair has been wetted and parted. His heavy legs pump hard and fast.

"Give him a little time to set hisself," Willie says.

"For what?"

"You'll see."

A silvery twilight leaks through the woods, and the first whippoorwill tunes up. When Willie stands to move off, Wayland follows. It's another half mile to the dairy. They step on the tracks the Rollaway Runner's tires has left in the dust.

By the time they reach the plank fence, night has eaten up the twilight. The darkness covers the road and fill the ditches like black water rising. Wayland smells the greasy sheep, the scent of manure, and hears them chewing their cuds.

"What we do now?" he whispers.

"We sneak behind the shearing shed to the house."

"Don't they got a dog?"

"Not at the house 'cause Lucy keeps a white cat. She don't want no dog around it."

Wayland climbs over the fence after Willie, and they walk softly among the sheep that herd together and bleat. Wayland brushes off flies as Willie curses. He's stepped into fresh-dropped pellets.

"Squished between my damn toes," he whispers.

A dog barks in the distance, scaring them. They stand motionless until it quiets and then make for the shearing shed, which is empty. They peek around it to lights of Lucy's father's shotgun house, a place owned by the Ballards. Willie studies it.

Because it's Ballard property, the Randolphs have electricity used not only for the house but also to supply current for the shears. The glow from a window gleams off Mud Dog's bicycle propped in the yard.

"They on the porch," Willie whispers.

"I don't see nothing."

"He ain't going to be far from that Rollaway Runner."

They work along the fence at the rear of the house and cross over to the yard.

"What now?" Wayland whispers.

"We going to crawl in the space under the porch and do the thing I the champ at."

There's only one thing Willie's the champ at. Most boys have tried and practiced it, but Willie's has a tone and trueness no others can match.

"We get caught, Mud Dog'll kill us," Wayland whispers.

"We run like hell in different directions. He can't catch both of us. You got half a chance of getting away."

"That how come you brung me?"

"It's your share of the plan. Now let's do it."

Crouching, they slip along beside the house avoiding patches of light from windows. Voices are talking inside. At the front corner, Willie sinks to his knees and has himself a slow look around the corner. Wayland hears squeaking from the chains that holds up the porch swing.

Willie inches forward and away to the blackness beneath the porch. Wayland thinks of allowing him to go on alone, but Willie's his closest friend and not sticking with him would make Wayland a yellow-bellied coward not fit to live. He'd take a beating before he'd allow that word to get around about him.

The wooden porch is a story high. As Wayland crawls toward it, he can just make out the faint ghosting of Willie's skin. Willie reaches back a hand to lead him under. They let down and wait.

Wayland tries to quiet his breathing by clamping a hand over his mouth. Surely sounds of his beating heart are so loud in his own ears it can be heard by others. The swing gives off rhythmic creaks, and shoes push and then drag across the porch floor.

He and Willie lie directly beneath the swing. Through slits of space between the boards, Wayland glimpses flickers of movement—light from a window catching the pass of Lucy's and Mud Dog's legs and feet. Wayland hates Lucy's legs being alongside Mud Dog's. It seems impure, like axle grease on a white dress.

"You ever been to a movie?" they hear Mud Dog ask Lucy. He talks different around her, the growl gone from his voice.

"The tent show, *Ten Nights in a Barroom*," she says. "Poor drunk man got sobered up and saved his family."

"Listen, they got a real movie theater now in Tobaccoton. You reckon your daddy'd let you go with me over there if I can borrow my daddy's car?"

"I don't guess unless you took him and my mama along."

"Wouldn't be as much fun, would it?"

"I don't know what you mean," she says and giggles.

"Not like when we out where nobody can see."

"Will you kindly watch where you putting your hand?"

"Your daddy's mending a boot, and your mamma's still in the kitchen. We could have us a little friendly kiss."

"I don't want you to think I go 'round kissing boys."

"I'd never tell a thing like that. I love you, Lucy."

"Maybe just a peck," she says.

The swing stops, and there is rustling. At that moment Willie sits up to do the thing he's the champ at. He cups a hand under an armpit and flaps his upper arm against the back of the hand. The compression produces a loud, lingering fart.

Silence overhead.

"About that peck," Mud Dog says after a time.

"Well," Lucy says.

Again the rustling. This time Willie gives it his best—three shorts and a long. Again the silence.

"I believe it's time for me to go in," Lucy says and stands.

"Wait, I don't hold it against you none what you did," Mud Dog says. "Hear it all the time 'round the house, my grandaddy 'specially."

"What I did? What you did."

"It wont me."

"Well it most certainly was not me."

"Just one of the things that happens to ever'body. Come on, sit back down here beside me."

"How can you say such a thing?" she asks. "I can tell you it does not happen to me."

She opens the screen door, walks inside the house, and lets the door slam. Mud Dog stands and knocks on it. Footsteps in the house.

"You get on away from here, Mud Dog," Mr. Randolph says.

"My name's Donald," Mud Dog says.

"You get on now, boy. I won't hear no backtalk from you. Lay your foot on the path."

"I never done nothing."

"You want trouble with me? Get now."

Mud Dog stomps down to his bicycle. He's talking to himself, cussing. He kicks up the stand, swings a leg over, and rides off fast down the lane.

Wayland and Willie cross back to the sheepfold fence and over before they let go to laughing. They about to bust. Wayland chokes, clutches his stomach, blinks tears. They stagger among the sheep, again climb a fence, and when they reach the lane, they hoot, holler, and roll in dust of the road.

"Just one of those things happens to ever'body," Wayland says.

"Don't hold it against you none," Willie says, rises to his knees, and again makes the sound three times so loud and right you had to believe stink would surely follow.

"Donald," they both call out, restarting the laughter, causing them to reel away into the night where the woods, road, and earth seem to pitch around them like fellow conspirators in their rollicking glory.

fourteen

Wayland heard the planes even though the Caddy's windows were shut. He opened the one on the driver's side and leaned out to see two F-16s sweeping across the sky, one apparently playing chase with the other. They flew low, and sounds of their jet engines boomed across the land and echoed in the direction of the river.

He thought of the first plane he'd ever seen, a two-winged Jenny that a barnstormer had landed in a mowed wheat field just east of Jericho Crossroads. He and Willie had gawked at the plane as well as the dashing pilot, a young man in boots, riding britches, and a leather helmet, his goggles pushed up on his forehead. He offered all comers a dollar ride. Times had been so tight the only persons who had the dollars were Eugene and Diana Ballard. Wayland heard Diana's excited laughter and girlish screams while she was airborne. The pilot had waited around half a day for more customers, and when none showed up, he flew on, the wings wobbling, toward Tobaccoton.

"You've hardly any trace of a southern accent now," Amy had told Wayland before they were married. "Just every now and again the hint of a Virginia planter slips out when you

127

drop your *r*s and *g*s and pronounce *fire* and *house* as if they're two-syllable words."

She didn't know how hard he'd worked on his pronunciation in the army by listening to the officers and while on guard or in the shower mimicking the way they talked. No more *cap'n* for *captain* or *'nough* for *sure enough*. He had begun to keep a penciled list of difficult words. And there had been also the Britannica encyclopedia in the Camp Blanding post library. The female desk clerk teased Wayland that he'd wear the volumes out.

"Actually I like the way you talk," Amy had said. "You smooth the edges off words. It's lulling."

"All along I thought it was my body not the way I talked that hooked you," he told Amy.

"That too. I still get hot and bothered seeing you work out using your weights. Those rippling abs belong to a much younger man."

"I should carry a barbell in the trunk," he said and reached across to slide a hand under her khaki skirt and along the soft warmth of her inner thigh. Until Jennifer was born, Amy had often accompanied him on business trips. "Use it in motels along the way."

"As quickly as you can reach a sporting goods store, stop," she said, her silken knees giving way to spreading, "and I'll buy you one for those beautiful . . .

. . . muscles hardening from the constant labor the Ballards demand in order to hold a job and survive. With his daddy gone and the family's need for money, Wayland doesn't even consider more schooling and speaks his goodbye to Miss Flowers, who is saddened and shakes her head.

The relentless sun browns him, and his shoulders broaden. He easily lifts and tosses seventy-pound alfalfa bales high to the hay wagons or up to barn lofts. He works so willingly that Mr. Wesley Rudd passes the word to Mr. Henry Ballard who agrees Wayland should be shifted from the fields to the sawmill.

It's a promotion that brings an extra ten cents an hour, yet not without danger. The shrieking blade, a height taller than his own, knows no mercy and passes through careless flesh as effortlessly as a knife through smoke.

"You pile slabs and stack ricks," Britt Mosley, the sawmill boss, tells him.

Britt is short, heavy, abrupt. Sawdust lodges in his dark beard as well as on his Big Boys and black-billed cap. Sometimes it coats his outsized teeth, and when he spits, a speckled brown blob arches and splatters on the ground. He oversees the steam engine and operates the clutch lever which slides pine logs on the hissing carriage to feed the ever-hungry blade.

The mill is set at the south end of a five-acre field rutted by wagon wheels and pocked by mud holes. Winding Branch bounds one side. A laggard, biting yellowish smoke rises from smoldering sawdust mounds. Mules skid in felled trees cut to length, which are rolled by darkies using cantdogs up a ramp and onto the log deck for debarking.

Live belts power the blade. A sagging revolving chain draws sawdust from beneath to a pile that builds and topples. Sized lumber leaving the blade rides on metal rollers to the trimmer. Slabs bypass the trimmer and slide on to the end of the conveyer where they dump to the ground.

His first day at the sawmill Wayland collects the slabs. They'll be sold to people for stoves and fireplaces come winter and are cheap but burn fast and must be carted away by buyers. He lifts lumber set aside at the trimmer, loads it on a wagon pulled by a mule named Dynamite, and hauls it across the lot to build ricks. The two-by-eights are clean and shiny as peeled apples and laid out in the full sun to season. They appear slick, yet feel raw and bristle with splinters. He's forgotten his gloves left across the railing of the cabin porch to dry.

He sweats under a flaming July sun that has boiled all blue from the sky and waits for Britt to holler, "Break," but rest comes only at noon when the sawmill gang is allowed thirty minutes to eat.

Wayland sits in shade of the corrugated metal roof that covers the stilled blade, the carriage, the live belts, and trimmer. He chews what he's brought for lunch—a potato sandwich, a bunch of coon grapes gathered in the woods, a Marglobe tomato from the garden. He crosses to and kneels beside Winding Branch to palm and suck up water.

He understands Britt's testing him. The foreman waits for Wayland to give out, slump, walk off, and never return. By mid-afternoon Wayland feels so dizzy he stumbles, and his sight wavers. His hands, though toughened from labor in the Ballard fields, bleed from splinters and keen edges.

"You spotting them boards with blood," Britt says. "Nobody'll want 'em."

"Don't have no gloves."

"I sure God see that. You got no brains either coming to a sawmill withouten gloves."

"I forgot 'em and woulda been late if I'd gone back."

"Let me tell you something, boy. There's ten men I can think of right off that would like your job. You work here, forget and forgot don't count. Got me?"

"Yes, sir."

"Now you take these gloves of mine. They 'bout worn out, and I keep an extra pair. And don't use them *forgot* words on me ever again."

"Thank you, Mr. Mosley."

"Thanks don't buy bird shit," he says and walks off to open the steam engine's fire box and toss in slabs. The iron stack shoots sparks among dark twisting smoke. Britt pumps up water to the boiler from the hose that dips into Winding Branch and again grasps the chest-high clutch lever in the cranny shack, which sends logs to give of themselves to the blade.

As he lays a rick, Wayland sees Josephus Blodgett driving a mule pulling a creaking wagon loaded with yellow poplar. It's choice work, and Wayland feels envy and anger. Josephus earns his beans, but it's wrong, Wayland believes, for coloreds to be put ahead of whites in the bestowing of jobs.

Josephus is shirtless, his blackness sweat-polished. His shoulders have become mighty, his thighs like legs of ham. He sits tall on the spring-supported driver's seat like he owns the Ballard rig as he reins in the mule and grins at Wayland.

"Think I stop at the store and buy me a cold Big Orange," he says. "Bottle with ice chips sliding down it. Rub the bottle against my head and chest 'fore I lets the drink slip on down my gullet to cool my belly."

"Git on away from here 'fore I hit you upside the head with a two-by-four."

"I think of you while I drinking it. I be feeling sorry for you, Wayland."

"I be thinking of you with a busted skull."

"My skull don't break easy," Josephus says and laughs. He clucks up the mule and drives away singing.

Wayland hates him and Mr. Wesley Rudd for transferring Josephus from the fields to mostly sitdown work hauling logs. Wayland pictures himself beating the burrhead, lying in wait holding the cocked LeFever, or burning the cabin where Josephus lives with his mama and daddy. Hating gives Wayland energy and helps pass the time.

He makes it through the twelve-hour days. At quitting time the sun still stands high as Britt shifts the clutch lever to neutral and the drive belts still. Before he releases the steam engine's pressure, he pulls a link chain that blows a whistle blast heard all the way to the river. The engine, like a tired animal, pants for hours before it quiets and red coals pulse under a white coat of ashes.

Saturday evening the whistle blasts loud and long, and the mill closes for the week. Wayland and the sawmill gang wait for their pay. Black Amos arrives driving a Reo bringing cash kept locked in a padlocked iron box. He watches as Britt counts the money into Wayland's cupped and blood-scabbed hands—two tattered ten-dollar bills, a five, three ones, two quarters, two dimes, and a nickel.

Wayland plods the mile and a half to the cabin where he strips off his clothes to wash at the well. He rubs down his body with soapsuds, draws up buckets of cooling water, and dumps them over his head. The lye soap burns his lacerated hands. He allows the sear air to dry his skin and slaps at greenies landing on his arms, face, and head.

He's alone. Emmett's still at the Ballard stable and been talking about joining the army. Ferdinand works late nights repairing equipment. Lottie pays ten cents each way for a ride with other women in a chugging old school bus to Tobaccoton where a shoe factory that hires females has opened. She sometimes stays over with a girlfriend after her shift.

The Ballards have hired Wayland's mama to do their baking in the big house's kitchen, and she won't return 'til her beaten biscuits or hot rolls are pulled from the oven. The Ballards eat late.

He spreads his wages across the kitchen table and sits waiting on the cabin steps. His mama will be bringing tote. Though the great blade no longer feeds, he continues to hear its shrill, and his nose still holds the stinging scent of the drifting yellow smoke from the burning sawdust mounds. To clear the smell, he snorts like a horse, and sawdust garnishes his snot.

His mama emerges through the pearly twilight along the lane to the cabin. She carries the tote in her string-handle shopping bag, which swings at her side. Her face is often powdered by Ballard flour, which is whiter and more finely ground than what's sold at their store. Ballard flour comes from Tobaccoton.

"You a good boy," she says when she sees and counts the money. A smile lifts the droop of her lips. After she washes herself, she lays out on the table a feast of Ballard leftovers—slices of lamb, a cheese soufflé which has fallen, two of her own beaten biscuits, and a heavy wedge of angel cake, its white icing mostly stripped off. Wayland thinks of it as being Diana Ballard's leavings.

Often his mama brings home clothing, pieces saved before reaching the pit, like the pair of trousers that has a snagged leg and easily patched by her deft fingers. The pants belonged to Mr. Henry's son Eugene, who continues to ride blooded horses across the fields and through the woods.

He also drives a yellow Ford coupé so fast it leaves behind red dust that rises twenty foot high and seems will never settle. Wayland glimpses him and the streaming hair of pretty laughing girls Eugene fetches from Tobaccoton to Bellepays.

Wayland's mama now owns a pair of lady's white gloves, a feathered hat, and a black party dress discarded after the death of the first Mrs. Ballard, who died of a reeling brain stroke while pruning roses in her garden. Black Amos tried to catch her before she toppled forward among blooms and angered bees.

At the funeral the road to the big house became so clogged a troop of state police helped Sheriff Calvin and his deputies direct traffic. Mourners left their cars parked along the secondary road's shoulders and walked to the family cemetery inside the wall. Wayland, Lottie, Pearl May, Emmett, Ferdinand, and their mama stood at the rear of the gathering alongside others who took Ballard pay. Wayland didn't even catch a glimpse of Diana.

Most nights Wayland's mama sits by the kerosene lamp and alters garments for herself, Lottie, and Pearl May—cast-off Ballard materials as fine and light as the passing touch of a breeze. Shadows of her hands rise and lower against the wall.

From the second Mrs. Ballard—who cantering past on Midnight Baron always waves to Wayland—his mama receives a soft, tan camel's-hair coat that has a moth hole in its silk lining and a torn fox fur at the collar. After she mends the hole and reattaches the fur, she stands before the mirror set on the dressing table Ferdinand has built, sanded, and stained for her. She turns right, left, and stares over her shoulder at her reflection, which quivers in light from the kerosene lamp's wick.

Wayland believes she pretends to see herself as a rich lady or a refined and painted model like those pictured on pages of discarded magazines brought from the big house—*Vogue*, *Cosmopolitan*, *Redbook*. She never wears the coat outside the cabin but draws it on only to dream in.

fifteen

Wayland drove past abandoned shacks and a timbered desolation along the winding dusty way. Like the human body, he thought, the land can be misused and bled until it gives forth only a feeble exhalation of life—a lingering, expiring breath. He pictured the sumptuous life he, Amy, and Jennifer lived in Florida— their four-bedroom house with its vined colonnade, the mosaic patio and dripping fountain, the lemon trees, the turquoise pool where each morning Wayland swam laps before he drove to his office, and the view across the bay to the white yachts sliding over their own reflections along the shimmering intercoastal.

From his air-conditioned office, part of a seventh-floor suite, he could look out over a blue- and red-roofed alabaster city to emerald fingers of tropical water winding among the royal palms. Frigate birds soared on thermals sent up from the sun-smacked metropolis that pulsated attainment, riches, and beauty.

Connie, his brunette secretary, carried him coffee and the morning's mail. His salesmen were so competent and loyal the business practically ran itself. At least once each day he turned to the broad, tinted window and reminded himself of what he'd achieved and where he'd come from—the other land, the other life.

Yet despite all he could lay his hand to, questions and doubts still remained and gnawed at him, mostly at odd hours of night but there were days . . .

. . . the sawmill labor requires different muscles, dispenses different aches and pains. Every job, Wayland learns, has a pace and rhythm, and the trick's to allow the body to find them and conform. Throughout the summer he pays out energy and brawn as if spending precious money, always holding back a reserve for the killing drains of large orders from the lumber buyers.

The second week of November Britt allows him to run the trimmer. Wayland hopes one day to tend the steam engine and operate the carriage, which clamps logs like bound captives and delivers them to the blade, the number one, most responsible job. He sees himself bossing a crew and like Britt counting out wages.

The December blizzard blows across the county from the northwest preceded by knockdown winds and temperature that drops so low the puddles collected in wagon ruts freeze over before noon. Snow begins as grit and changes into large, delicate wafers tossed ever' which away on turbulent air before finding purchase on the ground. They build fast into palls that round angles of land and drape the pine boughs. Sawdust smoke is weighed down by snow.

Wayland snakes timber from the reserve pile to the log deck by working Dynamite, who got his name because of a powerful kick that has broken men's legs. The snow collects so fast the mule lifts his hooves high and hunches against the harness to haul the loads. Dynamite don't like the snow and has to be smacked on his rump to keep him moving.

At four o'clock Britt studies the sky. Snow has lodged on his face and whitened his beard. He spits, again checks his dollar pocket watch, and shuts down the steam engine's drive wheel.

"Call it a day," he announces, sounds the whistle, and braces his body against wind, which flaps his pants and turns up the bill of his cap.

"We work tomorrow?" Wayland asks.

"If the world ain't ended," Britt hollers back and helps remove Dynamite's harness before swinging a leg over the mule to ride off. Their shapes merge into whirling flakes. Wayland and the other sawmill hands, bent forward into snow, follow by keeping to Dynamite's tracks.

Wayland breaks away to hike to the cabin until drifts block him. His legs tire from climbing over or pushing through them. He squints into the wildly shifting gale, which has again become grit that stings his face and forces him to clench his eyelids to slits.

The snow claims all landmarks, causing darkness to settle in early, and he can't make out the path he takes daily through the woods. Wind tips and staggers him, the blowing snow packs his eye sockets. He believes it best not to try for the cabin but double back with the wind behind him to the sawmill and wait for the storm to slacken.

He thinks of his mama. At breakfast Emmett has said he meant to take time off for a trip to Lynchburg and talk with an army recruiting sergeant. Ferdinand and Mr. Wesley Rudd were to drive to Danville and inspect a spanking new John Deere cultivator. Suppose the brothers and Lottie can't get home? Still his mama should be all right if she stays either in the Ballard kitchen or reaches the cabin where Wayland has stacked red oak slabs head high on the porch.

He backtracks to the sawmill, almost missing it, his footprints already filled and vanished, his vision shortened. The steam engine gives out heat that melts snow which refreezes to strung-out twisted ice. Despite the slamming, banging corrugated metal roof over them, the carriage, trimmer, blade, and belts are snow covered. The ricks and sawdust mounds are curtained and beyond his sight.

He wraps feed sacks that'd held grain for Dynamite around his body and legs before slumping back against planks of the cranny shack. He also pulls a sack over his head. It carries the good sweet smell of Ballard oats.

Snow blows through gaps in planks and collects on him. Gradually covered, his body warms, and the wind becomes distant. He snoozes, rouses, and lifts the sack from his head to peek out. Wind slashes the roof, and tin rips off spilling nails and flaps away like a huge tumbling wing.

He thinks of the Ballards comfortable before their great fireplaces in the big house with its many flared chimneys. Black Amos will carry logs to keep them burning hot. He also pictures Diana standing before the mirror of a pink silken bedroom. Using an ivory brush she strokes long strands of sheening black hair.

Head covered, Wayland sleeps through the night. The moment he wakes and removes the sack, the patting of snow on the last section of roof ceases suddenly as if a command to shut down has been obeyed. The wind too hushes, the sun works free, and the world becomes a dazzling white emptiness. He shades his eyes against the painful intensity of light.

He stands and beats his arms against his sides. The steam engine has cooled. No birds sing, and there's no sound except for the splintering of trees as boughs fracture under the weight of snow and ice, a procession like a giant's footsteps smashing through the forest.

Later in the day the sun's heat takes hold and causes a partial thawing. Rivulets begin to trickle under the snow. Limbs drop heavy dollops, the sounds of their plopping spreading among the piney woods. He hears ice cracking along the river as it gives way to warmth.

The drifts are still too high to make it to the cabin. He'll wait another night. As the sun sinks, cold spreads with darkness and all thawing ceases. Hunger wrenches his belly. He's finished half of the apple left from lunch the previous day and eats a handful of

Dynamite's oats. He sucks snow to wash down their scratchy dryness.

The second morning's sunlight outlines crisscrossed strands of the feed sack over his eyes. He uncovers them, pushes up, swings his arms, and stomps his feet. By noon water again runs beneath the snow. Life stirs too, crows ghosting among shrouded pines, cattle bawling, the rattle of a distant tractor, a hound barking.

He uses the handle of a broken cantdog as a staff to struggle and break through drifts. Partridges fly up, and he crosses prints of their tiny fleeing feet. Midafternoon while sweating and his breathing coming hard, he reaches the cabin. No smoke rises from its single chimney, but Reb bounds toward him and does his happy dance. His tail whips snow.

Inside the cabin no fire burns, and lids of the stove's top are cold. Dishes are stacked clean beside the sink's pitcher pump that Ferdinand has installed. Floors have been swept, the quilted beds are made.

Most likely his mama is with the servants at the big house. Wayland feeds Reb a ham bone that still has shreds of meat clinging to it, and Reb carries it under the house and gnaws away. Wayland eats a cold biscuit and partly frozen raw potato. His teeth crunch ice crystals.

The sun shines full, and the hackberry's shadow lies dark on the snow. Using his staff, Wayland slogs toward the big house. The stone pineapples on the gateposts are half revealed and dripping. He hears jingling. It's Eugene and Diana wearing coats, scarves, gloves, and knit caps. Eugene holds the reins as the trotting sorrel pulls the sled runners hissing along the drive.

Hooves sling snow, and Diana waves as they pass. The sound of bells attached to oiled leather harness recede. The sled's runners leave clean tracks, which straddle the sorrel's deep hoof prints.

Wayland smells smoke from the big house's chimneys. The walks and courtyard have been cleared, and snow knocked from the box bushes. Copper downspouts splash as gutters empty. An icicle drops from the dolphin's mouth and breaks on the ice of the fountain.

The house's rear entrance has a peaked roof over it. He knocks lightly, his knuckles against the wood more an apology than a demand. Black Amos opens the door. He is outfitted in a white shirt, a black bow tie, and a white apron. Those unlit bottomless dark eyes feed on Wayland and make him aware of his soggy, bedraggled appearance.

"Clean them boots," Black Amos orders, and Wayland wipes them on the mat. He keeps to sheets of newspaper spread across the kitchen floor and is allowed to stand near the stove. A copper ventilation hood covers it, and a battery of pots and pans hang from oak ceiling beams.

The iron cook stove is large enough for a hotel kitchen, this one itself so big it could hold all four rooms of the cabin. In the pantry a uniformed colored maid named Beulah stacks fruit in a glass bowl. She ignores Wayland.

"Your mother's not with us," Black Amos says, speaking the Ballard English he's learned from them and uses inside the big house. "And she failed to arrive today."

"She left during the snow?"

"I advised against it. She did as she wished."

Wayland thinks she must've stopped at Pearl May and Lonnie's to wait out the storm by their fire. He thanks Black Amos.

"You're growing, boy," Black Amos says. "One of these days you might even call yourself a man."

"I been hoping," Wayland says, not showing the resentment he feels at Black Amos for calling him *boy*.

"Take these to your mother," Black Amos says and lifts an orange, apple, and pear from the glass bowl. "She a good woman."

Wayland is surprised and confused by the fruit. He thinks of being dragged down from the tulip poplar because he looked over the wall. Never before has Black Amos shown him kindness.

As Wayland pushes toward Pearl May and Lonnie's, lengths of snow crumble free of tree limbs and fall. Ditches fill from the melting to overflowing. His boots draw up mud, which dirties the snow. He eats the pear.

Pearl May and Lonnie's is warmed by a wood-burning space heater set at the center of their cabin. Pearl May now has three children, the oldest five. They stop playing on the floor around the stove, alarmed by Wayland's entrance, their eyes large, stilled, and wary like fauns in the woods.

"She never come by here," Pearl May says, holding her youngest, a sickly baby girl who has a sugar tit stuck in her mouth. "She stayed somewheres else and prob'ly home by now."

They offer Wayland wedges of sorghum-sweetened corn bread and two mugs of hot black coffee before he starts off. He leaves the orange for the children. As he hikes, he hears the distant jingling of sleigh bells—Diana and Eugene returning to the big house.

A red fox chases a rabbit across the road into the woods. Wayland hears the rabbit's frantic death squeal. He runs after the fox hoping to scare it into dropping the rabbit he could carry home to cook up for a meal. The fox won't turn loose the rabbit, which has dripped drops of blood on the snow. Wayland gives up as the fox dodges under tangled laps left among stumps of cutover pines.

At the cabin Reb waits on the porch. Wayland has found no tracks left by his mama. Inside, nothing is changed. He walks into the yard, cups his hands around his mouth, and shouts "Mama." The snow absorbs and deadens his voice. There is no answer.

He crosses the yard to use the privy built by his father and kept in repair by Ferdinand. He needs to kick aside snow to open the door. His mama sits inside.

She's dressed as if for a journey—the ladylike gloves, the feathered hat, and the camel's-hair coat whose fur collar she has reattached. Her hands hold a *Saturday Evening Post* spread open across her lap to the advertisement of a silver Greyhound bus rolling along a palm-fringed highway that runs straight between Spanish-style mansions and waves of a pale green sea breaking gently on a salt-white beach.

Wayland's touch doesn't rouse her stiffened body. He takes hold of her with both hands, hugs her to warm her, but she's gone—traveled away on the Greyhound, the gentian blue eyes set on white spires of a sun-flooded city in the blue distance.

sixteen

In the distance a fire burned. He couldn't see the flames, but the black smoke formed its own nuclear-type cloud over the horizon. He smelled the charred wood and suspected that somebody was clearing land, but who would want to do that in this poor country? Well, maybe the Ballards. They never stopped acquiring property, which meant somebody else had to be giving it up.

Shortleaf pines grew in close to the road, their branches entwined and dropping a fragmented shade. Wayland had shot a racked deer in the bend of the road just ahead, the buck cautious, stepping softly, daintily, through the shadows, its nose quivering as it winded, its outsized ears alert and flicking forward. Hounds had driven it up from the bottom where mud had splotched its tawny dappled flanks.

His rifle had been a British Enfield .303, one of thousands imported into the country after the end of World War I and sold cheaply as surplus. His daddy had traded liquor for it, and the Enfield became the family's backup meat-hunting gun second to the LeFever used by him, Emmett, and Wayland. Ferdinand, however, had never taken to the killing of game.

Wayland's daddy later eventually sold the Enfield off for twenty dollars in order to buy time at the Ballards' store and fight a rearguard action against being forced by pressure of the relentless ledger to work in their fields.

During his boyhood Wayland's daddy had sent him out alone with the rifle and only a single cartridge with instructions to shoot at nothing he couldn't be certain of killing. Wayland arrived home at nightfall after missing a shot at a grunting, scampering razorback and received a whipping for the wasted shell. Strokes of a leather belt on his hind end had greatly improved his marksmanship.

He'd hit his first buck in the neck. As it bounded off spurting blood, he didn't hurry after it. He knew the animal would eventually spill out its life. He found it lying and breathing in an eddy of Wildcat Creek. Blood seeped away on the idle current, a last breath like a sigh escaped the deer, and the brown luster faded from eyes consenting to the arrival of death . . .

. . . that has taken Wayland's mama. She's held the family together, and after her burial at the Healing Spring Baptist Church, Wayland's sisters and brothers begin to pull and drift apart. Like chaff tossed into air, they are blown by winds of need and hunger.

Pearl May and Lonnie move to Blackstone where he lands a job at the shook factory. They rent a wind-honed company house that Lonnie paints yellow. Pearl May sews and hangs curtains. She has grown even heavier and is again full with child. Lonnie dreams of them one day owning a Chevrolet automobile.

Lottie is squired by a long-haired timberhick from Stony Point. She's been keeping up the cabin, but on a late April afternoon when Wayland returns from the sawmill he finds a penciled note telling him she's gone to live with the man, whose name is Buster Gauls. Lottie has a fine upright handwriting.

Wayland rides his thumb to Stony Point and confronts her as she hangs Buster's laundered work clothes on a wire strung between honey locust trees. She's too thin, the skin of her face, like their mama's, has pulled tight over bone. She seems to be straining even standing still.

The weedy yard behind the dilapidated shanty is strewn with rusting logging equipment, discarded tires, and overturned oil drums. A fiery-eyed black cat perches on a chain-hoisted engine block.

"You shaming Mama's memory the way you doing," Wayland says.

"Buster and me's going to marry," she answers, the tail of her oversized plaid shirt hanging loose almost to her knees. She jams clothespins taken from her mouth over a pair of heavy, big-bottomed corduroy pants. "Soon as things settle. I got his promise."

"Promise 'bout much account as a bucket of air."

"Well I love and believe him."

"Mama'd skin you, and Daddy'd shoot him."

"I'm old enough to do what I want."

"And be a damn fool."

"Just get out of my yard."

"It's his yard, not yours, and Mama's watching with her eyes and seeing you every minute you sin."

Lottie sniffles and presses a sleeveless undershirt she's lifted from the bushel basket to her face. Wayland talks her into gathering her belongings and returning to the cabin. He catches them a ride on a billet truck, and she stays home five days before she's gone again. He don't go after her a second time.

Ferdinand, the quiet brother, not only cares for the Ballards' machinery, he also secretly unearths the father's still. On payday field hands with deep thirsts know if they walk a crooked deer trail threading through the forest and purse their lips to a three-note partridge whistle, Ferdinand will limp from shadows and produce a Mason jar filled with honest white liquor.

He charges fifty cents a jar, meaning to save the money to build himself a garage, buy tools, and repair cars, trucks, and farm machinery. He does a good and growing business until a shaggy, bearded Fed from Richmond who wears Big Boys and a bandless slouch hat whistles the three notes and clamps handcuffs around Ferdinand's wrists. The government men joke and laugh as they tip over the mash and axe the jars and copper cooker.

Emmett is let go at Bellepays. Gossip is the beautiful woman from the north has left aging Mr. Henry Ballard and lives in Mexico. Days now, Emmett says, Mr. Henry don't leave the big house to inspect the fields. Eugene is away at school, and Diana still rides, but stalls wait empty in the stable.

Other more efficient sawmills using gasoline engines or electrically driven power belts begin to undercut the Ballard price for lumber. Some weeks Wayland works only three days. Mr. Henry should've spent more of his money on new machinery and the replanting of trees instead of horses and finery for his second wife. Britt Mosely, hat in hand, talks to him about needed improvements but says Mr. Henry doesn't really appear to be listening or much care.

"He was looking far away while I talked to him," Britt says.

Emmett thinks of finding work at Richmond. He's heard the Lucky Strike cigarette factory is hiring. He packs his clothes in a dented tin suitcase saved from the Ballards' pit, and Wayland stands beside him waiting for the bus that stops at Jericho Crossroads.

"If'en it's good, I'll send a postcard and tell you to come join me," Emmett says.

He climbs on the bus, takes a seat by the window, and waves. Wayland watches him leave. No postcard arrives, though Wayland late each afternoon stops by Ballards' store.

"Nothing today," Mr. Luther Blackburn says, a refrain.

Wayland hears that Lottie has left Buster Gauls and is living with a guano salesman. Before the county judge Ferdinand has pled guilty and from prison writes that he operates a lathe in its machine shop. For Ferdinand's birthday Wayland wraps and mails him a box of chocolate-covered cherries, a pack of Luckies, and a pair of white cotton socks.

In December Wayland finds old Reb curled up on the porch dead. He carries the hound to the garden plot he's only been half cultivating and buries him. He believes there's got to be a dog heaven. "He's been a fine hound," Wayland, standing with his cap removed, tells God.

At Christmas he sits alone by the stove. A north wind gusts over the flue, and sleet raps the roof and windowpanes. The most hurtful cold is the cabin's continuing emptiness. Neither Lottie nor Emmett has returned for the holiday. Pearl May's busy with her own family. Wayland tends to the cabin the best he can, but ever' room, board, and window curtain seems to have wilted or worn at the lack of a woman's touch. His mama's colorful bottles lining the windowsill throw only pale shadows on his hands at the kitchen sink.

He finally hears from Emmett, who's not at Richmond's American Tobacco but has joined the marines. He encloses a snapshot of himself, the sort snapped in carnival booths where you seat yourself and trigger your own picture after dropping a quarter down the slot. Emmett grins, appears cocky, his uniform cap set jauntily. He hopes for a posting to Hawaii.

The Philco radio on the counter at the Ballards' store talks of war in Europe and the draft. All men twenty-one to thirty-five are required to register. The government sends an official to set up a portable table on the Ballards' store porch and take signatures, which are often no more than *X*s carefully drawn.

"You need a deed," Mr. Luther Blackburn tells Wayland when he asks about selling the cabin.

Wayland lifts off the shelf his daddy's King Edward cigar box which holds the tarnished, notched button the father claimed is from Grandfather Winslow's Confederate uniform, the Ingersoll pocket watch that still works, the head of a buck deer carved into a knob of its leg bone, dice, the meerschaum pipe, and the copper coin advertising Green River whisky. He finds no deed.

He searches his mama's dresser drawers and fingers the combs of many colors she's collected, an empty bottle of perfume that has a glass stopper shaped like a lily, a curled, yellowed snapshot of her as a child. She's barefooted, wearing a dress that's little more than a flour sack with holes for her skinny arms, and sitting on a spotted ox. She smiles and offers a daisy toward the camera. The rope tied to the ox's halter is held by a hand and part of an arm that leads to a disconnected and unknown human being.

"Get yourself a lawyer," Mr. Luther Blackburn tells Wayland when he can't find the deed.

"Got no money for lawyers."

"A chance I can look it up at the courthouse next time I go to Tobaccoton," Mr. Luther Blackburn volunteers. "But lawyers into everything these days, including the grave."

The blade at the sawmill no longer shrills in Wayland's head. Mr. Henry sells the last of his timber holdings to lumber contractors from Drakes Branch and closes down the Ballard operation. Wayland and Britt are let go.

Mr. Wesley Rudd does what he can for Wayland, yet work in the fields is seasonal, and Wayland tries to join the CCC, which has a camp in neighboring Prince James County. The camp supervisor tells him their quota is filled.

"No record of your daddy ever owning that land," Mr. Luther Blackburn says of the cabin. "All the books was destroyed when the courthouse burned. You not been paying taxes. Looks to be a part of the original Ballard tract."

"Us Garnetts been living on the place ever since they come up from Tennessee," Wayland says.

"Fact is you got no paper and ownership's not writ down in the clerk's office."

"What I do?" Wayland asks.

"Without a lawyer, time for doing's gone," Mr. Luther Blackburn says and blinks in the rare way that makes people feel they've been touched. "Boy, nothing happening 'round here. Get yourself the hell out of Howell County."

Britt has been unable to find work and means to leave for Norfolk.

"They building ships down there fast as they can knock them together," he says. "They'll hire anything with one arm and two feet."

"Reckon I could tag along?" Wayland asks.

"Your shoe leather," Britt says.

Wayland owns no suitcase. He wears his go-to-meeting suit and packs a workshirt, a clean pair of Big Boy overalls, a change of underwear, and a razor in a blanket roll that he ties with bailer twine.

He looks through the Prince Edward cigar box. He takes the Ingersoll watch and Grandfather Winslow's notched uniform button, which he sticks in his pants pocket for a good-luck piece.

Pearl May kisses him. She'll tell Lottie. He calls on Mr. Wesley Rudd, Mr. Luther Blackburn, and Preacher Arbogast to speak his goodbyes.

"Keep you'self clean for the Lord," Preacher Arbogast says and lays a hand on Wayland's head. "And may our merciful God hold you safe and reach out His hand to you and guide your feet to the narrow paths of His righteousness."

Wayland walks toward the big house. He means to knock on the back door to speak to Black Amos and thinks maybe Mr. Henry Ballard himself might wish him well. He reaches the Kentucky gate at Bellepays's entrance and stops and stares down the paved drive flanked by magnolias and blooming dogwood.

Diana Ballard, on foot and holding reins, appears troubled as she leads her gimpy thoroughbred gelding along the lane's grassy shoulder.

seventeen

T he dirt road sloped downward, and Wayland passed a second cutover area—stumps and laps left among palls of sawdust that bleached the land. Ditches held empty tin cans, a sofa its stuffing exposed, a battered doorless refrigerator lying on its side, a bald truck tire, and a broken upside-down baby carriage, the wheels gone.

Had Amy been with him, she would have squinched up her sharp little nose, for she couldn't endure mess and had badgered him into giving up smoking because of ashes left around the house and a hole burned in a gray cashmere sweater. He felt relief she wasn't beside him and able to see the land's shameful care.

During his youth he'd never thought of land except in functional terms. It was there simply to be used—the forests, the fields, their crops, and most men born to Howell County took from it all they could with no thought or regard of consequences.

He spotted the iron bridge, a single span, the spidery superstructure once black now marred by chancres of rust. A sign that needed repainting warned the limit had been reduced to five tons of gross weight.

He'd once sat beside Mr. Wesley Rudd who drove a Ballard truck toward Tobaccoton in order to buy harrow tines used in preparing Ballard fields for spring planting. The Reo's truck tires had rattled planks laid across bridge girders, and Wayland had sat straight in the cab and felt proud of being chosen to help Mr. Wesley Rudd on an important job. It'd been evidence of approval and likely advancement.

"You saving any money?" Mr. Wesley Rudd had asked.

"I been trying."

"Trying ain't doing."

"I'm meaning to."

"Meaning to ain't either."

So long ago, Wayland thought, and Mr. Wesley Rudd had seemed lordly and wise.

"Shave a few cents off your pay ever' week and bury it in a coffee can," Mr. Wesley Rudd had advised him. "Never trust a bank. And keep you pecker in your pants except to pass water. You listen to what I'm telling you, Way- . . .

. . . -land withdraws his hand from the top plank of the Kentucky gate and watches Diana Ballard. He eyes her slim brown boots, tan riding britches, black leather gloves, yellow shirt, and the red kerchief knotted around her neck. Her black hair has been gathered and bound by a red ribbon and hangs down her back in a ponytail.

The black legs of her bay gelding appear to match Diana's hair. The horse has been fed nothing but sweet feed and timothy hay all its life, a diet that gives his coat a rich, glossy sheen. Maybe, Wayland thinks, she's chosen to ride the bay for that very reason— like an accessory, the way a girl might pick out shoes or a hat to go with certain frocks.

The bay's head dips with each step taken on his near front hoof. Diana stops, pats the horse's neck, strokes it. As she straightens she sees Wayland.

"Hey, come here and help me," she commands, not asks.

He opens the gate and jogs along the drive towards her. His pounding footsteps and quick approach spooks the bay and causes it to wheel and snort. As Diana holds out a hand to stop Wayland, she croons to the horse like a mother might to soothe a child.

"Now, Robin Hood, everything's good, so good, so good, yes-s-s, so good, Robin Hood."

She grips the reins close to the horse's mouth, again pats its neck, and the bay, who appears much too large and powerful to submit to her, quiets, though he's still wild of eye.

"This boy just doesn't understand you're not supposed to make sudden moves around a hot blood," she says.

Wayland has halted, his left leg planted back behind the right in midstride. He sets down his foot and says, "I'm sorry, Miss Diana."

"You can come closer but do it softly. Robin's spirited, not a plow animal."

"Yes'm."

"You look familiar."

Wayland knows she's near sixteen, his own age—slender, with green eyes so full and direct he can't look into them fully.

"Yes'm."

"You don't have to say 'yes'm' to me. I'm not an old hag."

"No'm, you surely not."

She laughs, a mocking sound from red lips that completely changes her mouth's usual pout.

"Not 'no'm' either," she says, studying him. "You favor Emmett Garnett."

"Emmett's my brother."

"Daddy says all you Garnetts look alike."

"Yes'm."

"There you go again. Yes and no are sufficient. We were sorry to see Emmett leave. He has a way with horses."

Wayland almost yes'ms her again but captures the word before it's out of his mouth.

"Emmett's smart all right."

"What about you, are you smart?"

"I'm pretty good with figures."

"But you don't know anything about horses?"

"I know a little."

"How little?"

"I been 'round 'em," he says and thinks of Hector the stud mounting and ravishing the mare at Uncle Allan's farm as well as the beautiful lady, the second Mrs. Ballard, who rode him on Midnight Baron and laid the silver dollar across his palm.

"How far around?" she asks and again laughs.

"Mam?"

"Never mind. Do you think you could possibly look at Robin's hoof and tell whether it's bruised?"

"Don't mind trying," he says, though he's never in his life fooled with any animal as fine as Robin Hood. A mule yes, Dynamite, but not a high-powered thoroughbred. He hesitates, thinking how best to go about it.

"Well?" she asks and impatiently taps the toe of a boot.

He moves in beside the bay, lays one hand on its withers, and runs the other down the horse's leg as he's seen Britt Mosely do when shoeing Dynamite. He strokes the leg before pinching the tendon behind the bone just above the fetlock. To his relief Robin obediently lifts the hoof. The bay turns its head to watch but stands easy. I must, Wayland thinks, look like I know what I'm doing.

He focuses on the hoof and runs his fingers over it but finds no damage to the sole, the frog, or the wall. He straddles the leg before pressing his thumbs against the sole. Robin doesn't respond.

"Don't seem bruised," Wayland says.

"Well it's bound to be something. Maybe in his knee or shoulder. Oh I hope not. I love my Robin Hood. I wish Emmett were here."

"I do too," Wayland says and runs his fingers around the inner side of the lightweight iron shoe. He feels an edge, leans close to peer at it, and lets down the hoof.

"What?" Diana asks.

"Maybe," he says and draws his Barlow from his pants pocket, opens the blade, and again pinches the bay's tendon. Robin raises the hoof. As Wayland works the tip of the blade under the shoe's edge, Robin tries to jerk free.

"Don't you dare hurt him," Diana says.

"Don't mean to," Wayland answers, and with a slight twist of the blade pops out a gravel. He releases the hoof, picks up the gravel, and holds it to Diana.

"That little thing?" she asks.

"Try him now."

She leads Robin along the shoulder, and the horse no longer favors the hoof. Diana brings him back to Wayland, who tosses the gravel aside and slaps at his pants legs, which spume dust.

"I bet you're like Emmett and have a way with horses," Diana says. "My father believes it's a gift some are born with. Come on, we'll go to the stable."

"I reckon," he says.

"The boy reckons. Help me mount."

He doesn't understand exactly how to go about it. She has looped the reins over Robin's head and stands with both hands on the saddle, her left leg lifted backwards.

"Well?" she asks and turns to him.

He's unsure where or how he should touch her. She's a Ballard, and the thought of contact both excites and unnerves him. He's glad he's washed up and well dressed. He decides he'll just take hold of her little waist and set her on the horse. His fingers cup and press the softness of her flesh.

"What are you doing?" she asks as he lifts her. She's no heavier than an alfalfa bale and starts laughing as he lets her down on the saddle. "My, you're strong. Haven't you ever helped a girl mount before?"

"I reckon not," he says, his face hot.

"Another reckon, and if you have to reckon, you haven't," she says and touches a heel to Robin's flank. The horse moves away in a fast walk. "Come on now," she calls back to Wayland.

He runs after them. He's wearing his black, box-toed leather shoes bought from the Ballards' store and used 'til this day only for preaching, weddings, and funerals. He believes his feet has pretty much stopped growing, and he expects the shoes to last a couple more years and then he'll have them half-soled. Not made for running, the shoes clumsily smack the paved drive.

The Ballard stable, located outside the wall southeast of the big house, is painted white with green trim around its doors and windows. The louvered steeple is topped by a galloping horse that serves as a weather vane. The roof slopes down and extends outward to a columned overhang that completely circles the building and allows riders to exercise the horses under cover when the weather's blowing, wet, or muddy.

Emmett has talked about the twenty oak-paneled stalls, each twelve by twelve and supplied with piped-in water and overhead cooling fans. The oak doors slide on roller tracks, and a concrete passageway large enough for a tractor to pull a feed wagon and manure spreader through extends the whole length. The loft where they store the timothy hay has a metal chute to send bales down to the wagon. Oats and other molasses-sweetened grains are kept in long wooden bins that have hinged tops.

To one side of the stable is the paddock, on the other the riding ring. Beyond and below a fenced pasture an acre pond half grown up with lily pads furnishes grazing animals drinking water. Two swans swim on it and leave wakes that disturb the reflected drifting clouds. The pond is fed and kept fresh by a bold branch, its overflow passing through an iron pipe and splashing downward to continue its course.

Diana walks Robin past the stable to the ring where sawdust surely hauled from the Ballards' sawmill covers and softens the ground. Near the fence a series of jumps has been arranged in a circle. Diana pulls her feet from the stirrups and slides down along the bay's flank to the ground. Her gloved fingers leave tracks along its sweaty glistening skin.

"Like to try him?" she asks.

"Guess not," he says.

"You don't have to guess. Either you do or don't."

"Not dressed for it," he said and holds out his arms as if showing his suit's jacket sleeves will demonstrate to her what she must've already seen.

"Look, I'm offering you the chance to ride a fine horse."

"Maybe some other time."

"You're frightened, aren't you?"

"No, I'm not."

"Then come on," she says and leads Robin to a stone mounting block and waits, her smile taunting him.

Wayland takes off his jacket and lays it over the fence. He is scared crossing to the horse. He's never ridden anything by himself except Dynamite, and this powerful animal is at least sixteen hands and seems to watch him from dark impenetrable eyes full of an evil intent. Wayland climbs the block, sticks his foot in a stirrup, and steps cautiously over onto the saddle, which is flat, seems way too small, and has no horn he can hold to.

His right foot attempts to find its place in the other stirrup, but it's set too short. Before he's ready, Diana releases the reins, allowing Robin to pass at a walk. Wayland squeezes his legs, calls "Whoa," but the horse moves into a jolting trot. Wayland tries to gain control by pulling at the reins while at the same time he holds to the saddle and tries to find footing. He bounces and begins to slip to the side.

Robin lunges into a canter, swerves, and heads for a jump—a red-and-black striped bar held between two white standards. Wayland can't turn him. The horse gathers, springs, and they're up and over. As they strike the ground, Wayland still slipping sideways lets go the reins and leans forward with both arms to clutch Robin around the neck. The horse takes two long strides and bucks. Wayland's flung free, twists in the air, and hits hard on his back. He lies stunned. Diana runs after Robin to catch his reins and is laughing.

"You won't be awarded any ribbons for that ride," she calls, her teeth bright in sunlight. All the Ballards have fine teeth.

"You knew he'd do that to me," Wayland says as he works to his feet and brushes sawdust off his clothes. His only white shirt is not only soiled but has a button ripped off.

"You told me you'd been around horses."

" 'Round, not on top them."

"If you could have seen yourself," she says and is still laughing.

"Real good joke on me, huh?"

"Now him's feelings are hurt."

"Guess I'll be moving on."

"Wait. I'll make you a deal. Since Emmett's left, we've needed stable help. You keep my tack clean and oiled and perform a few other chores, and I'll give you riding lessons."

He's reaching to the fence for his coat. She's smiling, has a knee bent inward like girls do, and he's actually touched and held her, a Ballard. Yet he doesn't trust her, and it's not much of a job without pay. Still she's beautiful and strange and he can no more say no than slow his beating heart.

"Guess I can give it a try," he says.

"Take away guessing you'd be practically out of words. Now climb back on Robin."

"Maybe some other day."

"Thought you weren't frightened."

"Not doing something dumb ain't the same as being scared."

"I promise he won't throw you."

He stares into those green eyes that remind him of a marble he'd once owned that had little gold flecks in it, and again lays his jacket across the fence. She lengthens the stirrups and holds the reins as he again steps from the mounting block to the saddle. He suspects a trick, but instead of turning loose of Robin Diana leads him. She wears silver earrings shaped like tiny horseshoes, and her perfume mixes with the horse's steamy scent.

"Now you take the reins," she orders when they complete a full circle. "I'll walk right here beside Robin, and you keep a light pressure on his mouth, just enough to let him know you've got him on the bit."

Wayland feels he's being talked to like a child, yet obeys. He's glad no one can see. He hears the cries of peacocks from within the wall around the big house and hounds barking in the kennel. The sun in a lemon color sky heats the ring. Diana unbinds the red kerchief and wipes her face. From above he's able to see down her shirt collar to a lacy fringe of a silky brassiere.

"Now try it alone," she says and stops to let him go on. "Don't tighten your legs. Robin'll think you want him to move out."

Wayland feels tense and rigid in the saddle. His knees want to clamp. With each stride Robin's head dips, and Wayland tries to catch the rhythm and fit himself to the pace. At the same time he thinks had he not come across Diana at the Kentucky gate, he would've said his goodbyes at the big house and been on his way to Jericho Crossroads and the Greyhound bus.

"You're a natural rider," Diana calls to him as he circles. "You have good hands, but your posture's bad. Sit forward in the saddle. Imagine a line dropping straight from your head, down through your hips to your heels. Allow your feet and ankles to flex like shock absorbers. It takes the pressure off Robin's back."

He tries to obey and continues to ride around the ring fearful that any moment the horse will bolt, but Robin is obedient to his fingers. Diana orders Wayland to circle in the opposite direction. He begins to feel more confident and looser on the horse. Robin has an easy, flowing stride not at all like the irregular and painful stabs of Dynamite's backbone against the crotch.

"All right, enough," Diana calls. "Dismount and I'll show you how to unsaddle Robin Hood, halter him, hose him down, groom him, and put him in his stall where he's to be fed a flake of hay. You don't water him 'til he's cooled out."

At the stable while holding Robin's lead line with one hand and the hose with the other, he follows Diana's directions and sprays the horse, who shakes himself and wets Wayland's clothes.

"Be careful with the currycomb where you can feel bone," Diana instructs him. She works on one side of horse, Wayland the other. She has removed her gloves, and her hands are small but proficient. She wears a ruby ring.

Robin's stall and others that are empty have names over them—Bellepays Champion, Ballerina, Missy, Midnight Baron, Black Wind. Of the twenty, only three are being used. Were the Ballards, Wayland wonders, feeling tight times like ordinary folks?

"Now I'll show you how to clean my tack," she says.

Tack's a word Wayland's not heard before. She has him carry her saddle, pad, and bridle to a paneled room at the end of the stable where red, blue, and yellow ribbons and framed pictures of horses have been hung from walls. Trophies line shelves, some tarnished and that could use a good polishing.

Racks hold two levels of saddles, and bridles dangle from hooks screwed into ceiling beams. At the center of the room is a wooden cleaning bench. Diana sits on a stool, crosses her legs, and with a booted foot swinging instructs him how to soap, wipe, and rub neatsfoot oil into leather. Wayland lastly rolls up his shirtsleeves to wash the saddle pad in a tub and hang it to dry on a line strung between columns of the walkway.

"I have to run," Diana says. "When you come back tomorrow, I'll teach you to post. Oh, what's your name?"

He tells her, and she leaves him. He stands a moment looking after her as she strides along the brick walk to the arched entrance through the stone wall.

He's a mess—wet, smelly, his clothes dirtied, his shirt torn, and feels he's been used. He doesn't care. *When you come back tomorrow*, she'd said, and he's touched and held her. Her perfume abides around him, the feel of her lingers in his fingers, and he raises his hands to stare at them as if they've been transformed. One thing for sure, he wont about to leave Howell County for Norfolk and the shipyards this day or maybe a while to come.

eighteen

ayland hesitated before crossing the bridge, worried that the Sedan de Ville's weight might be too much for the old span to bear. The state sign that announced the limit at five tons was not convincing, and it was a damn fool errand he was on anyhow—not even an errand but nothing more than a fruitless journey into an uneasy swamp of nostalgia. "Back up," he told himself. "Back up, turn around, and let it all go like the river flowing under this bridge." Yet when he removed his foot from the brake, the car moved not into reverse but forward, and the tires thumped onto the span in the direction of . . .

. . . the cabin where Wayland washes up and searches through his mama's wicker sewing baskets for a needle, thread, and thimble to sew his torn shirt. He sponges off and presses his suit using what were her irons, which he heats on the cook stove. He cleans and brushes his shoes.

Whenever Mr. Wesley Rudd can't use him in the fields, he slips over to the Ballard stable and is always careful about his Levi's and denim workshirt's neatness. The chores Diana instructs him about include mucking out stalls, watering the horses, slinging hay down the chute from the loft as well as keeping up her tack. She leaves her boots for him to wipe and oil.

He believes he's doing work her father has left to her and suspects she's not told Mr. Henry about him. Wayland doesn't care as long as he can be near her. He stands back in shadows and waits for her to walk fresh and perfumed from the big house to the stable, her stride often with a skip in it. He leans on the ring's fence to watch her ride and believes there's nothing finer to the eye than seeing a proud pretty girl joined to a blood horse. They move and merge in lazy arcs over jumps as if she has grown from Robin Hood's withers, the bay a glistening and powerful extension of her small thrusting body.

Her expression becomes removed, disconnected, like she's above physical caring about time or place—bored, about to yawn, and she fills him with so much wanting of her that he stands close to the fence so she can't notice the bulge in his Levi's.

She does teach him to post and canter, but not to jump. She carries him an old pair of riding boots, the leather cracked and sagging, that has belonged to Eugene. Wayland oils them up until the leather flexes. They are too small, but because they came from Diana's hand he wears them and ignores the pain.

Eugene returns home from the beach tanned, his off-blond hair curly and needing a cut. He's tall, has the same green eyes as Diana and Mr. Henry, and he moves easy, his muscles different from men who work in the fields, from Wayland's by being longer, smoother, built up on tennis courts and in swimming pools. His tan does not cease at his neckline.

He mistakes Wayland for Emmett when he strides out in the cool of the evening and asks for his horse. That's how close he's ever looked at people who've served him. He rides the chestnut named Warrior and lopes off with Diana on Robin Hood along Bellepays's trails. Wayland, hammer in hand, repairs a jump Diana calls a coop, though no chickens has ever lived in it. As he draws nails from his pocket, he sees Black Amos watching from the doorway through the wall to the big house. Wayland raises a hand. Black Amos turns away and closes the door.

Diana brings her cat named Claire to the stable. It's like a fluffy white powder puff with blue eyes. It also has a blue collar decorated with fake jewels. Diana kisses and talks to Claire. For the cat's safety, no dogs are allowed out of the kennel.

Wayland catches Diana smoking a cigarette. She stands behind the stable and holds it not cupped the way a man would but between two fingers in ladylike delicate fashion. She rests an elbow of one hand on the palm of the other. He's surprised her, and for an instant she looks both guilty and alarmed.

"All the girls smoke at St. Mary's by the Sea," she says.

"All?" he asks. He thinks she's probably swiped the cigarette from Mr. Henry or Eugene.

"All that count," she says and blows smoke at him.

"I won't tell on you."

"There's nothing to tell."

"You shouldn't light up around a stable."

"I'll smoke any damn place I please," she says, takes another draw on the cigarette, and drops it on the ground. She twists her boot heel over it.

On Wednesday afternoon while he's saddle soaping a leather girth, she stands by him, takes the girth from his hands to examine it, and as she gives it back her fingers touch his. Do they linger? She smiles, and Wayland's not certain.

Friday evening as he kneels before her to refasten a spur strap that has worked loose on her boot, she reaches down and takes off his cap. She runs her fingers over his head, spreads and pushes them through his hair and down the back of his neck.

"You have nice skin," she says when he looks up at her. "Don't you ever use shampoo?"

"Just regular soap."

"You should. You could have lovely hair."

She sets his cap back on and is smiling. Is she teasing him? Maybe he's only imagining she's attracted to him because he's been wanting it to happen.

Saturday evening when she and Eugene come in from riding, Wayland's removing timothy bales from last year's crop to make room for the new. The old hay will be fed to cattle. Ballard horses get only prime cuttings free of dust or mold.

Eugene walks on to the house after leaving Warrior with Wayland to cool out and put up. Maybe, Wayland thinks, he believes I'm getting paid. It's okay, though, as long as Diana stays around. She removes the ribbon from her ponytail and lets her hair fall over her back. It reaches the flair of hips shaped by the tight fit of her whipcord britches. As Wayland tosses bales on the wagon parked in the haulway, he realizes she's watching him. She stands leaning against a stall, one booted ankle crossed over the other. She shakes out and fingers back her hair.

"What you do on Saturday nights?" she asks.

"Nothing much. Probably walk down to the store."

"Big fun. Don't you get bored?"

"Usually I'm too tired."

"God, I'll be glad to get back to school. I've got a new dress for the Valentine Day tea dance."

"A T dance?"

"Boys from all the best prep schools are invited. This year I may be able to ride in the point-to-point."

"Point-to-point at what?"

"Never mind," she says and laughs. "At St. Mary's I sometimes have three or four young gentlemen waiting in the parlor."

"Waiting for what?"

"Ah me," she says and shakes her head. "So you go down to daddy's store, stand around, drink a Big Orange, and spit Brown's Mule off the porch."

Wayland stacks bales on the wagon without answering.

"You live an exciting life, I can tell that," she says and moves up behind him. She taps him between his shoulder blades.

"What?" he asks as he faces her.

"You ever kiss a girl?" she asks, and those green eyes fasten on him. Her smile uncovers the moist tips of her teeth.

"Sure," he says, only half a lie 'cause he'd kissed both Lottie and Pearl May at times in a family manner. He's dreamed too of Lucy Randolph and Miss Patricia Flowers who sent him home from school with head lice.

"Don't you want to kiss me?"

She waits, her hands held behind her. Oh, God, he wants to but can't seem to move 'til she lifts her face and brings those hands to fasten around his neck. He then grabs her and kisses her all over her face and eyes and finally her mouth. It's open, and her tongue darts at his. He's shocked, yet excited and on fire.

"Oh, you're rough and strong," she says and pushes free against his chest. She laughs as she leaves with a look back at him—not just at him but that place in his pants she has caused to bulge out. She walks off with him gaping like an idiot after her. He watches her pass through the wall and the door close.

He rubs a hand over his face, steadies himself against the wagon, turns confused, happy, scared. He's kissed not only a girl in that amazing way but a Ballard—perfumed, black hair down, green eyes agleam. Hoping she'll come back, he stays late at the stable. He lies on loft bales as the night takes hold and stares at the lighted windows in the big house. Maybe she's looking out from her pink room and thinking of him.

A thunderstorm moves up from the river. Lightning flashes make ghostly shapes of the blowing white oak. Not 'til the rain ceases drumming the stable roof does he make his way through the wet darkness to the cabin where he lies thinking. A Ballard girl.

Can it be that she's in love with him as much as he is with her? God Almighty, is such a thing possible?

On his skin he smells her and sniffs her lingering scent. I'll never wash it off, he thinks. He stretches out his arms as if she's bringing herself to him. In his mind he holds her, lifts her, carries her to the bed.

During the cool of morning before first light, he wakes calm and knowing he can never have her. He's got no money to care for her. Mr. Henry'd never allow it. Wayland leaves the bed for the cabin's steps. The crickets have quieted, and in the distance a whippoorwill only half completes its plaint. He eyes a shred of clouds sliding across the moon.

By dawn he hardly believes his touch of her has ever took place. He keeps reconstructing the moment. It happened, but the kiss was her mocking him, a little game she's playing with a poor white boy out of boredom until she can get back to her fancy school. Oh the terrible ache she causes in him. I might, he thinks, just go on lie down and die.

But he's at the stable by sunup. He tends the horses. Black Amos walks from the house. He has on his apron, and the sleeves of his white shirt are rolled up to his elbows, though he still wears his bow tie. His hands and arms are dusted with flour, likely because he's been mixing biscuit dough, the job once held by Wayland's mama.

"What you hanging 'round this place for?" Black Amos asks, scowling at Wayland.

"I mean to sweep out and clean up the tack room."

"Clean enough now to eat off the floor," Black Amos says. "You go on home now. You not needed around here no more."

"Miss Diana's never told me that."

"I do the telling 'round here. Now get on."

Wayland turns and walks off from the stable. Black Amos stands watching him. Wayland continues on 'til the house is out of sight and circles back through the woods to approach the stable from the rear. He half believes Black Amos must conjure and is able to see everything as he claims. Would he speak to Mr. Henry?

Wayland again settles on hay in the loft, the best place for him to watch the big house. The fountain has been cut off, and a peacock struts around it. Sunlight flashes off the glass of Diana's window. Black Amos backs the gray Cadillac from a garage bay and parks at the side entrance. Mr. Henry, Diana, and Eugene step from the house. Black Amos holds the door for them, and they sit in the rear. Black Amos is driving them to Tobaccoton and St. Luke's for morning church services. The car leaves through the front gate.

No breeze stirs the white oaks, and Bellepays's lawns remain stilled and empty. Not 'til midafternoon does the Cadillac return. Wayland catches sight of Diana's white hat and dress. She'll change her clothes before coming to the stable, yet nobody appears from the big house until evening, and that's Black Amos, who feeds and waters the horses. Buried under hay, Wayland lies quiet. Maybe Diana's in trouble and Mr. Henry's forbidden her to leave.

Monday morning again before daylight Wayland sneaks to the stable and hides. The big house is quiet. Black Amos cares for the horses. Wayland sees Eugene cross the lawn to the garage and drive off in the yellow Ford convertible. Finally Diana strides from the house. She looks fretted and glances behind her. She hesitates, hurries forward, and with every other step she smacks her riding crop against a boot.

He slips down the ladder from the loft and peeps at her as she leads Robin Hood from his stall. When Wayland shows himself, Robin Hood shies.

"I'll saddle up for you," Wayland says.

"No, you won't," she says and looks toward the house. "Go on home this minute and don't you come back."

"I love you," he says.

She don't even look at him as she fits the bit to Robin's mouth. Wayland offers his hands to help her mount, but she acts as if she doesn't notice and uses the block before riding off without speaking another word to him.

She canters away toward the woods and one of the riding trails. He thinks of running after her, but fast as he is, he wouldn't be able to catch up with Robin. Again Wayland asks himself did it really happen, did he ever hold and kiss her? Once more he waits in the loft. He sees Mr. Henry walk from the big house and cross the lawn. He holds a drink, strolls past the box bushes, and opens the gate in the iron fence around the family cemetery. He stands a while among the tombstones before returning to the house. He has emptied his glass.

Wayland watches the woods. Not 'til noon does Diana appear. She's walking Robin Hood to cool him off, and the horse's sweat catches sunlight. She rides him into the stable and slides from the saddle.

"Miss Diana, have I done something wrong?" he asks.

"I'm telling you you'd better leave," she says and glances toward the house.

"I'll hose Robin down for you."

"No you won't. Just go on now, and don't make trouble."

She's loosened the girth and has the saddle in her arms. He reaches out to touch her, but she slips aside to avoid his fingers. He glances toward the house and sees Eugene coming toward the stable. Wayland ducks out the rear. He runs to the woods, hides, and walks to the cabin. He lies on the bed hot and hurting so much from Diana he moans but believes it all has to mean something.

His wallet holds only three dollars. He's either got to use it to buy a bus ticket out of the county or find work. But there ain't no work in Howell County that would allow him to court a girl like Diana. Maybe there'd be a job in Norfolk at the shipyards, and if he could just get to Diana one more time, again tell her how much he loves her, and promise to come back for her.

During the night he returns to the stable. He lies hearing the horses stomp and swish their tails. Diana doesn't appear during the day. Black Amos and Eugene care for the horses. Wayland worries that maybe Diana's sick or gone off to school. Thursday morning she walks from the house. While she scoops sweet feed into a bucket, he begins watering the horses. She eyes him but doesn't speak.

"Why you treating me this way?" he asks.

"What way?" she answers and walks to Robin's stall. She spills grain into his feed box. "I'll tell you again you better leave."

Wayland doesn't see Mr. Henry until it's too late to run. He and Eugene stand in the stable doorway watching him. Mr. Henry has aged, his hair thinned and grayed, his paunch not entirely hidden by the rumpled drape of his white jacket, yet he stands erect as if on parade.

"Go to the house," he tells Diana.

"Oh, Daddy, you're being so silly."

"Now," Mr. Henry says.

"I'll do the horses," Eugene says and takes the bucket from her hand. He's dressed not for riding but in tennis shorts.

Diana leaves with a quick glance back at Wayland.

"You're not Emmett," Mr. Henry says to Wayland.

"His brother," Eugene says.

"A Garnett all right," Mr. Henry says. "Boy, you get on away from here now. We don't need your help."

"I don't mind, Mr. Henry. I like coming over and not asking pay or nothing."

"No, you stay away. Understand me?"

"I can't come here no more?"

"Best not to. Just go on now."

Wayland starts off and looks back toward the stable. Mr. Henry and Eugene stand watching him. As he leaves, his feet feel heavy, and he shuffles along the drive, walks through the Kentucky gate, and cries out, his voice disturbing crows, who flap squawking among the pines.

At the cabin he falls on the bed. He thinks of the last look Diana gave him. Maybe it meant that she cares for him, but they won't let her show it. He tosses on the bed and throws his arms aside. She cares for him, he believes that. No way he can give her up without one last try. If she loves him, she'll wait while he finds that shipyard job down in Norfolk where they pay big money. He'll save up, show people his worth, and in time make it right with Mr. Henry Ballard.

At first dark he pushes off the bed, washes himself, and changes into his mended shirt, suit, and sets on his fedora. He walks the drive between the dogwoods and looming magnolias toward the mansion. He stops to listen and hears a screech owl and hounds barking in the Ballard kennels. At the stable, Robin Hood nickers to him as Wayland squints towards windows of the big house. He watches the lights begin to switch off on the first floor. Diana's lamp burns. He crosses from the stable to the arched wooden door at the wall and tries its iron handle. The door's locked.

He climbs the wall by pulling himself up on ivy vines as thick as his wrist, balances on top, and jumps to the ground where he hunkers. Diana's pink second-floor lamp cuts off, but a last light still shines on the third. That, as Emmett has told him, is Black Amos's room.

Wayland believes if he can get Diana to come down where he can again tell how much he loves her, he'll be able to talk her into waiting for him. I'll be back, he'll swear, with a car and money, and they'll ride the horses on their own farm.

The turning circle behind the house is topped with white pebbles. He lifts a handful, stands back, and throws. The third pebble taps her window, the sound a loud crack. He crouches behind a box bush and waits, but she don't show herself. He again throws, and when the pebble strikes the pane, the pink glow switches on and tints grass of the lawn. A silhouette of Diana's head and nightgowned shoulders appear. She's let down her hair. He steps into the glow and beckons her.

She leaves the window. He moves behind a trunk of a white oak thinking she has to get past her father's and Eugene's rooms. He pictures her feet hurrying along carpets and descending steps. What's taking her so long? Maybe she has to put on a robe or dress. His heart pumps hard, and he's trembling.

When floodlights around the house switch on, he lifts a hand against the shattering brightness. A side door opens and out strides Eugene followed by Mr. Henry Ballard. Wayland starts to escape over the wall, then turns back to face them. Mr. Henry wears a bathrobe and slippers. He's bareheaded, his thin gray hair messed. Eugene has pulled on pants, tennis shoes, a sweatshirt.

"Boy, I told you not to come around here ever again," Mr. Henry says.

"Please, I need to talk to Miss Diana."

"You not talking to anybody but the sheriff if you don't get on away from here," Eugene says.

"Just let me see her a minute, and I'll go. I love her, Mr. Henry. I'd do anything in the world for her."

"Son, one lesson of this life you need to learn is that young ladies play games with you boys. It's how they test their powers, like a filly getting her legs and finding how fast she can run. Now my daughter doesn't want to talk to you. You got it all wrong in your head. Just go on home, and we'll forget about it."

"Mr. Henry, I want to hear it from her. I'll leave if she tells me, but I got to hear it from her mouth."

He sees Diana's silhouette again appear at the window and motions to her.

"Boy, I'm ordering you off the place," Mr. Henry says.

"She's got to tell me," Wayland says.

"Get Amos," Mr. Henry says to Eugene.

"Let me," Eugene says.

"Do it then," Mr. Henry says.

Eugene moves to Wayland and grips his upper right arm. His fingers press hard against the muscle.

"Leave quietly or be tossed out."

"If I hear it from her, I'll go," Wayland says.

"Your last chance," Eugene says.

"Why can't I talk to her?"

Eugene shoves him. Wayland rights himself and sets his feet as he looks up to the motionless silhouette.

"You're leaving," Eugene say and uses his shoulder to bump Wayland's back. Wayland stumbles, balances, and his arms raised he faces Eugene. He's heavier than Eugene and has got to be stronger from all the labor he's done for the Ballards.

Eugene steps back, his fists up, a boxer's stance. He dances on his toes from side to side and starts jabbing. The blows sting, their hurt lingering. Colored dots crisscross Wayland's vision. His fedora is knocked off as he covers his face and backs away.

Eugene keeps bobbing and punching. Likely he's been taught boxing at his fancy New England school. Wayland suffers the blows, waits until Eugene closes, and swings a right. Eugene sprawls backward on to the grass. He sits up, rises to a knee, and shakes his head.

"Get up and finish it," Mr. Henry orders him.

Eugene is careful now. He stays out of reach and darts in and out to punch. He bloodies Wayland's nose and causes an ear to ring and burn. He keeps circling. Again Wayland bides his time. He pretends to wilt, drops his arms, and accepts blows. Eugene draws closer. Wayland knocks him down a second time.

Hounds in the kennel are barking, and the peacocks too are disturbed and screeching. Black Amos, his nightgown flapping, hurries from the house. He runs across the grass toward Wayland 'til Mr. Henry stops him.

"Eugene will finish what he started," Mr. Henry says.

Again Eugene stands and squares off. Wayland sees Diana's still at the window. Her silhouette hasn't moved, and he wonders why don't she hurry down to help him? He believes he can rush and grab Eugene, rassle him down, use his knees to pin Eugene's arms, and smash him in the face. Yet rassling's not the Ballard way, not gentlemanly, and Wayland wants to appear that for Diana.

Eugene does not come at him but keeps circling. Wayland allows his hands to fall to his side and stands waiting. Eugene hits him once, twice, a third time. As he moves in, Wayland again knocks him to the grass. Mr. Henry restrains Black Amos, who waits ready. Eugene rises, his face now also bloody. He wipes a forearm across it. Blood drips on his sweatshirt. He raises his fists but is uncertain.

How many times do I have to do it? Wayland asks himself. If only Diana would come down she could stop it. He begins to feel not that he's losing but a draining of strength and a sort of helplessness—as if he's already defeated without being beaten. It's crazy he's gotten himself into fighting a Ballard. Howell County poor whites don't contend above their station. It's like his own blood's telling him that, the cells sending the message he'd lost even before he started, that one way or another the Ballards always win. And the silhouette at the window don't move.

He hits Eugene once more, sends him reeling to the side, but Eugene staggers back at him, and Wayland feels all ardor to fight leak away. It's not been given to him to be a winner. He backs off covering his head and allows Eugene to punch him at will from all sides.

Wayland takes a last look at the window. Diana's still there. He tries to raise a hand to her, and Eugene hits him in the mouth. Wayland tastes the blood.

"I love and would die for you," he tries to call to her, but the words are distorted by his choking.

Eugene follows him as Wayland turns toward the gate. Eugene hits him in the neck and on the back of his head.

"Enough," Mr. Henry calls.

Black Amos picks up Wayland's fedora and sails it after him. Wayland doesn't lift it but crosses through the wall's main gate, plods drunkenly to the cabin where by lantern light at the well he washes the blood off himself.

He rests a while before taking up his blanket roll. He padlocks the door, hides the key under edges of fieldstones that hold up a corner of the cabin, and looks back. In the ghostly moonlight the place already appears forsaken—no hound to bark, no lamp in the window, nothing to lift a hand to. Clouds again slide over the moon, and the cabin becomes one with the enfolding night.

"I'm through with you," Wayland says to it, to Diana, the Ballards, Howell County, the life he's lived here. "You'll never see me again ever, goddamn you. I'm finished for good and all."

nineteen

As the Caddy rolled onto the bridge, Wayland felt the sway of the narrow span and thought of the car dropping into the current and himself fighting to escape water pouring through windows. The worn planks still rattled across rusty girders. The Hidden River ran muddy from a recent rain upstream, and willow limbs dangled and dragged into the flow, streaking it as it parted around a single boulder whose spherical crown was crusted from dried debris of earlier floodings.

He thought of his fight with Josephus Blodgett, how they had hit, kicked, and bit along the length of the Ballard drainage ditch and tumbled into the river that washed away their sweat, dirt, and blood while other field hands stood on the bank and laughed.

He also envisioned his early baptism downstream, still on Ballard property, the congregation from the Healing Spring Baptist Church walking the path among pines to the edge of the stream. He'd worn a white sheet washed and starched by his mother, who had also combed and parted his hair.

Side by side with the Reverend Arbogast he'd walked hip deep into the warm murky stream, and the preacher had laid one calloused palm over Wayland's nose and mouth and the other at the base of Wayland's spine before bending him backward into the earthy tasting water and calling out, "Lord God, we bring You this child. Lord Jesus, pour out Your love and power on him that he may smite Satan at ever' turn." On the slippery bank the congregation had sung "Shall We Gather at the River" accompanied by Randall Fenton fluttering his fingers over his wailing harmonica.

Jesus had descended to Wayland that July day, had climbed dripping with him from the river, and stayed with him through the night and part of the next morning 'til in the Ballard fields the sun's fire boiled his blood while gnats, greenies, and ticks fattened on him and bled out his Jesus fever like drops of sweat falling onto and being drunk up by a thirsting weed-choked soil.

He'd been wetted by and crossed other waters since, one of them an ocean. Bedroll held by bailing twine over his shoulder, he'd left Howell County, hit the road hitchhiking, reached not Norfolk but Newport News where Britt Mosely shared a steamy boarding-house bed with him for a week 'til Wayland chose the course of unanchored men everywhere broken in pocket and heart. He joined the army.

Though only sixteen, because of his size he had no trouble lying to and convincing the recruiting sergeant about his age. The army was hungry for men . . .

. . . of the 19th Regimental Combat Team, which assembles and entrucks for the journey to Southampton, England. They wait three days on grimy, tar-patched docks fronting the harbor's oil-fouled water. Not able to drive stakes to pitch tents, they lounge with their gear, eat K-rations, sprawl onto full fieldpacks, and stare at scudding low clouds and mewing gulls, who themselves also appear filthy.

Rumor is the 19th will be part of the first wave, but it's dawn of D-3 before they board ship, each vessel with a swaying barrage balloon attached by cable to its stern. Navy gobs at twin 40mm antiaircraft guns raise binoculars and scan the sky. Second platoon of C Company crosses the deck and descends into the gloom of the cargo hold. They have been issued life preservers that can be inflated by crimping belt cartridges of compressed air. Only the hatch provides light, and the milling troops settle into the shadowed void, their backs leaned against rivet bolts of clammy bulkheads.

Hours they wait before the ship's engine changes pitch as it revs up. A slow wallowing takes hold, and within minutes men become seasick. Puke conquers all. They are allowed on deck singly to piss in pitching sheet-metal troughs that empty into swells of the disturbed sea.

Wayland's Liberty ship is third in line of the long bending convoy. He peers through a misty haze but sees no land either ahead or behind. The barrage balloon cable slants up into a wet grayness where at moments it seems to disappear.

Men of C Company are quiet. They listen to the creaking hull, check their weapons and the security of grenades attached to pack straps. A chaplain climbs down the pipe ladder, and in unison they recite the Lord's Prayer, even Kaminsky, a Jew and their platoon BAR man.

During the late afternoon, again a change of engine rpms. Orders shout down the hatch to assemble the platoon topside. As he emerges and blinks, Wayland makes out a faint shoreline partly obscured by an aroused overcast and drifting smoke. Muzzle blasts from a battleship's sixteen-inchers ignite the overcast. Black smoke billows forward into monstrous, leisurely rolling rings, the great ship reels, and with a slow, massive dignity rights herself, all before he hears the thunder of muzzle blasts.

The sea is tracked by destroyers. The wakes of LCTs, LCIs and Ducks leave disturbed furrows through steel-colored water. Crafts line the shore of the beach that the men hear the name of the first time—Utah. Nets unroll along sides of ships, and Higgins boats gather to offload units.

Lieutenant Sydney orders the platoon over. Wayland glances down as he holds to the net. The Higgins bounds and falls beneath him. A private named Burton has his leg crushed as the Higgins bangs against the Liberty's hull. Burton screams and is laid aside for others to spring free of the net and drop aboard.

Wayland judges the distance before releasing his grip just as the Higgins rises. The weight of rifle and gear topple him. Two helmeted navy gobs stand by and steady him by grabbing each arm. Burton continues to holler, yet no one attends him.

The loaded Higgins boats circle to assemble. More men become seasick. As engines roar, a young coxswain squats at the helm, his head raised to peer over a shield of armor plate, and steers full throttle toward the beach. The boat pounds, shakes, and rattles.

Wayland keeps low and prays. He sees the lips of others moving, and eyes stare from frightened darkened faces. Because of the engine's shrieking, he doesn't know whether they're under fire or not. Only the booming of the battleship's guns breaks through the tossing, deafening disorder.

Time needed to reach shore seems endless. Wayland clutches his M-1 so tightly his fingers ache. He fixes his bayonet for hand-to-hand combat. In the dull light the clean blade does not gleam. He hears someone sniffling.

The Higgins boat slams against and scrapes the coastline. The ramp clangs down. Wayland, M-1 held high, charges crouched into cold shallow water and splashes across the chaotic sandy beach before he realizes nobody or nothing's shooting at him.

A hip-booted landing officer uses a megaphone to direct them among barnacle-coated barbed wire and welded iron barriers the engineers have blasted aside. Wayland runs toward a gap in the sea wall and dunes. Life preservers lie about, thrown away by units of the 4th Infantry Division, which landed on D-1. Gas masks have been abandoned, and shell casings litter the sand. Wayland glimpses a bloody pack of Camels a boot has crushed.

Combat engineers work laying perforated, prefabricated sections of metal grids that will support trucks to offload ashore. A Sherman tank that has a bulldozer blade attached pushes aside debris. But where's the fighting?

Lieutenant Sydney rallies the platoon as C Company forms to move forward through a cut in dunes that grow a thin pale cover. Barbed wire has been rolled up, and Teller mines unearthed, disarmed, and heaped—more dirty work done by the engineers.

Wayland sees his first casualty, a paratrooper from the 101st Airborne who sits beside the road. His uniform's ragged, and bloody bandages cover the stump of a leg. A medic holding a plasma bottle kneels beside him. The paratrooper smokes a cigarette and gazes at Wayland as he passes, the man's bearded, begrimed face not showing pain but contempt for latecomers to the battle.

The company moves inland along the sandy road. Platoons keep a fifty-yard interval but still they've not come under fire. Behind they hear the battleship's sixteen-inchers, yet ahead only the rapid popping of small-arms fire. They glance at each other not believing it can be this easy.

They work around a destroyed, fire-blackened pillbox. Chunks have been torn off the thick concrete, the iron reinforcing bars exposed. A huge artillery piece hangs broken.

"Like my dick," somebody calls but brings no laughter.

Wayland sweats. He swigs water from his canteen and keeps checking the sky for planes. They fly over but are all American, mostly P-47s. The day remains leaden. They pass what must've been a beach cottage, all its windows shattered and the roof holed.

The terrain levels out among cultivated fields. Trees flank the road, some blasted, their branches and leaves scattered over a crop Wayland recognizes as wheat. Fences around a stone house have been flattened, and two dead draft horses lie in the yard, their tongues dangling. Flies swarm over astonished eyes.

German equipment has been shoved to both sides of the road— a heavy, clumsy-looking truck, its tires burning, a halftrack, treads broken, an overturned 88mm field cannon. Grenades, Mausers, and Panzerfausts are strewn about.

Wehrmacht prisoners straggle by, guarded by 4th Division MPs. The Krauts appear more weary and unshaven than dangerous. Mostly they are either young or old, and they smell like dirty socks. A German officer is among them, his black boots shiny, his uniform immaculate. He gives Wayland a haughty look.

The next Krauts are lying in a ditch where they've been laid out. Death has stiffened their arms and legs to awkward angles. A putrid greasy smell arises from bodies, an odor Wayland remembers from Howell County, Virginia, like dead cattle and hogs killed in the flood and left unburied. More flies, some flitting from the mouth of a boy whose gashed face has set into an expression of terror.

The column halts, and Captain Slayton, C Company commander, confers with MPs at a road junction. They unroll maps on the ground. Wayland and the men smoke and wait.

"My kind of war," MacNair says, but he too is thinking of the dead they've viewed. He's from Deltaville, Virginia—tall, limber, unhurried. He worked as a deck hand on his father's Chesapeake Bay dredge boat. He and Wayland are to share shelter halves.

Again the column moves forward into farm country that is well maintained and orderly. They stop, this time beside an orchard of undamaged apple trees heavy with unripened fruit. Captain Slayton assembles his platoon officers. Lieutenant Sydney brings word back to C Company.

"Spread out across the orchard and dig in," he orders. "Watch for mines. Battalion expects counterattacks."

As they scramble among the well-pruned and tended apple trees, they hear distant bursts of automatic fire and occasional eruptions of artillery. The orchard's soil easily gives way to Wayland's entrenching tool. He squats in his foxhole, keeps checking his M-1, feels his sweat's stickiness join the raw rubbing fabric of his uniform,

which is stiff from impregnated chemicals applied to make it resistant
to poison gas.

No counterattack strikes them. D-3 ends, and they've not
squeezed off a shot. The company's only casualty is Burton, who has
been returned by the Higgins to the Liberty ship. Wayland wonders
how that after all the briefings and warning of fanatical enemy
resistance a battle can be this effortless. Rumors spread the Germans
are in retreat and about to surrender. The war might already be over.

Sitting on their helmets, the men smoke the free cigarettes and eat
K-rations as a pale orange sunset colors a smeared skyline. They relax,
call to each other, dare to joke. They've made it and will live.

At dark Wayland spreads his shelter half beside the foxhole.
Lieutenant Sydney has set aside an area of the orchard for a latrine
ditch. They use entrenching tools to cover their feces. The lieutenant's
a proper low-country South Carolinian and does not say shit.

Wayland stretches out on his shelter half. The night's moistly
cool, and cloud cover masks the stars and moon. A scent of burnt
Sterno used to brew instant coffee remains. He touches the M-l at his
side to reassure himself. He will sleep. He's always been able to sleep.

A sparkling brightness wakes him. He believes it must be dawn
already before he realizes the sky has come painfully alight from flares
dropping slowly out of inflamed darkness. The orchard becomes so
radiant that apples tree stretch their long shadows across the ground.
Guns fire, small arms, then artillery rounds. The flares descend and
die, yet the shooting continues. A high-velocity shell shrieks over the
orchard and bursts in a treetop. Fifty-caliber tracers curve skyward,
and muzzle blasts flash as indistinct figures run about shouting. Men
are shooting but at what? Wayland jams on his helmet, tumbles into
his foxhole, and covers his head with his arms.

The whistling force smashes him. He's never felt such hot absolute
power. Jesus God. The night explodes, the darkness blazes. Erupting
soil rains over and blinds him. He can't stop his violent shaking. His

body balls of itself, and he realizes the whimpering he hears comes from his own mouth.

He's left his M-1 and entrenching tool outside the foxhole that he believes is not deep enough. He claws at it to dig. A .30-caliber machine gun opens up. He can't tell from what direction. Somebody's shouting. A grenade explodes. He feels the squish and smells the stink of his asshole letting go. He becomes wailing, cringing flesh nosed into defying earth.

twenty

The Caddy thumped twice off the end of the bridge onto the lowland road still unpaved after all these years. As the tires again roused dust, Wayland attempted to take in familiar but changed shapes of the land—its contours and fields no longer growing crops but claimed by thistles, Johnson grass, and climbing kudzu, which draped slash pines in green smothering shrouds.

Anxiety stiffened his body as he peered ahead for the cabin. He drove past the plot, hardly recognizing it because no structure stood, all fences were gone, and what had been the yard was now covered by stands of cedars and pines entwined by honeysuckle. A sickly locust tree dangled black scythe-like seedpods.

He stopped the car and backed two of the Caddy's wheels onto weeds of the shallow ditch. The old hackberry remained, a scabby corpse that had been split and partially charred by lightning. Gray-green patches of lichen were like crusted sores along haggard, leafless limbs.

He stepped carefully to keep his pants from snagging briars and methodically crisscrossed the area. He found not a rotted plank or wall stud from the cabin. Likely it'd been plundered and ripped down for any useful parts that could be carried off, the remainder decaying and shredding over the years to join the earth that'd supported it.

He skirted a patch of lustrous poison oak and searched among broomstraw, but his toe prodded not a cornerstone, broken rail, or rusted plow point. He nearly stepped into the old well, which had become overgrown with kudzu. He squatted beside the hackberry to finger up a clod of hard dry soil. He crushed and sifted it among his fingers.

As he stood, an object glittered among honeysuckle. He crossed to it and lifted a small shard of blue glass. He thought of his mother's colored bottles lined on the window ledge above her sink, the hues that fell upon hands tanned like cowhide as she snapped beans or washed a head of cabbage under the splashing flow of water from the pitcher pump.

He laid the shard back among the honeysuckle, its color buried from the intrusion of light . . .

. . . as Lieutenant Sydney coaxes Wayland from the foxhole. Guns have stopped firing, and no shells explode. Dawn breaks through darkness, a feeble streaking that spreads tentacles across the misted, cordite-stenched orchard. Arehart, a medic searching for wounded, has discovered Wayland.

"It's all right, son," Lieutenant Sydney says, kneeling by the foxhole. "It's over now."

Wayland doesn't unball. Shaking has given way to spastic jerks of his arms and legs. He clenches his eyes and gulps breaths through a choked throat. His mouth tastes of soil he's bitten into.

"You don't want to be sent back like this," the lieutenant says. "It'll mark you the rest of your life."

The lieutenant reaches down to grip the collar of Wayland's field jacket and raises him. He rubs dirt from Wayland's face and quiets him as you might a runaway horse by use of a gentle voice and the laying on of hands.

"Now straighten up," the lieutenant says. "We'll get you washed off. I need a radio man."

When Wayland inches from the hole, the lieutenant and Arehart walk him to a ditch that holds muddy water. They strip him and throw away his soiled undershorts and pants. Wayland thinks of the time he'd dirtied himself when Black Amos dragged him from the tulip poplar. Arehart uses his helmet to pour water over Wayland and wipes him down with swatches of grass snatched up from the orchard.

Wayland's so ashamed, yet still frightened. He's never before felt the devastation of absolute terror. It's seared him empty of all else. Arehart leaves and returns with fatigues that had to be taken from some other GI wounded or dead. Splattered blood has dried hard along the left leg. Wayland checks his Ingersoll pocket watch. It's still running.

Arehart rolls tent pins in the shelter half and straps it to Wayland's pack. The lieutenant hands Wayland the M-1. They steady him as he staggers between them among broken apple trees whose unripe fruit their boots squash or kick aside.

They pass the men of Wayland's platoon, who lounge smoking, their faces expressionless. Two medics tend a casualty, a private named Hoskins from Kentucky who's been the lieutenant's radioman. His stomach and chest are spotted with mortar fragments, which the medics pick out like removing meat from bloody walnut hulls. Hoskins will be sent to the aid station.

"Carry this and stay close to me," the lieutenant orders Wayland and turns over the weighty and bulky hand-held SCR. He explains how to use it. When Wayland raises it to his ear, he hears static and distorted jabberings.

Men of the platoon watch him. He can't meet their eyes. They believe me a yellow belly, Wayland thinks, and I am. He remembers how he gave up in the fight against Eugene Ballard. Yellowness in the blood or he would've won. Cowardice, he thinks, is given to a man like his height or the color of his hair or skin. He wants to flee, but the lieutenant watches him.

The SCR has a leather scabbard, which protects the antenna, and a sling for carrying. He bears the extra weight along with his M-1, pack, canteen, bayonet, ammo belt, and entrenching tool. Like the others, he's thrown away his gas mask but keeps the canvas case to hold his rations.

"Well I guess the Krauts ain't quite ready to surrender yet," MacNair says as he cleans his rifle. He has jammed it into the ground when he fell running for his foxhole.

MacNair and all members of the platoon are scared, but none, Wayland thinks, as bad as me. He knows talk of him will spread among the squads. He realizes he's been given the radio to carry so that Lieutenant Sydney can keep him under observation.

The outfit's confidence and swagger of yesterday have given way to wariness and shifty, darting expressions. The order to assemble and move out arrives down the line from Captain Slayton. They advance as skirmishers along both sides of the narrow tree-lined road. Wayland feels the great dread alive in his belly. He's been knocked up by fear and is carrying the baby.

The road passes above flooded fields where gliders crashed. Torn, twisted parts are scattered, and pieces of wrecked equipment float or are partly submerged among slack grassy stalks. Escaping ducks beat their wings to take flight.

More prisoners are escorted back. Some appear dazed, others smile, thankful to be captured by Americans and hopeful the war for them is over.

Wayland tends the radio that allows Lieutenant Sydney and Captain Slayton to confer. Foreign voices as well as high-pitch squeals interfere. The Krauts are jamming communications. Often the SCR doesn't work at all.

An artillery round strikes the rear of the company. Platoons break left and right off the road into the flooded fields. Wayland keeps the radio and his M-1 dry. The water is warm and has the odor of farmland—like the Ballard low grounds along the Hidden River.

Three Shermans rumble forward, their crews buttoned up. The company falls in behind. Farther down the road they pass around one of the tanks that has run over a mine and burns. Oily black smoke twists from its open hatch, and Wayland again scents the greasy odor of burnt flesh. A tanker's football-type helmet lies beside a broken tread.

The company bivouacs that night along the base of a hedgerow, and at dark they eat cold rations. The order comes down that nobody's to light Sterno. When matches are struck for cigarettes, palms cup the flames.

A plane flies over, identifiable as Kraut by the pulsing throb of its diesel engine. AA batteries fire, the muzzle blasts creating jittery lightning. Flares fall to the battalion's rear, and explosions rumble the ground. Over the tree line Wayland sees flashes of bomb detonations, the quaking yellowish white light, the pressure waves flowing outward like ripples in a pond. The sky is the pond.

Hedgerows used by farmers to fence their pastures favor the Krauts. As their units fall back, they retreat only a few hundred feet to another natural barrier. There seems no end to the rows. The Krauts dig in machine guns on the far sides and poke barrels through. Their artillery and mortars have all gaps and junctions zeroed in.

Though Wehrmacht troops and Panzers are always just another hedgerow or two away, Wayland hasn't yet fired his rifle. He's heard Kraut whistles and shouts. If any are wounded or killed, their medics bear them off.

"We winning?" he asks MacNair, who carries a folded Michelin tourist map of France and tries to figure out the division's deployments.

"Who knows except the generals?" MacNair answers. "Maybe not them either."

Dugan from Lima, Ohio, is killed. A tree burst hammers him flat as he rests his back against the trunk and gnaws on the hard chocolate bar from his K-ration. He lies with arms spread as if sunning himself on a beach, but there is no sun. Blood seeps from an empty eye socket. Arehart covers Dugan's face with his torn shelter half until stretcher bearers can carry him off.

Wayland stays dirty, skittish, frightened. He wakes curled around fear and hauls it with him day and night. He folds it into his fevered half sleep. He knows he can never be brave like the lieutenant. To survive, he believes, is the greatest feat of war.

Men die easily; a speck of steel no larger than a tick severs an unseen artery and a GI slips dreamily into the great beyond. Others survive wounds so slashing they reveal the red shimmer of intestines, the pumping of an uncovered heart, the flash of sunshine on jagged white bone. He remembers his daddy's arm.

Wayland moves low, a habitual crouch that feels natural even when they pull back and aren't under fire. Unlike MacNair, he doesn't check maps or try to pronounce the names of French villages they fight around or travel through—Mésiéres, Neuville au-Plain, Mere St. Eglise—some battered, others hardly touched, a few rubble.

The red blood of death contradicts the sweetness of summer, the weltering yellow flowers along the roads, the lush fragrance of the growing season. Beyond a collecting point for corpses, a farmer methodically cultivates his field of golden wheat, the heads filled out and heavy. What fine bread the wheat would make.

The regiment is reattached to the 30th Division at St. Lo, two battalions on the line, one in reserve. They pull back to make ready for an allied air bombardment. Wayland watches the flight of sun-glinting planes that fill all levels of clean blue sky—hundreds, maybe thousands, sweeping over in unswerving flights to release their death-dealing eggs. The horizon beyond the village becomes an obscuring curtain formed by convulsed earth flung upward and into itself.

The bombing continues, seemingly endless as he waits behind the protection of a weapons carrier. The earth quakes, and he wonders how anything can live under all this drumming death. MacNair glances at him, making Wayland aware he's been praying out loud.

When the planes complete their runs, the advance begins along the whole line. The first casualties are GIs from the 30th wounded by bombs dropped short on fallback positions. Medics lift bodies into meat wagons.

Wayland, carrying the radio, follows Lieutenant Sydney. The land is deeply pocked by bomb craters, German positions are flattened, artillery is overturned, tanks burn. C Company kicks stunned Krauts from their holes like rabbits from burrows. *Kamerad* is the cry of those able to speak, their quaking hands raised, their faces blackened and stunned, their eyes emptied of all except terror.

twenty-one

Among tangled sumac where the shed had once stood, Wayland collected branches broken from a cedar tree and used them to cover the old well so that no animal or hunter would fall in and be trapped. He tugged at briars, which had snagged a cuff of his trousers and wondered how he would explain the slight tear to Amy. Her quick eyes would certainly spot it. In the old days he might've used his mother's needle and thread to repair the damage.

He returned to the Caddy, but for a moment he gazed beyond the hackberry and saw his mother, father, sisters, brothers, and himself sitting on the cabin's steps, and he heard his father's voice talking of Granddaddy Winslow and his mother's mocking responses. What did it all mean if anything, he wondered, and twisted the key to start the engine . . .

. . . of a Jeep Lieutenant Sydney has secured, its driver named Petrie, an olive-skinned West Virginian who'd been a coal miner and grew up understanding the uses of black powder and other explosives. He becomes an expert blowing gaps in hedgerows. To crimp blasting caps to his fuses, he uses his strong yellowed teeth. Wayland rides in the rear with the radio and .50-caliber machine gun. The roads are jammed by barreling trucks carrying men, fuel, and ammunition forward in support of armor's breakthrough at the Malaise Pocket. It's a chase after Krauts fleeing to the Siegfried Line and Deutschland.

The regiment becomes strung out, and rations are scarce. Fear's baby within Wayland shrinks, yet still lives and squirms. Wayland jerks his head and squints as if Krauts might at any instant jump the unit. Sleep is fleeting, and even then dark forms lurk behind his eyelids.

The 19th Regimental Combat Team moves by fits and starts through France, meeting only disorderly resistance—ragtag units of bypassed Krauts, a lost Wehrmacht kitchen unit whose cooks are Russian, the crew of a camouflaged Mark IV tank eager to surrender. MPs herd hangdog lines of prisoners rearward.

Men of the 19th are wounded and killed not in great numbers but nibbled on by death, most often inflicted by mines rather than enemy fire until November when the Kraut counterattack strikes from the Hürtgen Forest. Their artillery has massed and fires the nights. Trees become part of shrapnel's shrieking rain. Mortar bursts and Screaming Meemies tear the ears. The hot jagged metal finds flesh, causing smoke to spiral upward like from burning meat.

The 19th loses 79 men killed, 310 casualties. A Bouncing Betty tripped by Captain Slayton's weary foot slashes off both legs at his thighs. His map case saves his balls. Lieutenant Sydney becomes company commander and seems to age ten years in a night.

Wayland at last fires his M-1 at a clumsy fleeing shape dodging among trees of the forest. The shape stumbles, rises, and continues on to become part of the agitated mist. Wayland finds blood spoor and thinks of deer he's tracked and killed back in Howell County.

The counterattack falters, the 19th is withdrawn. They transfer by trucks to a place Wayland first believes is "Our Dens" 'til he sees it as Ardennes on MacNair's map, a largely inactive front where units are quartered to rest, reorganize, top up their losses. Replacements who've not known fighting are seasoned in the area before being committed to combat.

Life is soft after the Hürtgen. Troops bivouac in commandeered houses that have stoves and dry, safe cellars. Even the bunkers, built from logs and sandbags, are snug. Hot food arrives daily, and at regimental headquarters platoons rotate to shower, get haircuts, receive mail, drink beer, dunk doughnuts, attend religious services, and see leggy Betty Grable in movies shown against the standing wall of a destroyed bakery.

Mostly it's waiting, routine reconnaissance, probing to establish the whereabouts of the shifting line, and occasional random artillery rounds whose sounds Wayland and others have learned to read so well they don't bother to take cover unless the shells are about to fall close. Replacements dive to the ground while veterans rarely glance up from card games.

Wayland hears from Pearl May. He's written her during basic to give her his address and to tell her he's fine. Her letter penciled on pink stationery has followed him. She's borne another child, her fourth, a daughter named Francine. She tells him Loretta has whooping cough and Lonnie's been deferred from the draft because of asthma but still works at the shook factory, which runs twenty-four hours a day and sells its entire production to the government. She's had no word from Lottie since Lottie left for Detroit to find a job in a defense factory. Pearl May does not mention Ferdinand.

Despite the Ardennes's easy living, Wayland's fear stirs. Sleep never brings him rest that reaches the bones. All veterans bear a constant weariness, their eyes hollowed out from the death they've fed upon—sights that have been seen too far too soon.

The line is static, six kilometers from the German West Wall. Divisional thrusts to the south have already breached it into the Fatherland, but the Roer holds up the advance. Krauts control the dams and are ready to flood the river when a crossing's attempted.

Still the feeling again is that Germany's finished and about to collapse.

Snow falls a soft sibilance and covers the land with its quiet, cold beauty. Later the freezing winds from the northeast bend the dark fir trees and spill snow from flogging branches. Wayland thinks of the blizzard at the Ballard sawmill. He also pictures Diana's silhouette in the pink window of the big house and his shameful giving up during his fight with Eugene.

The Ingersoll continues to tick. More Krauts surrender—bedraggled, wearing heavy greatcoats and cloddish boots. Once captured, they are obedient to authority. Directed by MPs, they tramp away unresisting and accepting. Wayland talks to a boyish Wehrmacht private from Cologne.

"My family made pianos until your bombers demolished our works," he says, his English better than Wayland's. All emblems have been torn from his uniform and his watch taken. GIs of the rifle companies strip prisoners of anything that can be sold or traded to rear-area commandos. The greatest find is a Luger or P-38.

"So learn to play the harmonica," Wayland says and thinks of the piano at the Ballard house and the singing of Diana's canary.

The Krauts use a new weapon, V-1 rockets directed at Liége. Wayland watches them fly over, and the loud banging of their primitive engines makes him recall the backfiring green Oliver tractors the Ballards used to plow, plant, and harvest.

The V-1s are of interest, yet no threat. None falls close to Battalion HQ. C Company moves up to relieve B on the perimeter, the unit bivouacked in a Belgian village named Schwarzhofen. Headquarters occupies a small, undamaged stone house that has a fireplace, a roof that doesn't leak, a well with good water.

Telephone wire has been strung to Battalion. Wayland tunes his new forty-pound backpack SCR to dance music broadcasts from Paris. MacNair jitterbugs with a broom.

Living remains warm and cozy. Snow hides scars of the village. Soon the Krauts will quit and allow unresisted entry into Germany. Arguments flare over whether the regiment will return stateside or become part of the forces slated to invade Japan.

"We done our part already," Petrie says and spits into the fire. The blob sizzles on a length of burning fir.

They hear action to the south, the faint rumble of artillery, and in the far distance the night sky flashes like a burning town. Captain Sydney reaches for the field phone.

"G-2 believes it's a diversionary attack to take pressure off the Roer dams and stall the Ninth Army's drive on Aachen," he explains.

Wayland remembers Aachen was the first word listed in the Funk & Wagnalls he studied while at Camp Blanding. He means to continue his reading of the encyclopedia when the war's over, starting with whatever follows Archimedes, which was as far as he got at the post library.

In the dark he accompanies Captain Sydney on a check of the perimeter and the placement of the three 57mm antitank guns, the two light machine guns, the three 60mm mortars. The night's hazy black, the dripping of melting snow ceasing as cold takes hold. Ice skims puddles collected in swags of cobblestones. He fingers great-grandfather Winslow's tarnished uniform button he's carried all this time for luck.

After they return to the billet, Wayland beds down on one of many mattresses dragged into headquarters from Belgian houses by B Company personnel. Men sprawl across the floor. The fire heats the room and causes shifting shadows. They've eaten well, smoked their last cigarettes, and listen to dance music on the SCR before edging into sleep.

Artillery east of Schwarzhofen wakes Wayland—not the 57mms on the perimeter but incoming 75mm high-velocity stuff with its female screeches. He fastens on his boots while Captain Sydney twirls the field phone's handle.

"Dead," he says. "Get Battalion on the radio."

Despite the static and intruding voices, Wayland raises Battalion. The captain learns I&R's checking with Regiment. The Krauts' strength and objectives are not known.

The shelling stops. A light snow falls through thick morning mist, which muffles sound. Peaceful again. Any attack, Wayland believes, can't be much. The Krauts just don't want the Yanks to sleep late.

C Company doesn't need to dig in. Foxholes and dugouts have been prepared by B Company. Some collect melting snow, and men curse combat boots that leak despite dubbing. Artillery and small arms commence firing to the southeast. Wayland can make out nothing beyond the curtain of mist.

From the northeast an eruption of mortar shells and Screaming Meemies. Snow falls, and muzzle blasts create an effect like heat lightning in the middle of winter. A command car comes busting down the road. It slows at the curve, and a helmeted head leans out to holler, "Fucking Krauts everywhere."

Captain Sydney wants to question the driver, but the command car speeds on through the village toward the rear.

The attack strikes straight at the center of C Company's perimeter. The 57mms and light machine guns open up. From the south men of the unit run toward the village to take cover in houses. Captain Sydney and platoon commanders sprint about trying to regroup them.

"We hold this line," the captain shouts.

"What line?" Arehart asks Wayland. He's fastened on his aid pouches and reset his helmet.

The Mark IVs rattle from snowy mist, their engines revved high, their dark rocking shapes visible in flashes of the 75mms. Machine guns flicker. The 57mm shells strike sparks as they bounce off thick armor. Where are the bazookas?

Krauts draped in white ponchos advance like ghosts out of mist. They are crouched targets and fire burp guns, MG-34s, and toss grenades as they dodge around tanks and half-tracks mounted with quad 20mm flak guns. Not all wear the white ponchos. Wayland glimpses the black jackets of *Waffen SS Panzers*.

The 19th's line gives way to rout. Exploding shells, flak guns, and Krauts' advancing shapes cause panic. C Company retreats through the village. Wayland doesn't know what they're fleeing to, but flight is the body's command. Fear riots in his belly.

The captain, Petrie, MacNair, and Wayland lugging the SCR snake through streets to the motor pool. Flames of a burning house brighten snow and cast wrenching contours. Black smoke from melting tires billows into falling snow. A 6x6 drives past, men hanging to it.

Petrie finds the Jeep and starts the engine as a bullet smashes the SCR. Wayland drops it away and dives among rubble still warm from a shell burst. Down the street against the background of flames he sees phantom GIs with arms held high. Shouts of *Kamerad*.

The captain raises his carbine and fires. MacNair tugs at him. A 75mm shell explodes against the side of a house, collapsing a wall. Stone and shrapnel zing past, and a white cat runs howling.

"No use, Captain," MacNair shouts.

The captain fires his carbine 'til the clip's empty. MacNair and Wayland drag him into the Jeep and hold him as Petrie gears them forward. They wind among streets and bounce over erupted cobblestones. A meat wagon, its doors hanging open, burns. Petrie skids the Jeep around it.

At the village's edge he bumps and zigzags them up a slope and across a snow-covered field. A mortar shell explodes, tips the Jeep, and hurls soil over them. Petrie, hunched forward, pumps the clutch and jams gears to keep them moving.

Wayland scrunches low and grips the captain who no longer tries to pull free but stares backward, flames glinting on his blackened, streaked face.

Petrie makes it to the forest. As he twists and turns the Jeep among fir trees, it nearly runs over a GI who lies face down in snow.

The captain orders Petrie to stop and swings out to kneel by the body. He turns it over and brushes snow from the GI's face to see the bullet-smashed forehead and scrambled brain gore.

"We take him," the captain says.

"Captain, they ain't gonna be room for all the bodies," Petrie says.

"The 19th doesn't leave its dead."

He orders Wayland to help load the body into the rear of the Jeep. The captain sits beside Petrie as he drives on. The body flops against Wayland and MacNair. They shove it off of themselves.

The forest light is pearly. The captain signals Petrie to stop. He turns back and listens to the shelling.

"Where'd they come from?" he asks but doesn't expect an answer. "We head west 'til we can cut back south to intercept the road."

"Which way's west?" Petrie asks.

The captain doesn't have his map case, but MacNair digs out his compass to set the direction. They hear more firing behind them. Petrie guns the Jeep among the precise rows of dark fir trees. Snow tumbles from limbs. Wayland and MacNair keep pushing the dead body off themselves. Blood is slimy on their hands. The Jeep sinks into a snowbank and becomes mired. Petrie works gears to free it.

The captain takes MacNair's compass and orders a change of direction south. The Jeep slews sideways. They reach the edge of the forest above the highway. GIs straggle in flight. Some have lost their rifles and helmets. Petrie maneuvers the Jeep bouncing down the rough slope.

Men cry out for a ride. They pile in and lie across the hood, hang on to the spare tire, the windshield, the frame as the Jeep dips, skids, and throws clods behind.

The high-velocity shell explodes behind them, an air burst of hot smashing brilliance. The Jeep pitches, lifts, overturns. Wayland's flung out. Punctured tires revolve and hiss. An arm from beneath the Jeep flaps against the snow.

He believes he's dying. Blood fills his mouth, and he has no sight in his left eye. Wavering fire burns through his vision. He wipes snow and blood from his face with a hand shaking so violently it batters his cheek.

He feels for his wounds. His uniform is ripped over a thigh, which is bleeding. He chokes from blood. He crawls to a steaming body drawn up as if clutching a ball—Petrie, his uniform scorched. His tobacco cud has blown from his mouth onto the snow. Wayland tries to rouse him. Petrie's head lolls. What Petrie clutches is the torn slithering gap that was his stomach.

The arm under the Jeep belongs to MacNair and stops moving. Wayland pushes to his feet and starts to run back up the slope for the protection of the forest. He thinks of the captain and stumbles back to the other side of the Jeep. Among bodies the blood-scummed captain lies unconscious but breathing. If Wayland is captured, there's a chance of better treatment if he survives in the presence of an officer.

All his life he's lugged weights. He lifts the captain and allows the body to flop forward over his shoulder. The captain's helmet drops away. Wayland scampers slew-footed up the slope toward cover. Shrapnel has peppered the snow. A frantic voice behind him calls, "Medic." Wayland doesn't turn back but stumbles after his faint deformed shadow. He falls, rises, and collects the captain.

When he reaches the line of firs, he runs into the forest until his knees give. His lungs feel they will tear from his chest, and he snaps at the air. The firing behind sounds remote. He lets the captain roll off into snow and searches for the compass. The captain's lost it. Wayland needs a bearing, but there's no sun in the forest, just the dim pearly light. He looks for moss on the side of the firs but finds none that will help him locate north.

He stands, again loads the captain, and moves toward what he believes is west. His field jacket is ripped, a sleeve almost gone. Blood from the captain's dangling fingers drips on Wayland's boots. Snow becomes calf deep, trips him, and he kicks his way through. He could be turned around in this fucking wilderness and headed back toward Schwarzhofen. He's able to carry the captain no farther and lowers him. The captain topples backwards, but he's not dead. A wisp of breath curls from his mouth.

Wayland abandons him. He pauses to listen for artillery or mortar fire and hears none. He has to keep moving even if wrong about the direction. With night will come freezing.

As he stops to rest and quiet his breathing, he hears a sound he can't believe—the lowing of a cow. He works through the snow until the forest gives way to open land and a barn that has a steeply pitched roof. Beyond a stone farmhouse at the edge of a road the Holstein stands in a fenced lot.

No sign of Krauts. Wayland starts toward the barn but again he thinks of the captain and retraces his tracks to gather him up. Wayland will have to trust the Belgians in the house not to turn them over to the Panzers.

The cow bawls. Wayland's top-heavy from the captain's shifting weight, and gravity pulls him sidestepping toward the barn where wind bangs doors. He peers inside to find all the stalls empty. He lets the captain slide as if boneless down onto matted straw. The captain bleeds from his face, throat, and chest. Wayland steps away to scan the house. No smoke from the chimney, meaning the Belgians have fled.

When he leaves the barn, the cow sees him, pushes against the fence, and bellows. Tits of her swollen udder squirt milk. Wayland hears engines and clanking treads and runs back to the barn. As he lies watching through the hinge side of a door, a Panther and armored car roll down the road and swerve toward the house. Panzer grenadiers ride them.

The grenadiers pile off and rush the house, rampage through it shouting and laughing. They find wine and stand outside drinking from long-necked bottles. The cow bawls. Krauts look toward the barn.

Three of them lope toward it, weapons held high. The stalls have a thin bedding of straw, not enough to hide under. No ladder reaches the loft. Wayland drags the captain behind the barn where stable droppings have been heaped. Steam rises, the heat of slow combustion, which has melted patches of snow. Using his hands, he digs deep into a side of the pile and drags the captain after him. He covers them with the shit-entwined bedding. When the cow bawls, the Krauts call to one another and begin shooting. The cow quiets. More laughter, as voices move away.

He waits in the manure's suffocating warmth. Slowly he fingers a breach for air. He hears shouts, engines rev up, the clash of gears. He sweeps an arm through the manure to crawl free and list to the barn.

The Krauts, some holding wine bottles, ride away on the clattering Panther and armored car in the direction of what he calculates must be east and Schwarzhofen. The house is burning. The cow, shot many times, lies on its side. Bullets have splattered the udder, causing milk and blood to fuse.

He uncovers the captain, rubs off the manure. The captain still breathes. Wayland shoulders him and moves straddle-legged past the house. Flames lick through smoke coiling from shattered windows. He hears distant small-arms fire. Bent under the captain's weight, he moves in the opposite direction taken by the grenadiers.

The road is sunken between rounded hills and flanked by forests. As he trudges onward, he becomes so weak he reels. He has to leave the captain and sets him upright in a snowbank at roadside where he hopes he'll be found by Belgians rather than the Panzers.

Wayland keeps moving, bowing into wind gusts, his left eye still closed, his mouth gaping. No tracks in the snow on the road which curves through forest until the way broadens. He lifts his face and wipes the good eye. Ahead a crossroads, a few houses, a small rounded stone church. No Krauts. No anybody.

A third time he returns for the captain. Under the load he totters. His wet combat boots crunch snow. The dwellings are shuttered, silent, no lights anywhere in the day's gathering grayness. He lurches house to house to knock on doors. None opens. When he listens he believes he hears life inside, calls out, begs. He turns to the church, reels toward it, climbs steps. He lowers the captain and tries the handle of a nail-studded entrance. It's locked.

He pitches down the steps and around the church where he finds a low, arched portal. He feebly beats the door. He backs against it and uses the heel of a combat boot to pound. Bloody snot drips from his nose. Everyone in the village must be fucking dead, and he wails.

When the door opens quickly, he sprawls backward and falls. What sounds like an iron bolt clangs. In darkness he struggles to work to his knee. A match strikes, a wick glows and enlarges to a meager yellow flame inside a lantern held by what he first believes is a black winged creature above him. They're not wings but a nun's elongated headdress which encloses an ancient, rutted face. Eyes gleam downward.

"The Cap'n," he says and pushes up along a cold stone wall. He fumbles to find the door.

The nun blows out the lantern. In the darkness he thinks she's left 'til he hears the slide of the bolt, and the door opens before him. He weaves out to the front of the church.

He no longer has strength enough to lift the captain and tugs at him until there are other hands. The nun has followed to help. They raise the captain's body between them and drag it back around the church. Inside they ease the captain down.

The nun shuts and bolts the door before again lighting the lantern. The glow pushes into darkness along the stone passageway. Holding the lantern over the captain, she gazes at him, her back humped. A bubble of spit on the captain's lips trembles, disturbed by his faint breath.

The nun starts away carrying the lantern. Wayland calls to her. She sets the lantern down beside him, and her long shadow moves ahead of her into darkness. He lets himself slip back against the stone wall. His head droops forward, his body gives way, and he lies beside the captain. Crusted blood and manure have stuck and stiffened his face. His jaw has lost the strength to close his mouth. He realizes he's pissing and can't stop it.

Shadows move, and the nun returns with a priest in a black cassock and beret who carries a brighter lantern. He's young, dark eyed, his skin fair, his face gaunt. He whispers to the nun and kneels at the captain's head where he works slender fingers under the slashed filthy shirt and presses his palm over the captain's heart.

"How brave and good to show such love for a comrade," he says to Wayland.

More nuns appear. At orders from the priest they carry the captain off. The ancient one helps Wayland stand and steadies him along the passageway. She guides him into a low windowless room where stone columns hold up intersecting wooden beams. The nuns are laying out the captain on a sheet spread over the floor beside a burning charcoal brazier.

The ancient nun assists Wayland to a wooden chair that has armrests as the priest and nuns remove the captain's boots and socks. They peel and cut away his uniform. They show no alarm or distaste, their faces intent and devotional.

When the captain lies naked, his skin reflects a luster from the brazier's coals. A nun balls his clothes and carries them off with his boots. The others wipe him using cloths dipped in a porcelain basin of water. The priest examines the captain's wounds—the worst a deep gash across his chest, a torn cheek, a flap of flesh hanging loose from his neck. Blood has caked his hair.

As they snip away the hair, the priest pours from an opaque bottle a liquid darker than iodine onto a gauze pad and dabs at the wounds. A nun begins to sew flesh of the captain's neck with a needle and thread. She has the patience of a woman hemming a skirt. Another nun adds charcoal to the brazier.

The priest turns to Wayland, examines his eye and the wound on his thigh before speaking to the ancient nun. She again helps Wayland stand. She carries the lantern as she assists him from the room and along another passageway into a chamber where a wooden tub has been filled with water. She dips fingers into it and motions to him he's to use it. She helps him lower himself to the bench and sets the lantern beside the tub before leaving.

He rests a time before painfully unfastening and toeing off his combat boots. He sheds the tattered stinking socks, his ripped uniform, the piss- and shit-fouled GI underwear.

He steps and lowers himself into heated water of the tub. Hooked to its side is a wire basket, which holds a sliver of pale soap. He cups his hands, pours water over his head, and moans from the goodness of the warmth as it streams down along his body. He lathers himself, fingers his bad eye, removes crud, and finds he can open the lid slightly, though his vision is still blurred. He attempts to immerse himself, but the tub's too confining. His filth floats on the water around him.

He drifts away until the nun returns and wakes him by softly touching his shoulder. She places a towel on the bench. She's taken his uniform and laid out a cassock, black socks, a pair of square-toed black shoes. She again leaves him.

Groaning, he works up from the tub, towels himself, sways. His skin is speckled from shrapnel, and he pinches out seeds of it as he might have Howell County ticks. The priest comes and lifts the lantern to examine him. He fingers a black salve from a jar and strokes it on Wayland's wounds. The salve is so thick it clogs the oozing blood.

"*Médecine fini,*" the priest says. "With this our farmers doctor their cattle. You may yourself dress."

Wayland painfully lifts the cassock and lets it settle around his body. The shoes are heavy and too large. As he sits forward on the bench to tie them, he tilts. The ancient nun hurries to him, rights his body, ties the shoes. He thanks her, but she keeps her face lowered and doesn't answer.

She supports him along the corridor to a vaulted room with large windows pointed at the top and covered by canvas. At its center under a black wrought-iron chandelier that holds candles is a long, plain oak table and benches. No candles are lit, and some have burned down while others are missing. She sets the lantern on the table. Bread and cheese wait on a wooden platter beside a cup and jug of pale milk.

Wayland tries not to wolf down food but can't stop himself from taking great gnawing bites. His cheeks bulge and ache with his chewing. He spills milk from his mouth over his chin. The nun places her hands in the sleeves of her habit and turns away.

"Want to thank you," Wayland says, his mouth full.

She doesn't answer, and he thinks she's deaf until he realizes no nuns have spoken. He guesses the order has some rule of silence and that the priest does their talking for them.

Wayland's weak, hurting, dizzy, and clutches the table to right himself. The nun again aids him as he stands and moves him along another corridor to a small chamber where white, red, and gold religious vestments hang on a rack in an alcove along a wall. Shelves hold folded linens, and banners are furled around flagpoles topped by brass crucifixes.

A thin gray pallet and a brown blanket are laid out behind the rack. As the nun settles him to the pallet, he again thanks her. Still no response from a face that is leached like eroded Howell County soil. She hands him something. It is the battered Ingersoll pocket watch still ticking.

She draws the vestments across the rack so that he's hidden by them. When he rises to look after her, she lays a finger across her lips, lifts the lantern, and pads away, closing the door.

He falls back and sinks into depths of sleep so black and deep he believes he will never stop falling and return to light.

❦

Rumbling and a trembling of the vestments wake him. He peeks from them. Close up they are clean, smell of soap, but are threadbare. He crawls from beneath them and stands on his toes to look through leaded glass of a window that is little more than a slit in the stone of the church's outer wall.

It's snowing, and the daylight is grimy. Tanks, motorcycles, and trucks pulling artillery roar and rattle through the village. Cobblestones are dislodged and crushed under treads, leaving furrows of upheaved earth. Krauts wearing the white ponchos advance slouching along both sides of the road, their slung weapons turned barrel downward, a ghost army passing through a ghost town.

SS grenadiers ride on the Mark Vs, and several gaze at the church. Wayland ducks away and checks the door. It has no lock. He drops down to squirm behind the vestments until he no longer hears the whining boogies and clanking treads or feels the pulsing of engines, the shuddering of earth.

When he dares push the vestments aside and again look from the window, the troops are gone. Falling snow partially covers their soiled tracks. The ancient nun appears and removes a hand from a sleeve of her habit to motion him to follow. A second time she leads him to the oak table under the wrought-iron chandelier where she offers him honey-sweetened porridge and thickly sliced black bread cut from a round loaf.

"The cap'n?" he asks as he finishes.

She nods, and he follows her. Captain Sydney lies on a narrow bed in a room cramped as a prison cell. He's covered by a gray blanket. Above him on the stone wall hangs a wooden crucifix. The captain's eyes are closed, and he breathes loudly through his mouth.

The nun lifts the blanket. The captain's chest and neck are bandaged. Stitches track his cheek. She lowers the blanket and leaves Wayland. He sits on a stool, leans against the wall, dozes. He pushes up only to use the Turkish toilet and when offered bread. He helps the nuns change dressings—not gauze but boiled white strips of clothes that have been torn to make the bandages. He thinks of his mama changing the dressings on the stump of his daddy's lost arm.

The captain stirs and tries to speak. Wayland can't understand the fevered words. When he holds up the captain's head to give him water, the captain reaches and takes hold of Wayland's arm. The fingers give out and release, the eyelids flutter, yet he still breathes.

During the night Wayland wakes to hear strange, otherworldly singing. He's unsure he's not sleeping and dreaming. He stands to feel his way through darkened passageways toward the sound and stops before a door around which are faint streaks of light.

He opens it just enough to see into a gilded chapel. The priest kneels before the altar on which a silver chalice glimmers. The nuns, who've never spoken in Wayland's presence, now sing, their faces raised in ivory candlelight. Belgian civilians stand among the shadowed pews. The statue of a loving Mary in a blue robe and holding the swaddled Jesus baby takes on life from fluttering flames.

Wayland backs away and returns to the captain. The singing stops. In time the priest appears carrying a lantern.

"The day of our Savior's birth," he says. "*Joyeux Noel.*"

"Pray for the cap'n?" Wayland asks.

"*Et vous, mon ami,*" the priest answers.

He and Wayland kneel by the bed, and the priest with bowed head speaks in his rapid language. When he finishes, he makes the sign of the cross. Wayland thinks of his own religion, surely no longer Baptist. He's called on the Lord and Jesus a thousand times, but what he senses is not the gentle Lamb of God but a fiercely hot, smashing, and devouring Power of an angry God hurling down bolts of red destruction and death. How can a man not bow and cringe before such a Being and beg mercy? Yet who could love Him?

Some Christmas, Wayland thinks. He wonders whether all the lights will be switched on by the Ballards at the big house. He feels old and has to calculate it's not until May will he be twenty. If he survives that long.

During the night the captain's fever rises and falls. He mumbles, shouts, calls out coordinates for artillery support. He opens his wild eyes to stare at Wayland, sweats, and turns his head away.

Each day is misted and snowy. Icicles hang from the church eaves, wind blows sprays of snow off the village's roofs. Kraut armor and troops continue to pass westward along the road.

A banging at the corridor door sends Wayland scurrying to his hiding place. He hears voices and approaching steps. Under the vestments he glimpses Kraut boots, one pair not clumsy but of finer quality, the calf-hugging leather worn by officers. All are wet and muddy around the soles.

Wayland doesn't move 'til the boots leave and the priest comes to say *Les Boches sont parti*. Wayland learns they took or destroyed nothing. They discovered the captain but did no more than look him over, and the captain slept through it.

Troop movements slow. There are hours of the day when no Kraut vehicles or armor clot the road. Belgians begin to open doors and go about their lives. Sunshine breaks through, fades, returns. Canvas is removed from windows. A Spitfire banks over so low Wayland sees the pilot's helmeted head.

He hears the drumming of artillery. Firing moves closer. A huge, black Mark VI Tiger roars and lumbers eastward through the village, grenadiers riding it, some holding to the 88mm cannon. It's followed by armored vehicles carrying Krauts, a truck hauling a *Nebelwerfer*, and a flak carrier, its quad guns pointing westward.

A shell zings back across the village and explodes east of it. Quiet follows. Icicles drip. Another plane flies over, a P-51, its shadow sweeping across the melting snow.

Wayland stays with the captain, who wakes and attempts to talk, the words too weak to form fully and be understood. He is pale, shrunken, but his fever has broken, and the redness of his wounds appears less angry.

Full sunlight at the windows is painful to the eyes. More Belgians move along the street. They talk and wave. A man leads a draft horse pulling a cart loaded with hay through the village. The Belgians look westward, hurry to their houses, and close the doors. Wayland hears small-arms fire, a burp gun, the explosion of a Panzerfaust. Krauts run along the road. A mortar round shatters the roof of a house. Wounded pigeons flutter in death throes on dirtied snow.

Wayland leaves the captain with the ancient nun and hides behind the vestments. He listens to gunfire beyond the church, a cannon blast, then a long, lingering silence. As he starts to crawl from under cover he hears the strike of hobnails along the passageway. He buries himself under the blanket.

Footsteps enter the chamber. They approach his curtain. Somebody's betrayed him. Jesus, oh Jesus. A gun barrel pokes through and sweeps aside vestments. He blinks into light and sits up to hold his hands high.

"*Kamerad*," he calls.

"No need to be formal, Yank," the limey dogface says, his netted helmet cocked at a jaunty angle over a smudged bony face. "You can just call me 'arry."

twenty-two

Again Wayland stopped the car, this time at the site of the Healing Spring Baptist Church. The structure stood scoured by wind and weather, the remaining clapboard loose and bowed, some pieces ripped off or lying flat on the ground.

Windowpanes were broken, all tin had been stripped from the roof, the field bell that had rung for services from the out-of-plumb belfry had vanished. Quarreling grackles swooped from gaps rotted in siding and circled to return.

The front door fell in as he touched it, causing dust to spiral through shafts of sunlight. The pine pews had been taken, the altar where Preacher Arbogast had implored the Lord God for mercy was gone. A single water-stained page from a hymnal had lodged in a cobwebbed corner—"Bringing in the Sheaves." The grackles had nested among rafters, and their droppings splattered the soft, decomposing floorboards.

He crossed out and around the building. Kudzu had claimed not only the surrounding pines but also the cemetery itself, a knee-deep leafy sea of vines that strangled all other growth. A blacksnake slid away beneath them with sinuous speed. Wayland searched for plots, few ever commemorated by paid-for markers. When he left Howell County, tight times had still held sway, and who had money to spend on death except the Ballards? Most graves were headed by the slabs of fieldstone with names and dates lettered on them in the church-owned Sears gallon of white oil-base house paint.

He trampled kudzu until he found the patch of ground where his one-armed father lay buried beside the mother wearing her mended coat with its fur collar. He pulled at kudzu, straightened the markers, and stomped his heels to tighten the soil around them.

Clearing and burning the kudzu would require a team of men using bush axes, but he could somehow arrange it. He felt guilt and anger. The whole county might go to hell, yet the Ballards with their money had stayed rich and secure behind stones of their walls.

Rains had washed away lettering on many markers leaving only scraps of decipherable identification. With a finger he traced flakes of curled, darkened paint on the small one he set upright:

Baby Ell n

Ju   7   36

God Wan ed Her

So Ba He To k

er E rly

He turned away thinking of Pearl May and Lonnie's child born at the cabin, the baby so tiny she hardly filled a shoe box, Preacher Arbogast's spindly hands lifting the box as if presenting an offering to God.

Wayland remembered the evening he carried his own daughter Jennifer home and left Amy nursing the baby while he stood on his darkening Florida lawn before their new Mediterranean house with its solid walls and red tile roof. A salty breeze blew off the bay where red and green channel markers flashed, rustling the palms, and lights from the house's windows shone on the Bermuda grass of his watered lawn.

I will love and protect you, Wayland had whispered, his face raised to Polaris in the night's purple sky, his promise to Jennifer. My house is strong and tight. You will never know want or terror . . .

. . . that he still carries even freed. Before leaving the Belgian church he changes the cassock for his uniform. The nuns have darned his socks, sewed his shirt and field jacket, dried and polished his boots. He thanks the priest, who kisses each side of Wayland's face.

"*Aimez Dieu et tout sera bien*," the priest tells him.

The ancient nun has another thing for him—the confederate button from Granddad Winslow's uniform. Wayland pockets it with the dollar Ingersoll watch, which has survived all and continues to run. He wants to take hold of the nun's hand, but she holds her palms toward him and shakes her head as she backs away into shadows of the corridor. For an instant he sees a fleeting vision of a pretty face buried under the mask of her eroded, downcast eyelids.

A British lieutenant arranges for a lorry. Captain Sydney's strapped to a stretcher and loaded on. Wayland sits beside him as they pass a crippled 6x6 that reeks of oil and burnt rubber, the air so thick with the stinks they become a taste in Wayland's mouth. The snow's been trampled black.

Dead frozen Krauts have been arranged head to head at the side of the road waiting to be carried off. Many are young, and some of the bodies have been splashed by truck tires. He glimpses a boy with bled-fair skin that has a sheen like polished marble. That could be me, he thinks.

At a crossroads American MPs direct traffic and flag down a meat wagon for Wayland and the captain. The ride is bumpy and lurching, causing the captain to blink wildly. Wayland steadies him. When the ambulance stops at an 84th Division aid station, the captain receives plasma and morphine before he's routed to an evac hospital. He's gone before Wayland can say goodbye.

A medic examines Wayland's scabbed thigh and finds no infection. He swabs the wound and sprinkles sulfur powder over it, tapes on gauze, and shoots Wayland with tetanus antitoxin. Wayland is sent to a field hospital where he showers, shaves, and eats hot Spam diced into powdered scrambled eggs. A nurse smelling of perfume and alcohol tends him. He rests two nights on a ward cot beside casualties suffering from fiery, stinking trench foot. The nurse salvages bits of untorn uniforms for him, the parts, including the boots, likely taken from the dead.

MPs help him locate the 19th Regimental Combat Team and catch him a ride on a weapons carrier to Liége. The 19th is quartered in a block of civilian houses. A yet unknown number of men are still missing—captured, wounded, dead. A few who became lost at Schwarzhofen continue to straggle in.

Company C has a new lieutenant named Wilburn, who promotes Wayland to platoon sergeant. Replacements arrive, young like the German dead at the side of the road. He fills out his three squads, and the replacements treat him like an old-timer. He doesn't allow himself to think of MacNair, Petrie, or legless Captain Slayton. He feels ancient at nearly twenty.

He's ordered to dress in his Class A uniform and jeeped to Regimental Headquarters located in a white stone mansion that has a golden chandelier under a central dome. Colonel Stanton pins a bronze star on Wayland's freshly issued Eisenhower jacket. The citation read by a major speaks of Sergeant Wayland Garnett who performed the valorous act of rescuing his commanding officer while under intense enemy fire, meaning Captain Sydney, who's been ZI'd after medical treatment in England. Wayland's wounds also earn him a purple heart.

The colonel's aide slips him a bottle of Scotch. Wayland hates the taste and divides it among his squad leaders. He knows himself to be no hero. Most of the brave are dead.

When all units of the 19th are up to strength, the regiment again moves forward. The Krauts still have fight, and there are rivers to cross—the Roer, the Ruhr, the Rhine. Casualties are light, mostly replacements. At the dark waters of the Elbe the fighting stops, but men of the 19th are suspicious of word the Krauts have surrendered 'til on the far side they see Russian soldiers waving.

Unauthorized celebrations erupt. Wayland and a husky Russian private armed with a rifle dance and kiss. She smells of sweat, cordite, and onions. They drink vodka from her canteen as soldiers fall laughing and whooping into the river. He screws her standing up beside a tank that has a red star painted on it. It's the first woman whose body he's ever known.

The warmth of May expands. The regiment holes up in Magdeburg after kicking civilians from their houses to provide quarters. The belief is the 19th will be sent to the Pacific. There's beer, movies, and hungry German girls who wait smiling and milling around the kitchen and mess hall. Some are children with sweet urgent faces, their cheeks rouged, and their lips grotesquely painted. He wants to scrub off what the war has done to them.

When the atomic bomb finishes the Japs, the point system determines who leaves Europe first for stateside. Because of his length of service, campaign ribbons, bronze star, and purple heart, Wayland has enough points to be sent home and discharged early.

The 19th begins to break up. He shakes hands with Lieutenant Wilburn, Kaminsky, Arehart, and a few replacements before turning in his helmet, M-1, ammo belt, and bayonet, which he's used mainly to open C rations. Quartermasters ship him out on a military train through Germany and France to Le Havre.

A gray ship waits, its bow high and sharp. He's assigned to a four-bunk compartment topside, plenty of space, sheets, a porthole to breathe sea air instead of the foulness below deck. The troops eat steaks, vegetables, and real eggs. Before embarking, they've been paid, and liquor can be bought from the ship's crew. Poker and craps games run twenty-four hours. Money is plentiful and fast, but Wayland saves his.

Eight days to New York harbor. Men assemble on deck and stare at the Statue of Liberty lit by a thin October sun. Colorful unit flags have been hung from the rafters of the dock sheds where smiling matronly ladies meet them to hand out cigarettes and candy.

He lays over thirty-six hours at Fort Dix, where he has his hair cut and buys a new wallet, a comb, and a wristwatch at the PX. The old Ingersoll has finally given out and is honorably retired. Kaminsky, who's from Chicago, is still with him. He teaches Wayland the rudiments of playing chess.

"It orders the mind," Kaminsky says.

At Fort Meade Wayland rejects an offer to reenlist. The discharge process requires three days. He receives a physical and has his teeth fixed in a long narrow building where a row of twenty dental chairs is bolted to the floor. He's issued a new, well-fitting uniform, which has a ruptured duck sewn to the Eisenhower jacket, and he receives his final pay.

"We can ticket you on a Greyhound to Jericho Crossroads," the transportation corporal says.

"No," Wayland says.

"That's your address, right?" the corporal asks, looking up after again checking Wayland's records.

"I'm headed down to Florida. Never mean to be cold again."

As he rides the Greyhound south, he can't accept the truth he's shut of the army. That life lives inside him. The fear he's carried all these months has shrunk to pea size, yet survives, its heart beating quietly.

twenty-three

Wayland drove toward Bellepays thinking he'd come so far not just from Fort Lauderdale, not geographical measurements and miles, but in what he'd made of himself and his life. He no longer had any reason to feel intimidated by his Howell County past. He'd proved himself, surmounted the disadvantages of his origin, and won the game, hadn't he?

He thought of Tampa where he'd worked on a construction gang during the day and used the GI Bill to attend Excel Business College at night. The school had been on the second floor above a dry cleaning establishment off Cigar Street, a 1920s brick building that lacked an elevator and where the office had . . .

. . . frosted windows, and he talks with the dean, an elderly man whose false teeth appear much too large and loose. Dean Moss gives him a test, basic math, which Wayland handles easily, though he blanks many multiple-choice questions in the vocabulary section.

"You know your figures well enough but you'll need our beginner's English course," the dean tells him.

He enrolls Wayland and assigns him a student desk among precisely lined rows across the mustard-colored loft.

A battery of bluish fluorescent lights buzzes overhead. Wayland's books, pencils, and exercise sheets, also paid for by Uncle Sam, he keeps in the drawer, which has a lock.

He studies accounting and business English. The precise, middle-aged Miss Bernice Waters walks the aisles between the desks to check assignments. She leans over his shoulder to make corrections and has beautiful handwriting, her fingers quick, the nails painted a faint pink and squared off as precisely as if measured by calipers.

English is taught in a boxlike classroom that is surrounded by blackboards. Wayland's anxious about his courses but finds he's no worse off than many other students—Italians, Hispanics, and a wild-eyed brooding veteran who fought in the Pacific. While Miss Waters explains the parts of speech, the vet, named Floyd, stands, screams, and walks out never to return.

"You're doing well on written assignments, but your oral delivery and pronunciation are frightful," Miss Waters tells Wayland. "We'll concentrate on those aspects of your education."

He receives seventy-five dollars a month from the government and averages forty a week at Gulf Building and Supply, which specializes in steel erections. At a co-op near Ybor City he's found a room that lacks a closet and provides a rack made of plumber's pipe to hang his few clothes. When lights are switched on in the community kitchen, roaches scurry, and he hurries about even when barefooted to stomp them.

His view is to the back of a sooty brick building, an industrial operation where men in overalls stand among power belts and before clacking machinery. Iron bars cover grimy windows. Steam and smoke coil from black metal chimneys sticking from the roof and are blown away by wind off Tampa Bay.

He does his own cooking—hamburgers, chicken, Aunt Jemima pancake mix. He studies whenever he can seize minutes and solves accounting problems mentally while pounding nails to install siding or mixing mortar mud to push in the wheelbarrow to the bricklayers hollering for it.

"You have remarkable powers of concentration," Miss Waters tells him at his graduation where he's handed a printed Certificate of Accomplishment. She has dinner with him that night, a celebration during which they drink wine, and afterward she permits him in her bed. She teaches him another course.

He studies the want ads and lands a clerical job with Florida Power & Light, a daily grind with no chance of advancement among college-boy types on executive tracks, yet it's an opportunity that allows him to observe, study, and learn from people of substance how to dress correctly, carry himself, use the proper table etiquette. He goes to school on those around him.

It's the small things, he realizes, that declare one's caste like the way a fork is held, the soup eaten, the tone used addressing waiters as well as the cut of one's lapels, the choice of a religious denomination, above all how one speaks and uses the language.

Recognizing he's like a starving man with a hunger for learning, Miss Waters continues to work and sleep with him. She stands him before her and orders him to converse politely as she corrects his pronunciation. She requires him to write reports, uses a red pencil on his grammar, and directs the organization of his thoughts. He follows her suggestion that he practice speaking before her mirror. He borrows one of Florida Power's dictation machines to listen to his own voice, realizing his country accent has to be remodeled and submerged. He might as well be learning a new tongue.

For a man with his limited education and contacts, he believes the best money's to be found in sales and applies for a job with Palmetto Auto Parts, where after training he's given designated territory that covers six Florida counties. He will sink or swim on commissions because though he has a drawing account, there's no salary, medical, or retirement benefits.

He develops a soft selling manner as well as persistence, refusing to be turned away or insulted by potential customers. To complete a sale he outsits purchasing agents 'til they surrender and give him orders to write up just to be rid of him. He learns to smile in the face of rejection, think out moves ahead of presentations, have refutations ready on his lips. It is said of him he can outsit stones.

Sales, he feels, are a sort of hunting, tracking, and the taking of game. Instead of bringing home the meat, he stalks commissions and dollars—paper victuals that needn't be skinned, gutted, and washed before cooking.

All goes increasingly well until Mr. Gorman, his boss and the owner of Palmetto Auto Parts, brings his college-boy son into the business and awards him choice areas of Wayland's selling territory. The boy's given Jacksonville, Orlando, and St. Petersburg as well as other major cities while Wayland has to make his beans around the fringes of the most populated regions. His commissions drop, and he confronts Mr. Gorman in his well-appointed office on the third floor above the company warehouse. Mr. Gorman's desk displays a colored photograph of his wife, his son, and himself smiling at the camera from beside their turquoise swimming pool.

"I know you're feeling bad about how things have turned out," Mr. Gorman says. He's bald, gaining weight, and has a golfer's tan. He also owns a Bertram sports fishing boat with twin outriggers and a tuna tower.

"You told me your son was going to be a lawyer," Wayland says.

"He doesn't feel the law's right for him, and as I explained to you before this is a family business."

"I had this feeling I was part of the family."

"You got to understand." He rubbed his shiny bald spot as if to polish it. "If you had a wife and son you would."

"I worked hard to develop those territories. Your son just walks in and picks up my money."

"Wayland, I'm sorry but you need to get it through your head that this is the way it has to be."

"You never told me there was any chance of you sticking your son ahead of me. You knew all along he'd be coming into the business. You been using and lying to me."

"Look, I take exception to the tone of your voice and the way you're talking to me," Gorman says and swings forward in his chair. "If you don't like this job, you know where the door is."

Wayland doesn't quit that afternoon. Instead he broods. He's been nursing an idea that took shape while he studied competitors' price lists and discovered that small hydraulic presses primarily used for removing auto and truck wheel bearings were being manufactured in Japan and sold from California. He examines one, takes it apart, reassembles it. He's astonished at its simplicity. It's merely a few steel I-beams welded to make a rigid frame to which the hand-operated hydraulic component can be bolted. He investigates further and finds hydraulics themselves are such basic mechanical apparatuses that no patents hold sway. The principle, the encyclopedia reveals, is as old as Archimedes. If the presses can be produced locally instead of buying them from California and paying the heavy freight charges, significant money could be saved.

While continuing to work for Palmetto he stops by machine shops and requests bids on a simple model he designs himself. He can find none that will do the work for a price he can afford. He'll also need a pickup truck to haul the model around for demonstrations and display. Just gearing up for the venture will take all the money he's worked so hard to sock away. He feels fear at the thought of loss.

Running out of hope, he pulls up before a small independent shop named Peerless Machine on the outskirts of Gainesville, the place a converted army surplus Quonset hut that appears unpromising for what he wants, yet he's surprised at the interior, which is well laid out, the lathes, power drills, and workbenches orderly and wiped clean. It's owned by a hairy man who gives his name as Max Freeman. He has an outsized head, a small body, and the stub of a cigar clamped in his teeth. His gray coveralls and billed cap are grease spotted. He sits behind a desk made from a sheet of plywood laid over sawhorses. Despite the heat, he wears work gloves.

"Why you looking at my nose?" he asks after Wayland has introduced himself, shaken hands, and seated himself before the desk.

"Didn't realize I was," Wayland answers, a lie. The nose is hooked.

"Yeah you did. You're thinking I'm a Jew, right?"

"It crossed my mind but makes no difference to me."

"Oh hell no. You're thinking this damn Jew will try to screw me. I know the routine. Okay, let's see what you got on your mind if you got any mind at all. Sketch it out for me."

Wayland does on the back of a soiled envelope the man shoves across the desk. Max studies it and grunts. He needs a shave. He uses his tongue to shift the cigar stub from one side of his mouth to the other.

"All right, I'll make you a model for seventeen hundred bucks."

Wayland shakes his head. That's too much. He's prepared to go twelve hundred. More than that would eat up the working capitol needed to sustain himself on the road. He stands and starts away. He thinks it's no use and he might as well give up the idea for good.

"Hold it a second," Max says. "I'll come down a hundred."

"Still too much," Wayland says and reaches the door.

"You're thinking I'm a dirty Jew trying to Shylock you."

"I'm thinking I got to get back to work."

"You're a vet, ain't you?"

"What makes you think so?"

"I can read it on you, especially the eyes. For those that's seen combat, it's always in the eyes. How much can you afford to pay me for doing the job?"

"Twelve hundred."

"I'm a vet myself. Left a piece of myself at Salerno."

"What piece of yourself?"

Max stands, fingers and twists a wrist, and detaches a gloved hand. He tosses it to the desk. It thumps against the plywood.

"That piece," he says, picks up the artificial hand, and reattaches it. "We got us a deal or not?"

"We do."

"I'll want six hundred down."

"I'll write you a check."

"I'll wait 'til it clears before I start work on your press. Let's fine-tune your sketch for the precise specs. You know, I can see what you're aiming to do here, what you have in mind for the press. I could steal the idea. You'd have no proof, couldn't take me to court with any hope of winning. But I won't. I admire enterprise, especially in vets. You still think I'm a dirty Jew?"

"No, sir, I don't," Wayland says and writes the check. When he gives it to Max, he holds the man's good hand in both of his own and squeezes it in a lingering thanks.

"Hell, don't overdo it," Max says and again shifts the cigar stub to the other side of his mouth.

❧

Wayland quits his job with Palmetto, trades his Ford for a Chevy pickup, and is equipped this time not with an auto parts catalogue but the beautifully built and brightly painted demonstrator model turned out for him by Max Freeman. Wayland's already acquainted with all the wholesalers in his old territory, has established relationships with many, and offers a product they can buy at nearly half the imported price and sell at higher profit margins.

On the road again weeks at a stretch he husbands his money by searching out and staying in deteriorating hotels where he asks for a commercial rate on the cheapest rooms. He fixes meals of soda crackers and canned soups using hot water drawn from bathroom faucets. For dessert he unwraps Butterfingers or Baby Ruths. He packs a GE iron to keep his suits pressed and hangs his cotton shirts on radiators after washing them in the sink. He sneaks his two-burner hotplate past desk clerks. It blows fuses, and he pretends innocence. He works so late his footsteps often sound to him like drum knells along lonely halls where bulbs burn so feebly they cast hardly a shadow before him.

He puts every cent he has in the venture. Driving the secondhand Chevy pickup, he visits not only major car dealerships but also every jackleg garage he happens upon in dusty sun-blasted towns of the Deep South. He demonstrates the press sometimes three and four times the same day and makes an oral guarantee that it can be sold retail for at least a 35% profit margin—a promise at this stage of funds in his bank account he couldn't possibly keep.

He's not asked to keep it. His customers are pleased, the word gets around, and he's able to claw increasing bites of the market pie from his major competitors, including Palmetto Auto Parts. At the end of eighteen months his costs give way to solid profits, and he begins to bank significant money. The second year he rents Fort Lauderdale office space for his headquarters, and when he makes deposits at the Florida National, the bankers begin to notice him, stand, speak his name, and shake his hand.

He reveals as little as possible about his background but lets people know he's from Virginia, his modified manner of speaking convincing them he's talking genteel southern, not a redneck dialect. When his pronunciation or grammar slips or falters, it's taken to be a good-humored mocking of the local crackers.

He first dreams about and then succeeds in increasing his line of offerings to include hydraulic lifts, racks, tools, and wheel alignment equipment. Max, who's been given as much of the hydraulic press business as he could handle, dies at one of his lathes, and Wayland attends the Gainesville funeral. By then Wayland has amassed enough capital and credit to break free of subcontractors and build his own small manufacturing plant. He's able to hire a salesman, then two, and three as well as keep extending his territory. Part of the year he allows himself to stay off the road except for meetings with his most profitable customers. Palmetto Auto Parts is not one of them. It's gone out of business.

And finally Amy surrenders to him, they are married, and she gives birth to Jennifer. He contracts with an architect and contractor to build their palm-shaded, white stucco Mediterranean house with its red tile roof. I finally have it all, he thinks when he stretches out a chaise beside the pool or swings a golf club with friends at the Le Cielo Club, yet unbidden forms from the past rise in his mind like great predatory fish swimming up from dark depths to disturb the sun-smacked waters.

He thinks of Lottie, Pearl May, Emmett, Ferdinand, Lonnie and feels guilt he hasn't sought them out, but what if they show up at his door? They might well be a shock and embarrassment to Amy if taken out to dinner or introduced to their friends. She would rightly feel he has deceived her about his past.

And there is Eugene Ballard. Wayland goes for months without thoughts of him, then wakes during nights to recreate Diana's valentine-like silhouette at the pink window of the big house and his humiliation before her. He should have fought on and won. In the genes? He again wonders about his. Is one's life all foreordained, as some of his Presbyterian acquaintances suggest?

I'm all right, he tells himself over the years. I've proved myself in a thousand ways. I'm not the same ignorant youth I was in Howell County. I've made it, and there's nothing I'd back down from today. Yet the threatening shapes of memory continue to glide from the deep and swirl in the darkness of his mind.

twenty-four

He swallowed and flexed his fingers on the Caddy's steering wheel. Bellepays was close now. The road curved left between shedding pines, and he glimpsed the Kentucky gate hung between the white brick posts topped by the stone pineapples.

A Private Property sign had been tacked to the top plank of the gate. In his youth no such warning would've been required, the name Ballard being sufficiently spread and a warning of itself. The fence appeared freshly painted, denoting that somebody in the family still cared for the estate.

He experienced trepidations of his boyhood—the closed throat, the tightened lump of his stomach, a drawing in of his shoulders as if he were shrinking. Despite traveling so far to be in this place, he again felt the urge to reverse course, return to Richmond, and fly home to Florida.

Well he'd drive in at least as far as the stone wall around the big house. Chances of his being recognized were remote, for surely he no longer resembled in any fashion whatsoever the ragtag young hick who'd shaken the dust of Howell County from his feet forty-seven years earlier. If challenged, he'd appear to be prosperous and respectable, the type of person welcomed and treated with respect by Black Amos or whoever was in residence.

He set the parking brake, stepped from the car, and pulled the wooden handle dangling from its chain to open the Kentucky gate. He latched it until he drove through, then waited for it to be drawn shut by its cannonball counterweight. Old habits still held. In the country you always closed gates.

The dogwoods and magnolias bordering the drive stood in order, grass along the shoulder had been clipped, no potholes impaired the pavement, all further evidence Bellepays was being well maintained. He again wondered what members of the family might be living here. Surely Mr. Henry Ballard had died by this time. Likely Eugene himself, heir apparent and squire, resided in splendor, or perhaps Diana had become grand dame of the manor. How would the years have treated her? God, she'd once been so haughty and beautiful. Little chance she'd remember even his name.

He drove slowly and thought of the time he'd believed the very air of Bellepays to be special, purified, each breath refined. Only later did he understand that air knew no boundaries, not in Florida, Germany, or protected by ivy-covered stone walls.

The black iron gates stood open. Wisteria long past blooming twisted snake-like around the immense white oaks and dangled from their ponderous limbs. He thought of himself as a boy climbing the tulip poplar and peering over to see the house like a resplendent vision the summer evening Black Amos had dragged him down the trunk.

Three deer, a buck and two does, ran in front of the car, their hooves clattering on pavement, their eyes bright with alarm, their white tails flung upward. They bounded into shadows of the forest. The buck would've been an easy shot with the old Enfield .303 his daddy had traded for. Meat on the table.

His Amy disapproved of hunting, though he'd tried to explain to her that hungry men might need to kill to eat or because deer destroyed gardens and stripped bark from the fruit trees, causing them to wither and die.

"That was then, not now," she had said and of course was right, though she never in her life had known tight times. Her father's protected federal income had kept her safe from want and dirt.

He drove close to the iron gate and stopped. A drape of deep shade subdued the white granite mansion and its louvered, black-green shutters. Cobblestones of the courtyard could've used a sweeping. Black Amos would've not allowed leaves to collect over them or clog the storm drains.

Wayland realized he'd pushed his foot hard against the brake pedal, evidence he was definitely still intimidated by the place. Of course Bellepays might have changed ownership after all these years, strangers now living inside. No, he could not imagine that. The Ballards were forever.

He allowed the Caddy to drift forward over cobblestones that caused the tires to thump softly. A black Ford pickup was parked under shade of the porte-cochere. He stopped the Caddy, and this time he waited for somebody to emerge from the house, which appeared in good repair, no gutters hanging loose, no shutters askew, yet he sensed a stillness and somnolent lack of activity.

He didn't dare honk the horn, an act which might be interpreted by the dwellers as a demand for attention. Instead he cut the engine, opened the door, and set on his Panama hat as he moved toward the house. He almost veered to the kitchen, which had always been his point of entry. Never had he stood at the front door. Old habits again directing him.

He kept his feet on the path's river-washed pebbles and circled to the mansion's formal entrance. Nine marble steps broad at the bottom narrowed toward the top, where they passed between massive stone flower urns to the veranda and oak double doors. He noted the urns were empty of soil and that the doors had outsized knobs and preening brass swans for knockers that could've used a shine. He thought of Black Amos wearing his denim apron and carrying polish and his clean cotton rag.

Wayland raised the lowered head of a swan, tentatively tapped it, and waited. He heard no response. Irritated by his timidity, he lifted the knocker higher and released it fully. The house swallowed an echoing bang. He shifted his weight. Nobody home, and he didn't try to fool himself about what he felt, which was relief. At the same time he became further annoyed about his anxiety. The truth was he was more than intimidated, even a bit frightened. Would the Ballards' power never release him?

He walked to a high broad window to the right of the door and peeked in. Probably this would be the parlor, but a drawn curtain partially covered the panes. He made out the legs of what appeared to be a workbench. Perhaps the house was undergoing remodeling or repairs.

He turned and laid a hand on the outswept railing to walk down the steps. With no one about, he could at least look around outside. He set off across the lawn toward the garden enclosed by a rectangle of English boxwoods that wanted trimming. The grass had been mowed, but the flower beds appeared neglected. Weeds grew among drooping chrysanthemums, honeysuckle entangled a butterfly bush, and the grape arbor needed pruning, the vines so heavy the bower sagged under their weight.

The fountain had been cut off and held a puddle of yellowish rainwater in its scalloped bowl. The curved dolphin's copper mouth was darkly tarnished. A dead grasshopper floated on the surface. It had flown too high.

A voice shouted, and from the side of the house hurried a man in laced-up leather boots, camouflaged coveralls, and a blaze orange cap that had a long bill. Authority paced his stride. "Private Property. Didn't you see the sign?"

"I saw it," Wayland said, "but I didn't think anyone would object. As a boy I lived close by and used to come to this house."

The man scowled and reset his cap.

"The owners don't want nobody on the place," he said.

"Well I apologize for intruding. I couldn't just pass on by without stopping. Are any of the Ballards at home?"

What would Wayland say to them, that he'd returned to see where he and his family had been used and in his case humiliated?

"The Ballards is gone," the man answered. His square-jawed face was darkened by a short growth of ratty brown beard. "Timber company owns this property. I'm Barker, the caretaker."

"Mr. Henry Ballard, his daughter Diana?"

"Never seen them," Barker said. "This place a hunting lodge now. Company officers fly down from Richmond to shoot quail, deer, and ducks along the river. Expecting a bunch this evening for dove season."

"There are no Ballards left in Howell County?"

"They gone. All the Ballards is, except them lying in the graveyard."

And Lottie, Pearl May, Lonnie, Emmett, and Ferdinand, were they even in the land of the living?

"May I cross over to the cemetery?"

"Don't guess it can hurt," Barker said. "Just don't touch nothing."

He didn't follow as Wayland walked west of the house toward the wall. A fence of iron pickets crowned with arrowhead finials surrounded the graves. At the center rose a marble obelisk with the name Ballard chiseled into it. Around it were jutted headstones, the oldest with its inscription worn but readable:

John Caleb Ballard

1785-1843

Mr. Henry Ballard lay alongside his first wife Isabelle. There were no flowers or wreaths, but Mr. Henry's had a small American flag, the kind children waved at parades, stuck in the ground at the foot. The flag was tilted and faded. Wayland stopped abruptly before the next marker. Another flag, and the name shocked him:

Lieutenant Eugene Fontaine Ballard

1925-1945

He Died For His Country

There was also a representation of the Air Medal carved into the tombstone. Eugene a pilot and hero. For an instant Wayland felt resentment at the flyboys who wore fur-collared leather jackets and floppy caps, who knew nothing of mud's taste or the daily stink of their own shit, who lounged in ready rooms to be waited on by orderlies, whose feet in combat never had to touch the earth—a gentleman's kind of war just perfect for the Ballards of this world.

Then he felt shame. Death didn't come genteel or pretty even in the cockpit of a P-47 or B-24. There would be fire and screaming pain and the lash of terror. How could he resent any man who'd encountered death bravely? God's grace to them all.

Diana? He found no plot for her. Dead, would she be buried here or in some more exotic place? Maybe she had brought the flags. The cemetery, like the flowers, needed care. Dandelions spread among the shaded grass, and honeysuckle reached from pickets to gravestones. If not rooted up, the vines would claim all because nature hated man-made order.

At the rear corner of the wall was a second cemetery, this one for the Ballards' favorite animals—dogs, cats, a canary, Diana's white pony Missy, Mr. Henry's chestnut stallion Windlord. Each had a hewn marker with name and date. Wayland thought of kudzu-tangled, overturned fieldstones at the Healing Spring Baptist Church.

When he walked back across the lawn, he stood in front of the house and called up the sound of a piano, a canary singing, the flame-shaped bulbs of a parlor chandelier glinting off a silver bowl of fruit at a curtained window.

Barker reappeared pushing a wheelbarrow loaded with oak logs sawed to uniform lengths. Company officers would want a fire during the cool of night after their dove hunt. They'd need a place to gather, drink liquor, spin tales.

"Who put the flags at the foot of the graves?" Wayland asked.

"Me. Part of the deal is the company agreed to preserve the cemetery and stick flags in. Don't tell me them plots need weeding. I'll get to them."

"Would you know where Miss Diana Ballard might be?"

"Nope."

"Look, Mr. Barker, I'd very much like a look inside. I've driven a long way to be here."

"Not open to the public," Barker said and let down legs of the wheelbarrow at the foot of the steps.

"I knew these people and feel like family, not public."

"Timber companies got owners, not family," Barker said.

"I'll make a contribution," Wayland said and reached for his wallet. "Twenty dollars."

Barker eyed the money, reached for it, and slipped it fast into a breast pocket of his coveralls.

"Since I going in myself, I reckon I can let you take a quick look-see."

He lifted an armful of logs and climbed the steps. At the top he balanced the wood while he drew a large brass key from a pocket to fit into the massive lock of the door, surely the original installed when the house was built. The latch slid free, the sound no sissy little click but a clang like a rifle's bolt sprung forward into firing position.

"Don't touch or take nothing," Barker said as he opened one of the double doors. He preceded Wayland into the great hall, high and empty now, the chandelier gone, taped tag ends of electrical wires exposed, the plaster intact but dusty. Rectangular shadings checkered walls where portraits had once hung. Along the wainscoted baseboard a mousetrap had been set, the cheese dry and shrunken.

To the right and left were spacious rooms, the one Barker entered furnished with stuffed armchairs arranged in a semicircle before the fireplace. He knelt to stack logs on black andirons topped by brass fox faces. These walls too were bare, and a second chandelier was missing. Lamps had been set about, their cords trailing over uncarpeted heart-of-pine floorboards.

Across the hall in the dining room the yellow damask curtains were drawn but let in a slice of light through wavy glass that distorted vision. No huntboard held candelabra, chafing dishes, or delicate china. A picnic bench of the sort that might be seen at a roadside park had replaced the grand cherry dining table his mother had talked of, and centered on it were salt and pepper shakers, not silver but aluminum.

Wayland looked into what had been a library, the shelves empty of books, the room furnished with a round table surrounded by straight chairs and covered with green felt on which lay several decks of cards and stacks of poker chips.

The music room still held an old Bechstein grand piano and nothing else. The closed piano's winglike top had been stained and scared by drinks and cigarettes. Age-curled pages of sheet music survived propped above the keyboard, the first opened to Cole Porter's "I Get a Kick Out of You." Despite Barker's instruction not to touch anything, Wayland softly pressed middle C. The note sounded sourly lost.

Barker left for more wood. Without waiting to ask permission, Wayland climbed the left arm of the staircase that rose above both sides of the entrance to join at the landing. Along the hallway he opened doors. Made-up cots waited in some of the large rooms, but he also found others abandoned in which egg-and-dart molding strung cobwebs and dripping faucets had discolored enamel sinks and claw-foot bathtubs.

The walls of Diana's room though empty were still painted pink. The only sign of her he could find was a hairpin on the dusty mantel supported by fluted Ionic columns. Wayland lifted it to take with him but set it back gently before backing off and closing the door.

He walked down the steps and at the bottom turned into the wainscoted hall, boards of which creaked underfoot and echoed. He pushed through a swinging door to the pantry where a GE refrigerator emitted a rattling hum. Washed cocktail glasses, heavy white plates, and mugs of the kind he'd drunk from at Camp Blanding filled shelves of a cabinet. Bright and exotic liquor bottles had been arranged rank upon rank beneath the counter.

A second swinging door opened into the kitchen. The great Kalamazoo wood stove with its copper hood had been removed and left a large gap along the wall. The replacement was a Whirlpool electric range of the kind found in any suburban house, and it appeared dwarfed and pitiful in the vacant space surrounding it.

The man-high fireplace still held an iron spit, recently greased, perhaps used to barbecue a pig, fat likely dripping and causing smoldering hickory to flare. The hunters would've eaten thick slabs of meat, hash browns, corn on the cob, and if venison the taste of the forest might've resided in the animal's lean flesh.

Hooks remained screwed in ceiling beams from which pots, pans, and skillets had hung. A meat clever lay on the butcher block, the blade clean, deep slashes in the wood tainted with old blood from pork, lamb, and beef that had given way under Black Amos's violent downstrokes.

Wayland moved toward the bakery at the rear of the kitchen. Firebrick encased the wall oven and its hinged iron door. Loaves had been set in and taken out on a long-handled wooden paddle. He looked for it, but the paddle was gone. His mother had cast flour on the counter at the side of the oven before rolling out her dough. No flour now but another haze of dust.

On the windowsill lay a biscuit cutter, a round one she would've used to stamp out the dough. Wayland pictured his mother walking home carrying her tote, her body tipped by the drag of its weight, her feet all but scuffing the lane. He saw her spare worn hands as she set food before him and the family at the cabin table covered with oilcloth wiped to a faded green. Mostly she had brought home bread, often still warm, and flour lodged in hairs of her wrist and arms.

He reached to the biscuit cutter. It felt light and insubstantial. Was it all that was left, this little more than a discarded scrap of base metal a monument to a life? He looked out the window to the brick smokehouse shaded by a white oak. Doves fluttered down to a stone birdbath. He remembered his daddy had told him doves were the only birds that drank without bobbing their heads to swallow. Soon these might be shot at and end up torn-out breasts and clumps of bloody feathers. He felt sorrow for them.

A cruising hawk caused the doves to fly upward into shafts of sunlight, the white stripes of tail feathers flashing before fusing among branches of the oak's wine-dark shadows.

He again thought of his mother and father, of Lottie, Pearl May, Emmett, Ferdinand, Lonnie, and his eyes dimmed as if looking through a rainy day's wetness. Their lives, the time his people had walked this earth, had to have carried meaning, yet they had vanished leaving no more testimony to their worth than chaff tossed up to the wind.

The sense of loss bowed him, and he touched at his eyes before placing the biscuit cutter on the windowsill in the exact spot where it had left its circular imprint among dust. He turned back through the empty hall, walked from the house, and met Barker at the bottom of the steps. Barker was carrying in more logs.

"Been wondering about you," he said. "Seen all you want?"

"I have and thanks."

"You didn't take nothing?"

"No, I took nothing."

Wayland walked around the house to the car, started the engine, and steered over cobblestones through the gateway. In his rearview mirror he had a final glimpse of Bellepays before a bend of dogwoods and magnolias obscured the house and wall. Gone, he thought. All gone.

twenty-five

He drove back to the Kentucky gate, closed it behind him, and once again slowed along the dusty road to look at the Healing Spring Baptist Church and the kudzu-choked graveyard. He'd do something about the latter, arrange with a lawyer or bank in Tobaccoton to set up a trust fund and annually pay men to clean away the growth as well as to raise upright and cement into the earth all the markers. Would he try to search out Lottie, Pearl May, Lonnie, Emmett, and Ferdinand? What could be gained now by trying to reestablish lasting and meaningful relationships? Surely those were beyond repair, and most important of all Amy had to be considered.

He crossed the rusted bridge over the muddy swollen river to Jericho Crossroads and the Ballards' swaybacked, vine-captured store. A white panel truck had the right-of-way at the narrow intersection, and on its side was painted MEEKUMS PLUMBING, HEATING & APPLIANCES as well as representation of a joyous golden-haired child gazing at a TV screen that shot out lightning-like streaks interspersed with stars directly into her face.

Wayland blew his horn as he turned left to follow the truck. It swerved to the side of the road, and the driver stuck his head from the window to look back. Wayland opened the Caddy's door and hurried to the Ford.

He couldn't be sure it was Willie Meekums. This person had a full and fleshy face while Willie had been skinny with freckles. Still the man's incisors protruded like Willie's had, and his thinning hair was red.

"Willie?"

He looked Wayland over, unlatched the door, and stepped down from the truck.

"Well I'll be pig in slop," he said and extended his hand. His grip was hard, and his arm kept pumping. "Wayland, I figured the earth had done swallowed you up a long time ago."

"I wasn't certain anyone I knew still lived around here."

"Ah yeah. Some of us too trifling to leave. Though it's not the same. It's sure as hell not the same. Now you follow me to the house. I want you to meet Mary Ellen. I got me four kids and seven grandchildren. You look like you carrying a thirst. We'll drink us some mint tea."

Wayland started to explain he was late and had to move on, but then calculated he could take another hour and still make Richmond and his plane before dark. He followed the panel truck south along a secondary road that wound down toward the river. At the edge of a pine grove a mailbox had the name Meekums painted on it, and red roses twined around the post. The truck turned into a gravel drive bordered by crepe myrtles with tawny flaking trunks, some branches still flowering purple blooms.

The drive ran an eighth of a mile through the woods to a clearing where a brick ranch house with a two-car garage sat above the river. Beyond a white outbuilding a vegetable garden grew a late crop of corn. The orchard held peach and apple trees. Verbena and azaleas circled the house.

Willie would easily weigh in at two hundred pounds now. His Levi's sagged, and a sweaty white T-shirt proclaimed his allegiance to the Redskins. He moved heavily on Nikes and used his cap to wipe sweat off his forehead.

"Mary Ellen," he hollered at the house.

She pushed the screen door open, a short, plump woman wearing a yellow halter, yellow shorts, and yellow flipflops. Plastic curlers speckled her blond hair. She had a broad, friendly smile.

"I heard enough about you," she said to Wayland and hugged him as if she'd known him all his life. "Lucky both of you didn't end up in the jail."

"No jail big enough to hold us," Willie said and led Wayland through the house where on tables, mantles, and the TV set were framed color photographs of children. The screen porch at the front held matching blue chairs and a glider.

"Always get a breeze here," Willie said. "Though I'd sell you an air conditioner and got a unit right here in the house, I don't like 'em. There's nothing like the coolness that comes off the water. And who even ever had a unit when we was growing up?"

"The Ballards," Wayland said.

"Oh sure, them. What didn't they have?"

A set of wooden steps led down the slope to the laggardly flowing river where in a quiet eddy Willie had a dock and an aluminum johnboat. A bait can and fishing rods lay athwart a cushion seat.

"Willie, looks to me like you've done all right for yourself."

"Oh for a poor boy I get by. Me and Mary Ellen had to hump it a few years when we first got started, but now we got a little money in the bank and carry life insurance. I worked in Tobaccoton 'til I learned the business. I like being on my own. Mary Ellen and I can slip away to Nag's Head whenever we take a notion, and I got my young'uns to remind me I ain't wasted all my time."

As Mary Ellen came out with a tray, her flipflops patted the porch's concrete floor. Sprigs of mint floated in the pitcher of iced tea. The glasses also held ice and had sunflowers painted on their sides. She next offered Wayland a plate of shortbread cookies, each topped with half a pecan.

"Let me tell you I got me a woman who's the champion cook of this whole wide world," Willie said.

"He wants something or he wouldn't be talking that way," Mary Ellen said, and when she straightened, she had to readjust her halter, which had been dragged down by the heaviness of her breasts. Willie undoubtedly knew those breasts well.

Smiling, she padded back inside the house. A radio played, and Wayland heard the announcer identify the station as Tobaccoton. When he grew up, Tobaccoton hadn't had any such thing, and he thought of the Philco he'd listened to at the Ballards' store, the voices distant and staticky. He'd been awed and believed radio a miracle.

"Look like you done okay yourself," Willie said. He drank a full glass of tea with one lifting of the glass to his mouth and filled it a second time. "Hell, I first thought this man in the Cadillac car and go-to-meeting suit must be a lawyer or banker at least. You ain't, are you?"

"No, I have a small business down Florida way."

"You talk different now, that's for sure. What kind of business?"

"Automotive products."

"You own it?"

"Every nut and bolt."

"That's the only way. You can eye every dollar that passes by. Hey, Wayland, you ever believe either one of us would ever 'mount to anything? All you wanted was to drive a Ballard tractor, and I hoped to breed Belgians. Now we got money and brick houses. Yours is brick, ain't it?"

"It's stucco over block but solid."

"Never thought I'd have a brick house of my own or a wife like Mary Ellen or even a bank account. She's a Steadman from over in Halifax County. Let me tell you the damn world's sure God changed."

He looked down toward willows along the river as if he was seeing more pass there than the flow of water. A fish broke the surface, a smallmouth bass likely after a snake doctor, and the current carried the ripples downstream. Wayland remembered his father and how the river had taken him.

He thought also of his mother and the way she would've loved a house like this with electricity, a modern kitchen, a furnace controlled by a thermostat, indoor plumbing. He envisioned her parading before her mirror while wearing a coat, not Mrs. Ballard's castoff one with the mended fur collar but it all new and fashionable.

"You remember old Mud Dog?" Willie asked. "Would you believe he's in the legislature? Came back from the army and used his GI Bill to go to college and become a lawyer. Had his picture in the paper with the governor."

"Any chance you hear anything of Pearl May, Lottie, Emmett, Ferdinand, or Lonnie?"

"You not knowed about Emmett?" Willie said, staring at him. "Bought it in the Pacific. A Marine. Buried in a military cemetery over there in Guam. Pearl May tried to get in touch with you. Letter she sent you come back. She didn't have your right address or something. Where was you?"

"For a number of years I traveled and had no permanent address," Wayland said. He pictured Emmett barefooted, wearing little more than a feed sack with holes in it for his arms and head, fishing with him at the river and hauling out a catfish so large they both wrestled it on the bank. They'd fed the whole family that night and had enough left over for a meal the next day.

"Lottie's supposed to have gone up to Detroit for a war job," Willie said. "Never been seen around here since. Pearl May and Lonnie headed for Cincinnati. They come back once three or four years ago for a Big Meeting at the church. Had kids and drove a Buick automobile. Lonnie had found him a good job in a brewery."

"Ferdinand?"

"When he got out the jail he took off for Texas. He ain't showed his face 'round here from that time to this."

Like the feathery seeds of the milkweed pods floating on wind that carried them wherever it blew. There were detective agencies Wayland could hire to track them and maybe bring them together one more time, but not without revealing to Amy the many lies he'd told her about his past.

Mary Ellen returned from the kitchen carrying on a platter a loaf of bread still warm from her oven. She deftly sliced it and set tub butter and a pot of honey beside it.

"Sourwood," she said. "I found us a bee tree."

She and Willie were so obviously suited to each other. Their accents had once been Wayland's own, and he felt himself being drawn back to it as if his mouth had been loosened and freed.

"The Ballards," he said. "I stopped by the big house and found the whole place had been sold."

"You didn't know that neither?" Willie asked. "You must've been in some far distant country not to hear. Yep, everything sold. Nothing's the same, Wayland. It's all changed. Ever'thing has."

"I felt pulled there, Willie. You remember I worked at the stable a spell."

"I remember you mooning 'round sick for something you couldn't get. Well, Mr. Henry kind of slipped downhill after you was gone. Couldn't seem to get it together the way he used to. Word was he suffered the high blood."

"Wont high blood," Mary Ellen called from the kitchen. "Was that second wife of his, that Stephanie. With her fine horses, clothes, and jewels. She used him up and emptied his moneybags. What I heard is she went to live with the frogs."

"Frogs?" Wayland asked.

"Somewhere in France with all them mustached men that has slicked-down black hair," Mary Ellen said. "Can't even speak English."

Wayland thought of Midnight Baron and the wild ride the lady had taken him on. She surely had never belonged in Howell County.

"Squeezed him dry," Mary Ellen said.

"Mr. Henry did seem to kind of dry up," Willie said, finishing a second glass of tea. "Started carrying a cane and dragged a foot. Found him dead on the terrace in front of his house where he liked to sit looking out over his land. Big funeral, the governor and all, and the National Guard sent a unit and played "Taps." Nothing but timber company's loblolly pines planted in that land now. They got machines to keep the ditches cleared."

"I left a lot of my sweat there," Wayland said.

"We sure God humped it. I still got my hoe. When Mr. Wesley Rudd left, he never called for it. He started himself a hardware store in Danville. Reckon he's dead now too."

"Black Amos."

"He stayed at the house 'til it was sold," Willie said. "Kept it up pretty good by hisself after Mr. Henry died. Left driving that old LaSalle. Mr. Henry had willed that to him and some money. Black Amos said he'd always wanted to see the Grand Canyon. He never come back."

"I saw Eugene's grave."

"Oh, yeah. He got writ up on the front page of the Tobaccoton *Bee*. An ace. He flew a Hellcat and shot down seven Jap planes before they punched his ticket. Another high-powered funeral, a general and bunch of navy big dogs, yet they never found his body. Somewheres deep in the sea. They put his dress uniform and saber alongside one another inside the casket. Shot off rifles above it."

I apologize to you, Eugene, Wayland thought. I wish I could have known you man to man, and I still envy your blue-blooded ways, which I'll never possess. It will take more time for that in my family, though my daughter Jennifer is well on her way to a stylish assurance that arises from the certainty of her worth.

"Diana?" Wayland said.

"She died," Mary Ellen called.

"I didn't see her grave," Wayland said, turning around in his chair to look toward the kitchen.

"Oh I mean on the TV," Mary Ellen said. She appeared smoking a cigarette in the kitchen doorway. "You never saw her on the tube? *The World Turns*. They killed her off the program her second year. She played this slinky unfaithful wife who tried to take her best friend's husband."

"She's never come back to Howell County?"

"She came for the two funerals," Mary Ellen said. "The big house and land got left to her. She's the one who sold out. Word is she flew back to California. Haven't heard anything since."

Feathery seeds from the milkweed pods floating on the wind to wherever it blew. Mighty and seemingly beyond the touch of ordinary people but the Ballards too had been brought down to the earth from which they sprang. They'd shared the fellowship of suffering and loss, and who ever escaped those? If Diana still lived, he wished her well. He experienced an eerie sensation that his hands, which all those years belonged to the Ballards and Howell County, had opened and at last released him from their grip.

"She was a heart-pounding beauty," Willie said. "She never passed by I didn't get a hard-on."

"Willie," Mary Ellen said.

"Getting one now just thinking 'bout her."

"This what you getting," Mary Anne said and slapped him playfully on his head.

"Just fooling," he said, ducking and laughing. "I know when I got it good."

"You better behave or your good ain't going to be getting," she said and flounced into the kitchen.

"So long ago," Wayland said. "So different a day."

"Me, I like it one hell of a lot better now than then," Willie said. "Lots of people look back on old times as if that was the life. Man, it was damn money grubbing, cat-scratching fight for my bread, and many a night my belly rubbed my backbone. Don't never talk to me about how good it was in the old days. No way I'd ever go back if I could."

Nor would Wayland, yet he felt a sadness and reluctance to let go. He wished he could bring together the scattered seeds one last time, speak some sort of blessing over them as Preacher Arbogast would've as he stood behind the painted pulpit at the Healing Spring Baptist Church:

> *May the Good Lord keep and protect you,*
> *And make His face shine upon you,*
> *And grant you peace.*

"Willie, I got to move along. It's been fine seeing you and meeting Mary Ellen."

"You're not leaving without eating," she hollered.

"That's all I've been doing back here in Virginia. I best be going."

"We got plenty of beds. You stay here with us, and I'll stick a pork loin in the oven that'll make your taste buds think they gone to Heaven."

"Wish I could do that thing. Maybe when I come back?"

"You coming back?" she asked from the kitchen doorway.

"I'll try," Wayland said. It was a lie. He wouldn't be back.

When he stood, Mary Ellen hugged him and kissed his mouth. She'd wrapped shortbread cookies in a Glad Wrap bag for him to carry along. Willie walked out to the car with him.

"You think you could hire somebody to clear and keep up the Healing Spring Baptist Cemetery?" Wayland asked. "I'll foot the bill."

"I'll see to it," Willie said. "Should've done it myself, but my folks mostly buried over at Pisgah Baptist."

"It's been good being here with you, Willie."

"Yeah it has, Wayland. We done all right, ain't we?"

"Not bad for country boys."

"Reckon you'll really be coming back?" Willie asked. He'd sensed the truth.

"Hard to tell, Willie. I got lots yanking at me."

"Well you welcome, Wayland. Always got a bed for you and a seat at the table."

"Bless you, Willie."

"I can always use a blessing. Man can't get too many of them in this life."

twenty-six

He left Willie's, headed back to Jericho Crossroads, and turned west along the state secondary that would join the four-lane highway that led east to Richmond and his flight south to Florida and another world. Hot asphalt popped and crackled beneath his tires. He felt the years dragging at him and couldn't shed his sense of loss, not for himself alone so much as the passages of humanity, the paths taken, the destinations unknown except for the final one in the grave.

No, he wouldn't reveal to Amy how he'd deceived her by claiming he had no blood kin left. The Confederate captain's portrait would remain over the living-room fireplace, the polished ladle stay nestled in a curl of black velvet behind the clean glass of Amy's silver cabinet. He couldn't take the chance she'd never again trust him, that out of hurt and her high sense of integrity she might stop loving him and even consider leaving. Surely their years of good marriage justified his lies to her. There was an intent and higher truth that surpassed them.

He braked at the sight of a car parked ahead among Queen Anne's lace off the road's shoulder, a four-door Dodge, its blighted gray paint flaking from a rear fender, the glass of a taillight smashed, the radio antenna broken. The hood was raised.

Hands balled on his hips, a young black man gazed at the engine before suddenly ducking so far forward over the radiator that his feet lifted from the ground. Wayland started to pass on by. Too much violence in the world now, and Florida had become particularly infected with it, causing him to have had an intricate and expensive alarm system installed in his Fort Lauderdale home. This junker at the side of the road could be a decoy set out to waylay and rob him of his money and the Sedan de Ville.

No, this is Howell County, he thought, surely not as perilous as the towered cities where life could be taken as quickly and casually as the slicing of a melon. He pulled to the shoulder ahead of the car, shifted to park, and stepped to the pavement as the youth rocked back from the engine well. He had a long, intelligent face, corn-rowed hair, and wore harness-strap boots, snug jeans, and a midnight blue shirt that wound curlicues of golden thread across his chest, shoulders, and collar.

He cursed because he'd smeared a spot of grease on a cuff. Steam hissed not from the radiator but the block itself. Wayland again thought of Josephus Blodgett, their fight and brawling tumble down the riverbank, their washing off blood in the cooling, mud-roused current.

"Looks like you got you a cracked cylinder head," Wayland said. "Expect you'll need a tow. I can give you a lift to your garage."

"I don't happen to own no garage," the youth answered and kicked a fender. From beneath it a clod of caked red clay fell and broke. "The garages, they own me. Let me tell you, man, anything got tits or wheels on it is trouble."

Wayland scanned the Dodge's interior. It was packed for a journey—clothes piled on seats along with a boom box, pearl-colored cowboy hat, an iron frypan, a red-white-and-blue five-string guitar, and the wooden handle to what? In this day and age surely not a hoe.

"You know how far I got down this damn road?" the youth asked. "Less than two miles down this goddamn road is how far I got. Once you in Howell County, you never get out."

He again kicked the fender laced by rust. The Mexican steel buckle of his black belt was shaped like a horseshoe. He punched at the air, slumped away, and with a long, slim hand covered his eyes.

Why, Wayland thought, he's close to breaking, to giving in to defeat, maybe weeping. The sight caused Wayland's heart to grip, and he pictured youths leaving all over the world, hundreds, thousands, tens of thousands headed down alien roads to find what life had waiting at the far end. Seeds on the wind.

He reached into his jacket's inner pocket to draw out the book of traveller's checks. He unclipped his pen, walked to the Caddy to sign one on its hot metal trunk, and crossed back to the youth.

"Any bank will cash it," he said.

"You fucking with me, man?" the youth asked, his ripe plum-colored eyes enlarged and fixed on the check.

"Not silver dollars but as good. You ever know a Josephus Blodgett?"

"Yeah, I know that planter but don't want to up close," he answered and studied the check, his brow furrowed.

"Josephus a planter now?"

"Not tobacco. Sell you insurance, a cemetery plot, and plant you in it. Rides around in a big-ass Lincoln so long it can't turn a tight corner. Got him a three-story house, a wife who owns a flower shop down Halifax way, and sends his drop to William and Mary. How I know this check good?"

"Unless all the banks burned down, it's money in your pocket," Wayland said, feeling glad about Josephus. "Best of luck on your trip."

He walked back to the Caddy, and as he drove away, he sighted the youth looking after him and holding the check with both hands as if it might take wing and fly.

Wayland pictured his daughter Jennifer. She too would be leaving soon. She'd given up her dream of becoming a ballet dancer, had graduated from Agnes Scott in political science.

"Fact is, I'm not built for leaping around," she'd said. "My legs are okay, but I'm heavy boned. Guess I got those from you, Pop."

"My apologies."

"Hey, listen, I also got your smarts. I'll become a lawyer, join Legal Services, help the common man. How's that?"

"You'll find the common man's not so common," he'd told her.

At the highway he paused at the stop sign and twisted around against the restraint of the seat belt to gaze behind him—a last look down the black, shimmering road before entering a break in the racing traffic. His eyes lingered an instant on an expanse of wildly flourishing trumpet vine that dangled fiery blooms from askew locust fence posts and entwined strands of rusty, broken barbed wire.

The End.